NE~~VER~~ renewed

BE TOLD

MICHELLE ANGHARAD
PASHLEY

Cinnamon Press
:: small miracles from distinctive voices ::

Published by Cinnamon Press
Meirion House
Tanygrisiau
Blaenau Ffestiniog
Gwynedd
LL41 3SU
www.cinnamonpress.com

Lyrics of 'Run' by Wildwood Kin used with kind permission of the band. © Wildwood Kin.

The quotes from Felicity Dawe are excerpts from her blog, *My words my ocean—my ongoing journey with cancer.* © Felicity Dawe,

Designed and typeset in Garamond by Cinnamon Press. Cover design by Adam Craig © Adam Craig.

Cinnamon Press is represented by Inpress and by the Welsh Books Council in Wales. Printed in Poland.

The publisher gratefully acknowledges the support of the Welsh Books Council.

Acknowledgements

To my husband, Peter Ingham, for his constant love, for being there for me, always, and for the incredible bravery shown when he agreed to proof read the manuscript for this book; a daunting task!

And to Adam Craig, not only for his stunning cover design, but for his much valued friendship.

And, last, but by no means least, to my editor, Jan Fortune. Her support and encouragement have kept me going, kept me afloat, kept me sane; a true and loving friend.

To my daughter, Felicity Dawe,
for her strength, her courage and her compassion
through the darkest of times.

We'll go on together. We'll go on together.
I'll hold you close to me, I promise. Won't let go.
Sometimes we break but never notice how far we've run...

'Run' by Wildwood Kin.

Look to the stars
To light up the dark.
Look to the stars
To brighten the night.
Look to the stars
To bring you back home.
Look to the stars
And you'll find them in you.

Felicity Dawe.
From *My words my ocean—my ongoing journey with cancer*

She focused on that tiny
drop of hope still left in
her heart and she
dreamt it turned into an
ocean...

Felicity Dawe.
From *My words my ocean—my ongoing journey with cancer*

NEVER TO BE TOLD

Chapter 1
London, Bexleyheath, April 2013

He'd gone on about it for months now. In her opinion, he either had to do something or let it go. She leaned forward, her reflection peered back at her, looking decisive. She would broach the subject tonight. She tilted her head, tousled her short blonde hair and decided that she needed a touch more mascara and perhaps some blusher. Clicking shut the compact she stood, took one last look in the mirror, and made her way downstairs.

'At last,' her father said. 'I feared you'd locked yourself in the loo.'

'For God's sake, Dad, I was six when that happened.'

'You're still my little girl, sweetheart.'

She planted a kiss on her father's bald head. 'I'll see you later.'

'Have fun.'

'Always,' she said. 'But don't be surprised if I get back early.'

'Trouble in the love nest?'

'Not yet, but that might change soon.'

'Is your father allowed to ask what you're talking about, or should I speak to your mother?'

'Ask Mum. Must dash, bye.'

Paul looked up as the restaurant door banged shut again, checked his watch and sighed. He took another sip of wine and proceeded to dismantle a carefully-crafted swan napkin.

'You've killed it,' exclaimed Julia, collapsing into the seat opposite. 'Sorry I'm late.'

'I should be used to it by now, but I always get a knot of anxiety.'

Julia reached across, dislodged the mangled swan from his fingers and squeezed his hand.

He squeezed her hand back. 'Shall we order?'

Paul refilled Julia's glass as the waiter cleared away the plates. 'You've been very quiet, is everything alright?'

'With us, yes,' said Julia, staring intently into Paul's eyes.

'There was a 'but' there.'

Julia took a gulp of wine and banged the glass down. 'I know it's none of my business, but you've been wittering, no sorry that's not fair, worrying about, no that's not right either.' She took a huge breath in. 'You've been discussing the possibility of searching for your biological mum for some time now, and I just...'

'You just thought I should do something about it and, if not, just shut up and forget about it?'

'Well, not forget about it, obviously. But how are you going to find her? She could have changed her name, her appearance or both. She could be living in a different country, for God's sake.' Julia pushed her hands through her hair. 'There could be months, years even, of stress and disappointment ahead for you.'

'I know, you're probably right, but I need to understand why she did what she did. What drove her away? Has she ever regretted her action? Does she even think about me? Can she...?'

The waiter reappeared.

Paul whirled round. 'What?'

'The dessert menu, sir?'

'Not now,' exclaimed Paul.

Julia smiled sweetly. 'I don't think so, no. Could we have the bill, please.'

'Certainly,' said the waiter, as he backed away at speed.

'He was only doing his job, Paul.'

'Oh, Julia what am I going to do?'

'Have you spoken to your father?'

Paul nodded. 'He thinks I should leave well alone.'

'What about Barbara?'

'She says it's up to me.'

Julia nodded. 'I agree.'

'But she also said that part of her agreed with Dad.'

A small, white plate was slid onto the table. Paul clamped his hand on the waiter's arm. 'Apologies for my rudeness; I was, well, I was…'

'No need to explain, sir. I hope you enjoyed your meal.'

'We did, thank you.'

The waiter nodded and bowed, backing away at a more sedate speed

James looked up from the kitchen table. 'Morning. Barbara's just brewed a fresh pot of coffee.' He put the Sunday newspaper down and held his mug out. 'While you're there, thanks.'

Paul plonked the mugs down and sat. 'Dad, can we talk?'

James abandoned his newspaper again. 'About?'

'I've decided I'm going to do it and I thought you should know.'

James sighed. 'By *do it* I assume you're talking about looking for your mother. I did try to find her, Paul, I told you. I even hired a private detective, but it was hopeless. She obviously didn't want to be found. I fail to see what you're going to achieve, it's been over twenty years. Let it go.'

'Well that's just it, Dad. It was a long time ago and maybe, just maybe, she wants to be found now.'

'If she'd wanted to get back in touch all she had to do was pick up the phone. She could me ring here or contact Camberwell College.

'I know that! But isn't it possible she'd feel just a tad awkward doing that; she probably assumes you'd hang up.'

'I would.'

'Well, there you are.'

'Well, there I am, what?'

'Don't be obtuse, you know what I mean.'

'Fine. It's up to you, but I warn you, it'll only end in heartache.'

'You can't possibly know that.'

His father gave a small shrug and took a sip of coffee.

'Will you help?'

'Jesus, why the hell would you ask me that? She broke my heart, and if it hadn't been for you, so tiny and so helpless, I would have curled up and died.'

'All I want is the name of the detective you used.'

James rubbed his eyes. 'His name was Adam Trent, but I've no idea if he's still working.'

'Have you got a contact number?'

'I did, but I can't remember it now.'

'An address?'

'It was a PO box number.'

'Didn't you keep any correspondence from back then?'

James stood and shoved his chair backwards. 'Wait there.'

Paul flinched as his father snatched open the kitchen door and stomped along the hallway. He heard the study door creak open and heard the click as it was shut. He closed his eyes and waited.

James leaned on the door, surveying his study. He clenched his fists and made his way towards the bookcase. He opened a small silver box, removed a key from within it and unlocked the bottom drawer of his desk. Within the drawer there lay one file. He stared at that file for several moments before he reached towards it. His hand touched the file; he froze. He closed his eyes, took a deep breath, grabbed it and tossed it onto the desk. He slumped down and opened it. Her letter stared out at him. He slipped the single sheet from the envelope and re-read it. He sighed, and, with a quick glance towards the door, returned the letter to the drawer, slammed it shut and locked it.

Paul sensed his father's presence behind him.

A manila folder landed on the table. 'This is all I have.'

'And you're alright about it?'

'Not really, but I understand why you want to try.'

Paul scooped up the file. 'I appreciate it, really I do.'

James laid his hand on his son's shoulder and, in a hushed tone, added, 'Just be careful. She might not be the person you want her to be.'

'What's that supposed to mean?'

'She abandoned you, Paul, abandoned you when you were a small, defenceless baby.'

'But why, Dad? There must have been a reason.'

'If there was, she never told me.'

'Surely she left a note, something?'

James swallowed. 'Nothing.'

'Was there...?' Paul cleared his throat. 'Was there...?'

'Another man?'

Paul nodded.

'I've no idea.'

'But...'

'Paul, there's nothing more I can tell you, sorry.'

Picking up his coffee, Paul made his way to his room and settled down at his desk. He set the folder down, placed his coffee next to it and took a deep breath.

Stapled to the folder's front cover was Adam Trent's card with his PO Box address. Scrawled underneath was a mobile phone number. Paul opened the folder. Inside, there were a few sheets of typed notes from Adam Trent and some scraps of paper covered in notes written in his father's hand, information he'd probably received over the phone, judging by the doodles.

Paul picked up the typed sheets and scanned through them. Adam Trent had managed to locate his mother, but then she'd disappeared again. The last letter, dated 10.08.1992, detailed his fees and an acknowledgement that his services were no longer required. There was a report attached. Paul picked up his coffee and took sips as he read.

The final paragraph read,

It is my firm opinion, Mr Sharp, that your wife has adopted a new identity. As you know, I spoke again to the people in the village and the hotel, but nobody seemed to know anything. They all said she'd simply disappeared. I showed her photograph again to the taxi driver, the train and bus station staff. The taxi driver did remember giving her a lift when she'd first arrived, but he said he'd not seen her since. My advice is for you to inform the police. I fear they will tell you she's an adult and entitled to disappear. The fact that she emptied your joint savings account implies she had a plan...

Paul lowered the sheet and leaned back. A flicker of a frown crossed his face. He peered out of the window. 'Where are you now, Mum? Have you got a family of your own? Are you happy? Do you ever think about me?'

He returned his attention to the letter and continued reading... *had a plan. If you did wish me to continue the search, there are several lines of enquiry that I could follow, but this would entail an open-ended search and I appreciate...*

His phone vibrated across his desk.

'Hi, Julia, I was just about to ring you. Dad's given me the go-ahead. I'm going to do it, Julia, I'm really going to do it. Am I crazy? I'm not, am I? I've got the address and number for Adam Trent, the detective guy, and I suppose, oh shit, I...'

'I'm coming over, Paul. Please, don't do anything till I get there. Do you understand?'

Paul stood up and went across to the window.

'Paul, are you still there? Paul!'

'Yes, yes, I'm still here.'

'Did you hear what I said?'

'Don't do anything till you get here, right?'

'Good, I'll be there in fifteen. Love you.'

When Julia arrived, Paul was still in his dressing gown, sitting at his desk, surrounded by files and text books. 'The last sighting of my mum was in a place called Strontian in Scotland, she was working in a hotel, but by the time Dad got there, she'd vanished. Come and look at this,' he said. 'What do you think?'

'And hello to you, too,' said Julia.

'Sorry, hi, thanks for coming over.'

Julia pulled up a chair, gave him a kiss and peered at Paul's notes. 'Am I supposed to be able to read this? It looks like the work of a drunken spider.'

Paul frowned and adjusted his glasses. 'Point taken. I'll summarise.'

'Good plan.'

'I've been reviewing my second-year notes on identity theft.'

'And?'

'Do you know what that is?'

She thumped him with the back of her hand. 'Jesus, Paul, I know I'm not a bloody genius, but credit me with some intelligence.'

'Sorry—again.'

'I'm assuming that's what you think your mum did, not for the purpose of fraud, but to hide.'

'That's exactly right, yes,' said Paul, nodding with such vigour that his glasses slipped towards the tip of his nose. After pushing them back into position, he dragged one of the books from the pile and stabbed at the open page. 'It explains it all here.'

Julia scanned the page. 'I don't wish to be discouraging, but wouldn't the private detective have thought of that?'

Paul swivelled round in his chair, bent down, retrieved the folder from the floor and took out Adam's letter. 'He did, look. He specifically says—*it is my firm opinion, Mr Sharp, that your wife has adopted a new identity*.'

'Again, I don't wish to be discouraging, but if he couldn't...'

'But that's just it, Julia,' said Paul. 'He never got the chance to continue his search because Dad dismissed him.'

'Why?'

'I'm almost certain it was because Dad couldn't afford it.'

'I find that hard to believe, I mean...'

'I know, but in Adam Trent's letter it says that Mum emptied the joint savings account before she ran away.'

'Did you know about that?'

Paul shook his head.

Julia reached across and took his hand.

'The point is, Adam Trent found her.'

'Yes, so you said. But then he lost her again,' said Julia.

'In Strontian.'

'Yes, and?'

'Well, I thought we could go there.'

'To Scotland?' exclaimed Julia.

'That's where Strontian is, so, yes.'

'But why? She's hardly likely to have gone back there.'

'I know that, Julia, I'm not an idiot either.'

'Explain why you want to go there, then.'

'I'll tell you when we get there.'

'Why can't you tell me now?'

'Humour me.'

Julia shrugged. 'Fine. When?'

'The sooner the better,' said Paul, as he entered the hotel's number into his mobile.

'*Kilcamb Lodge.* Can I help you?'

'Yes, I hope so,' said Paul. 'I was hoping to book a double room.'

'When for, sir?'

'Is there one available now?'

'I'll just check, but this is one of our busiest months.'

'Is it? I didn't realise that, surely you have…'

'I'm sorry, sir, there are no double rooms available.'

'What about…?'

'I'm sorry, sir. We're fully booked.'

'I see. Is there another hotel in the village?'

'There is, but I've been informed that it's also fully booked. As I said, it's one of our busiest months—sorry, could you hold the line a moment?'

Paul covered the mouthpiece. 'They're fully booked.'

'I heard,' said Julia. 'So, what's happening now?'

Paul shrugged. 'No idea, she asked me to hang on. We could take a tent.'

'You're joking, I hope.'

'Oh, I don't know; think about it, you and me under the stars by the Loch.'

'Plagued by midges and other creepy crawlies, I think not.'

'Where's your sense of…?'

'Hello, are you still there, sir?'

'Hello, yes, I'm still here,' said Paul.

'Well, it seems you're in luck. My colleague has just informed me that a cancellation for a mid-week to mid-week booking came through this morning.'

'Which week?'

'Next week. Wednesday, the twenty-fourth of April to Wednesday, the first of May. Is that any good?'

'Yes, that's brilliant,' exclaimed Paul. 'I think I love you.'

'We aim to please, sir. If I could just take your details.'

He punched the air. 'We're in.'

'Excellent. I think,' said Julie, with a wry smile.

Paul flicked open the file and frowned.

'What?'

'There's no point ringing this mobile number, is there?'

'Why not?'

'It's twenty-one years old.'

17

'I wouldn't bother.'

'No, you're probably right,' he said, as he punched in the number and hit the speaker button. An automated voice responded; *Please check the number and try again.*

'Told you.'

'I'll write a note to this PO Box address. Hopefully, he'll be prepared to take on the case again.'

Chapter 2
Yorkshire, The Previous Month, March 2013

Evie stepped out into the bright sunshine of Northallerton train station and, map in hand, made her way towards Willow Road. Ten minutes later, she was standing on the pavement looking across at number 16, a detached house with wisteria growing up the brickwork around the front door and windows. There was a side gate to the right leading, Evie assumed, to the courtyard mentioned in the property details. On either side of the front door stood two stone flowerpots containing *Iberis sempervirens*, their crisp, white flowers trailing down the steps. Smiling, Evie stuffed the map into her bag, made her way towards the front door and rang the bell.

The door opened almost immediately. 'Hi there, I'm Sarah Watson and you, I assume, must be Evie Morgan. Come in, come in, the kettle's on.'

Sarah pointed to the first door on the right. 'That's the living room. It has French windows that look out over the courtyard. I was tempted to have that room for myself, but Dad pointed out the difficulty of installing an en-suite, something about moving pipework from across the hall, where the loo used to be. So, I took the other room.' She nodded towards the left. 'That one. The loo is now the en-suite. Luckily Dad's a whiz with DIY, otherwise it would no doubt have cost a fortune. Your room,' she said, pointing to another door on the right, 'if you want it that is, hasn't got en-suite facilities, but the bathroom is directly opposite.' She pushed open the door at the far end of the hall. 'And this, as you can see, is the kitchen. Sit down, make yourself comfortable. I'll show you round properly in a tick. Coffee or tea?'

'Coffee please.'

'Sorry, was I gabbling? Dad's always telling me to slow down, I don't want to put you off before you've even seen the place, not that seeing the place will put you off, I mean —I'll just shut up, shall I?'

Evie giggled. 'Looking at the outside didn't put me off.'

'Well that's something, I suppose,' said Sarah. 'Cover your ears.'

'Sorry?'

'Coffee grinder; noisy,' said Sarah, as she flicked the switch.

Evie watched as Sarah continued to talk, every word lost.

Coffee grinding complete, Sarah's words finally reached Evie. '...I was sad, of course, but...'

'Sorry, I didn't catch what you were saying, what happened? Why were you sad?'

'Because my nan died. This was her home. Obviously, it didn't look like this when she lived here. It was all chintz and patterned wallpaper, frightful. Anyway, my dad and his brother converted it into two flats. The upstairs is a one-bed place, separate front door, access via steps up the side, Simon Trent lives there, a nice bloke, mid-forties. He's been here from the beginning, moved up here from London. He's a private investigator, of all things. I work at the library, not quite so exciting, although Simon tells me that a lot of his work is mundane; still, he would say that I suppose, he can't be blabbing to all and sundry about what cases he's working on, client confidentiality and—I'm doing it again, sorry. Milk and sugar?'

'Milk, no sugar.'

Sarah set the mugs down and sat opposite Evie. 'So, what do you do?'

'Nothing at the moment. I was a PA up in Edinburgh, but the company went bust and I was made redundant.'

'So, this is a fresh start.'

'It is, yes.'

'Come on, bring your coffee,' said Sarah. 'I'll show you round properly.' She threw open the door on the left. 'This is the room for rent.'

Evie stepped into the L-shaped room. There were two windows; a large one on the left, overlooking the back garden and, opposite it, another that overlooked the courtyard. 'This is lovely; the two windows make it so bright and airy,' she said.

'That was Dad's idea, the double aspect. I especially like the view of the courtyard. So, what do you think?'

Evie took another swig of coffee and peered at Sarah across the rim. 'And it's £300 per month. Is that right?'

'With the first two months in advance but, if that's a problem, you know, what with you not working at the moment, then...'

'It's not a problem,' said Evie. 'The redundancy money will keep me going for a while.'

Sarah swept her hand through her tangled mass of black hair. 'Come and see the rest of the place.'

A short while later they were sat in the courtyard. Sarah poured two glasses of wine. 'Here's to your fresh start.'

'Cheers,' said Evie, clinking glasses. 'When can I move in?'

'Whenever you want—now, if you like.'

'Don't you need to do checks first?'

'Probably, but I trust you. Am I mad?'

'Probably,' said Evie. 'Look, are you serious?'

'What, about being mad?'

'No, about me moving in.'

Sarah nodded.

'Brilliant. Would a week today be OK?'

'Saturday the ninth?'

'Yes.'

'Perfect. So, where's all your stuff?'

'At my dad's house,' said Evie. 'He lives in York with Charlotte, my sister.'

'Older or younger?'

'Younger. She's eleven, no sorry, she's eleven years and seven months; she likes to be precise. She'll be twelve in August.'

'Wow, that's a big gap.'

'Yes, Mum announced her pregnancy when I was fourteen.' Evie took a sip of wine. 'I wasn't impressed.'

'Such a charming time of one's life, being fourteen.'

'Quite; it's all me, me, me.'

'Listen, do you fancy bunking down here for the night? We could get a takeaway, there's an excellent Indian, or a Chinese, whatever you fancy, and then you'd get a proper feel for the place. I'll ring Dad and, if you're certain, you can sign whatever it is you have to sign in the morning. Oh, I'm sure we're going to have fun. I know I work in a library, but don't believe everything you hear and read about librarians. We have hidden depths.'

'Should I be worried?'

'About what?'

'Your hidden depths.'

'Oh, right, yes, I mean, no, I'm quite normal,' said Sarah. 'Actually, that's not entirely true.'

Evie took a gulp of wine. 'What, you mean you *are* mad?'

'According to Dad, I'm completely loopy. He's amazed I get through single days let alone life in general.'

'I think that applies to all of us really, don't you?'

'Absobloomingutely.'

Evie was stood at the back of the van, hands on hips, as her father loaded another box of books. She glanced at her watch. 'My God, it's gone 12,' she exclaimed. 'Is that everything?'

'Apart from your mother's bookcase,' he said, massaging his lower back.

'Are you sure you don't mind me having it?'

'Where else are you going to put all those books?' he said. 'And I thought you might like to have her old writing slope, too.'

Evie flung her arms around her father's neck. 'Love you.'

'Love you, too,' he said. 'Now, come on, I dismantled the bookcase yesterday.'

The moment they drew up outside, Sarah threw open the front door. 'Thank goodness; I was beginning to get worried.'

'Good morning, young lady. Our late arrival is entirely down to my daughter's extensive book collection,' Evie's father said, exiting the van and doffing his hat.

'Hi, Sarah. This is my father.'

'Gerry Morgan at your service; Miss Evie Morgan's driver and skivvy for the day.'

Sarah extended her hand. 'Hi there.'

'Right, come on, Dad, boxes to unload.'

'Do you need a hand?'

'A coffee would be very much appreciated,' said Gerry, glancing at Evie, 'in about an hour?'

Evie nodded. 'Would that be alright, Sarah.'

'Coffee in an hour; duly noted,' said Sarah, giving a modest curtsey. 'Look, are you sure I can't help? I don't mind.'

'You could give me a hand with my desk while Dad concentrates on the boxes.'

'No problem.'

Gerry grunted as he dumped another box in Evie's room. 'That's it, thank God. Now where's that girl got to with the coffee?'

Sarah poked her head round the door. 'How's it going?'

'Excellent timing, we've just finished.'

'The coffee's brewed.'

Gerry's face lit up. 'Brewed?'

'I'm not keen on instant, it tastes like the dried scrapings from the factory floor,' said Sarah.

'I quite agree. One shudders to think what's in it,' said Gerry.

'I thought we'd have it in the courtyard,' said Sarah. 'This way.'

They followed her down a small corridor leading off from the hallway and stepped through a glass door at the end. There was a rusting, cream-painted bistro table and four chairs situated beneath the shade of a magnolia tree; Sarah plonked the tray down, collapsed onto one of the chairs and extracted several small packages from the top pocket of her tie-dyed dungarees. 'Sugar?'

Gerry shook his head. 'Evie mentioned that you worked at the library.'

'That's right. I work in Archives, the historical section, the Seventeenth Century to be precise,' said Sarah, depressing the plunger of the cafetière.

'Well, I never. What a small world. You must be the SW who deals with my requests for articles, then,' said Gerry. 'I lecture in seventeenth century history at the university.'

Sarah's eyes widened. 'Gosh, you mean you're *the* Dr Morgan.'

'I am he.'

'Goodness.'

'So, you must know Martha Green,' said Gerry.

'She's the Chief Librarian.'

'Wasn't she Mum's old friend?' said Evie.

Gerry nodded. 'That's right. Jean, my wife, and Martha were at Cambridge together. Jean's death was a terrible blow to her.'

'Oh, I'm sorry, I didn't, well I didn't realise that Evie's mum was…'

'No reason why you should, my dear, no reason at all,' said Gerry, patting Sarah's arm. 'Jean was a great support to

Martha when Martha's mum was diagnosed with dementia. It must have been, what? Ten years ago? It's what Jean's father died from, you see, so Jean knew what to expect. Jean's father was only in his fifties when he was diagnosed; terrible disease, terrible. He died when Evie was a little tot.'

'Martha's mother died last year, did you know?'

Gerry started. 'No, I didn't know that. Poor Martha.'

'She never talked about it. I only know that Martha's mum was in the hospice at the end because my aunt works there. She told me Martha visited every day, but her mum never recognised her. It must have been awful.'

Gerry shuddered, glanced at his watch and downed his coffee. 'That was lovely, but I fear time marches on and I need to get the van back before they get it into their heads to charge us for another day.'

'Thanks, Dad.'

He bent and kissed Evie on the top of her head. 'Be a good girl and I'll see you soon.'

'I'll show you out,' said Sarah.

'No need,' said Gerry, 'You two have fun. Bye.'

'I'm so sorry about your mum,' said Sarah, as they heard the van pull away.

'Thanks; it was—anyway, fancy you working for Martha, it really *is* a small world.'

'I know, weird or what?' said Sarah. 'I don't know her very well. She's a good-looking woman, keeps very much to herself, not married, which is sad.'

'I suppose she had her mum to look after for all those years,' said Evie.

'True. Mind you, I get the impression she's found herself a man at last.'

'Oh?'

'Yes, little things like a new hairstyle, new shoes and the like.'

'Well, good for her.'

'Anyway, do you want some help with that bookcase?'

Evie swigged the last of the coffee. 'If you're offering, I'm accepting.'

Simon Trent was sat at his desk in the upstairs flat, going through case notes, pencil clamped between his teeth as his fingers hovered over a page within the file. Something was nagging at him. He snatched the pencil from his mouth and began to underline sections. Halfway through the process, loud banging and hammering from below caused him to lose his train of thought. Swearing, he flung the pencil at the wall, scraped back his chair, snatched his jacket from its hook by the front door and, having shoved it on, slammed the door, stomped down the steps and banged on Sarah's front door.

'Oh hi, Simon,' trilled Sarah. 'You look flustered, is everything alright?'

'It was, until whatever major renovation work you're carrying out down here shattered the peace.'

'Oh, dear, were we disturbing you?'

'I imagine you've disturbed the entire bloody street, the racket you were making.'

Sarah lowered her eyes and muttered an apology.

'Oh, give over,' said Simon. 'What exactly *are* you doing?'

'Nothing now, as it happens. I was just about to make a coffee. Do you want one?'

'Might as well.'

'No need to overwhelm me with your enthusiasm.'

'A coffee sounds absolutely delightful. I cannot thank you enough for such a …'

Sarah thumped him. 'Right, well, come on in, you can meet Evie.' She pushed open the door to Evie's room and Simon marched in. 'Good God,' he exclaimed, as he surveyed the scene.

The bookcase occupied most of the far wall and there was a large oak desk positioned beneath the window overlooking the courtyard. A wrought-iron bed was under the window on the left. There were books, clothes, various soft toys and framed photographs scattered across the floor, the bed and the desk, as well as at least ten boxes sealed with heavy-duty tape and labelled 'Books', stacked in the middle of the room.

Evie followed Simon's gaze. 'I accept the room's not looking its best at the moment,' she said, 'but once I've sorted the books out, it'll be fine.' She collapsed back onto the bed, landing on a hard copy of *Gray's Anatomy*. Her expletive followed her as she tumbled sideways onto the floor.

Simon rushed over.

Evie struggled to regain an upright posture, just as Simon bent down towards her. Their heads met in a sickening thud. Evie fell again, and Simon reeled backwards.

Sarah hooted with laughter.

Pulling herself into a sitting position and peering over her bed, Evie said, 'I'm fine, Sarah. Thanks for asking.' She looked up at Simon. 'Are *you* OK?'

'I'll live.'

'I'll make that coffee, shall I?' said Sarah.

'Good idea,' said Simon, rubbing his head with exaggerated force. He stepped towards Evie and extended his hand. 'Simon Trent, I live upstairs. You must be Sarah's new tenant, Evie. Pleased to meet you.'

Evie grabbed hold of Simon's hand, hauled herself upright, dusted herself down and smiled. 'A pleasure to meet you.'

Simon glanced around the room again. 'Do you need any help?'

'Well, that's very kind, but I couldn't possibly impose…'

'Oh, give over, you look knackered.'

Evie caught sight of her reflection. 'Good grief, I look a complete wreck.'

'Not a complete wreck, but…'

'Were you being serious?'

'About?'

'Helping.'

'Absolutely.'

'Fantastic. You can make a start on this,' said Evie, shoving a box towards him.

He saluted and ripped open the box just as Sarah dashed into the room. 'Sorry, change of plan. Mum's just rung. I'm supposed to be at theirs; family gathering, I'd completely forgotten. The coffee's brewing. Help yourself. Awful welcome for your first night as my official flatmate, I know, but I can't get out of it. The takeout menus are pinned up behind the microwave. Will you be alright? I feel terrible, but…'

'Don't worry, have fun and I'll see you later.'

'I was going to help with all those books.'

'I'm going to give her a hand,' said Simon.

'Such a gentleman under that stern exterior,' said Sarah. 'OK, so, Simon Trent this is Evie Morgan, Evie…'

'We've done that bit,' said Simon.

'Good, good, yes, well, I'd better get a move on, sorry again.'

There was a deathly quiet as the reverberations from the front door died down. Evie cleared her throat. 'Right then, coffee?'

'Smashing, milk no sugar,' said Simon. 'I'll press on.'

'Here we are. Where shall I put your mug?'

Simon looked around and nodded towards the floor at his feet. 'Here seems to be the only available space.'

Evie smiled. 'It'll be fine once…'

'Once you get all these books unpacked and shelved, yes, you said,' remarked Simon, holding up three framed pictures. 'So, what about these? Where shall I…?'

'Oh, you clever man, you found them,' she said. 'I thought I'd put all the photographs together, but I couldn't find those. I'll put them on my desk.'

'So, who's the curly-haired little blonde cherub?'

'That's my kid sister, Charlotte. And for information, she hates being called a cherub.'

He pointed to the woman holding her hand. 'Your mum?'

Evie nodded.

He looked at the other photograph. 'You, with your mum?'

Evie nodded again.

Lifting up the final one, he said, 'And the whole happy family group.'

Evie burst into tears.

'Shit, sorry, what have I said? Jesus.'

The tears continued to flow. 'Sorry, sorry.'

'No, I'm sorry.' He moved towards Evie, hesitated, clenched his fists and backed off. 'I'm hopeless when women cry,' he said. 'I never know what to do. I'd offer to make tea but we already have coffee so that would be ridiculous. I'll put these on your desk and then I'll, I'll oh, shit, no, you'll want to do that.'

Wiping her eyes, a giggle escaped as she watched Simon advance and retreat from her desk, hopping from foot to foot, clutching the photographs to his chest. She stood and walked towards him. 'Give them here.'

He shoved them into her hands and took a step back, banging into the corner of the desk.

'They're not about to explode you know.'

'No, right, sorry.'

'Not your fault. It's just that, it's just…'

'You don't have to say anything.'

She placed the photographs on her desk and took hold of Simon's hand. 'Come and sit back down.'

He sat.

Evie handed him his coffee.

'Thanks,' he said, staring down into the mug.

Evie took a deep breath and blurted. 'It was in 2004, two months before Charlotte's third birthday. Mum died in a car accident.'

'Oh, God. How awful.'

Evie examined the pattern on the carpet.

Simon kept quiet.

She looked up. 'When it happened, my first thought was about me. Isn't that appalling? I thought that's it, my life's over, Dad will expect me to stay home and be a replacement mum for Charlotte.'

Simon sipped his coffee.

'He didn't, of course. He was amazing. He advertised for a Nanny and asked me to help him vet the applicants. We couldn't believe how awful some of them were. The moment they left the house we'd collapse into hysterics and then feel guilty for laughing because, well because...'

'Because your mum was dead.'

Evie nodded.

'Did you find one?'

'Yes, a woman called Mandy. She's still the Nanny.' Evie smiled. 'But she reckons it's Dad who needs looking after these days, rather than Charlotte.'

''Tis ever the way.'

'The accident occurred on some B-road, in North Wales of all places. I've always wondered what the hell Mum was doing there.'

'Doesn't your dad know?'

'He doesn't talk about it.'

'That's understandable.'

'I suppose, but—well—oh, I don't know. Dad and I are very close. He and I talk about anything and everything, but whenever I try and broach the subject, he clams up.' She stared into Simon's eyes. 'I've no idea why I'm telling you all this. You only offered to help me with the books and now I'm burdening you with all this baggage. Sorry.'

'No need to apologise. It's been fun.'

Evie's eyes widened.

Simon groaned. 'Fun? Did I just say, this has been fun? Jesus! What a fucking idiotic thing to say. I can't believe I said that. I just meant, well, I'm not sure *what* I meant.'

'It's entirely your own fault, you know. You're easy to talk to.'

Simon gave Evie a dazzling smile. 'At your service.'

'You charmer, you.'

'Listen, I hope you don't think I'm being presumptions, but, given that Sarah's abandoned you on your first night, do you fancy joining me for a meal?'

'Why sir, are you asking me out on a date?'

'I'm simply asking if you fancy a meal.'

'Right, of course, sorry,' said Evie.

'So, do you?'

'What?'

'Fancy a meal?'

'Yes, that would be lovely.'

'What time?'

Evie glanced across at the mirror and emitted a strangled gasp. 'I'm going to need at least forty-five minutes,' she exclaimed.

Chapter 3
Yorkshire, Friday 29th March 2013

On her way to meet Sarah for lunch at Betty's Café, Evie picked up a couple of thin envelopes from the hall mat. 'More shitty rejections,' she said, as she slammed the door shut.

Sitting at their usual table, surrounded by the familiar bustle of the café, Sarah asked, 'So, how many is it now?'

'Four applications. Four rejections.'

'You don't seem that bothered.'

'None of them appealed to me, not really. No doubt my lack of enthusiasm shone through in my covering letters,' she said, biting down on her chicken sandwich.

'So why apply?'

She shrugged, chewed and swallowed. 'I'm bored.'

'Have you spoken to Simon?'

'About?'

'A job. He's been saying for ages he could do with some help.'

'He hasn't said.'

'I'm amazed. You've been out with him on enough dates, and so I'd...'

'*Three* times, I've been out with him *three* times, that's all,' she took a sip of tea. '*And*, none of them were dates.'

'Oh, come on. I detect romance in the air.'

'Don't be ridiculous, he's nearly twenty years older than me, for God's sake.'

'Seventeen, to be exact,' said Sarah, 'and what's that got to do with anything? It's obvious he fancies you. Don't tell me you haven't noticed.'

'Nonsense.'

'OK, I'll let that pass for now, but you should ask him about a job. It could be fun.'

Back at the flat, later that evening, Evie's phone rang. 'Hello, sweetheart, haven't heard from you for at least three weeks. How's it going?'

'Oh hi Dad,' said Evie. 'Yeah, all good.'

'I take it you managed to assemble the bookcase. To be honest, I was expecting you to call for assistance.'

'Easy-peasy.'

'Really?'

'I simply followed your instructions; all very straightforward.'

'Well, that's a first,' he exclaimed. 'You've never listened to instructions given to you before, let alone followed them.'

'Anyway, you rang?'

'I did.'

'Was there a particular reason, or were you merely checking up on my DIY proficiency?'

'Oh right, yes. We've been invited to lunch. That's you, me and Charlotte.'

'When and where, Dad?'

'Next month, Sunday.'

'*Which* Sunday, Dad?'

'Hang on, let me check.'

Evie held the phone away from her ear and heard the familiar clunk as her father dropped the phone onto his desk.'

'April the twenty-eighth. Are you free?'

'I've no idea, Dad, probably. So, where is this lunch?'

'At *Honeypot Cottage*.'

'Don't tell me Alex has got *another* new girlfriend.'

Gerry sighed. 'What can I say? The man just can't seem to find what he's looking for.'

'The last one was a complete bimbo; thick as custard.'

'That's rather harsh.'

'Hah!—so, what's this latest one like?'

'Well, that's the strange thing,' said Gerry. 'You know what he's normally like, going on and on about their attributes, but this time he's hardly said a word about her.'

'And you're telling me this lunch isn't until April the twenty-eighth; a whole four weeks away?'

'Yes, I know. It'll be a record if he keeps one for that long,' said Gerry. 'Anyway, can you come?'

'I have to say I'm intrigued but, oh, I don't know, Dad, his girlfriends are such hard work.'

'Oh darling, please don't abandon your father in his hour of need.'

'*Fine*, but can I bring a guest?'

'Sarah would be most…'

'Not Sarah.'

'Who then?'

'Simon.'

'The man in the upstairs flat?'

'Yes.'

'I don't see why not. Will you need a lift?'

'No, Simon has a car.'

'The invitation says one o'clock.'

Evie dashed out of the front door and shot up the steps to Simon's flat.

'Dad's just been on the phone. I've committed you to lunch at *Honeypot* on Sunday, not this Sunday, Sunday the twenty-eighth next month, so plenty of time to reorganise your social calendar.'

A frazzled-looking Simon finished pulling on his jacket and grabbed his keys from the side table. 'What a kind invitation, delivered with such grace and charm. Now let me think, am I able to reorganise my hectic social calendar? Not sure, could be tricky.'

'Oh, shut up. God, you *are* free, aren't you? Please say you are.'

A wide grin spread across Simon's face.

She grabbed his shoulders and pushed him back inside. 'This is serious, Simon.'

He closed his eyes and took a deep breath. 'Right. Serious, you say.'

Evie nodded.

'Sunday lunch at *Honeypot*. I've never heard of it. Is it a new restaurant?'

'No, it's where Alex lives.'

'And he is?'

'A professor at York University, an old friend of Mum; works in the same department as Dad. Anyway, he has yet another new girlfriend he wants us to meet. No doubt she'll be at least half his age, they usually are.'

'Your sour expression tells me you don't approve. Strange, I never saw you as a prude.'

'I am *not* a prude.' She paused. 'Well, perhaps I am, just slightly.'

'You can't be slightly prude in the same way that you can't be slightly pregnant. You either are, or you aren't.'

'Fine, but it doesn't change the fact that Alex has been working his way through the entire airhead population of Ripon,' said Evie. 'And trust me, much as I love Ripon, there seem to be an awful lot of them.'

'Anyway, although I'd love to stay and chat, I really must dash. I'm already late.' He glanced at his watch. 'Very late. I need to speak to, to— sorry, I've got to go.'

'You need to speak to?'

'Someone.'

'Ah, someone.'

'Yes.'

'And this someone is?'

'A client.'

'You're working on a case! How exciting.'

'Not really. Look, I don't wish to be rude, but I must get on.'

Evie stood aside. 'So, will you be able to…?'

Simon dashed down the stairs. 'Just pull the door to. Bye.'

'…join me?'

Evie stepped outside and was about to shut the door when a movement caught her eye. She pushed the door fully open as a small black cat, tail up, came tripping down the hallway towards her. 'Well, hello there and who are you?'

The cat miaowed and dashed back down the hallway. Evie followed. 'Here kitty, kitty.'

It skittered off to the right, skidded left over the wooden flooring into the living room and jumped onto Simon's desk. It sat surveying her as she approached. 'I'm not entirely convinced you should be up there,' said Evie.

The phone rang. The cat sprang down, its back paws slipping on a pile of paperwork, sending several sheets slithering off the desk into the waste bin below.

'Oh, that's not good,' laughed Evie, delving into the bin.

As she began to reassemble the sheets into a neat pile, Simon's voice filled the room asking the caller to leave a message. There was a loud beep. Evie started and a sheet of paper fell back towards the floor. 'Bugger,' she exclaimed, bending to retrieve it.

A woman's breathless voice rang out. 'Oh, Mr Trent, it's me, Mrs Ferris. Do you hear me? Please pick up. It's happened again. Exactly the same as before. I'm not imagining it, I'm not.'—There was a catch in her voice. —'My sister thinks I'm going doolally. She's told me not to bother you. Well, bother you I shall. She'll be gone next week, so please come, Mr Trent, please. Next Friday, the fifth of April, at noon, I'm not…oh, blast and damnation, she's coming.' The line went dead.

Evie stared at the phone. It sat there, motionless and silent. 'So, what was that all about?' she asked it.

About to replace the sheet, she hesitated and began to read. *Mr Trent, PO Box…* 'Shit, what am I doing?' She slapped the sheet down onto the top of the pile and looked around. There was no sign of the cat. She heard running footsteps. She gasped and made a move away from the desk. A figure dashed in, waving a heavy wooden walking stick. Evie threw herself behind the settee.

'Evie?'

Evie popped her head above the settee. 'Simon?'

'What *are* you doing?'

'It was the cat, I just...'

'What cat, I don't have a bloody cat,' said Simon. 'And come out from there, for God's sake.'

'I can explain.'

Simon took a step forward. Evie backed up. He chucked the walking stick onto the settee. 'I was just going to the drinks cabinet. You look pale.'

'Do I? Can't think why.'

He handed her a glass. 'Here, drink this.'

She sniffed. 'I don't drink whisky.'

'Make an exception.'

She took a sip and started coughing. Simon thumped her back. Evie pointed towards the hatch. 'There,' she spluttered.

The cat was sat on the hatch counter, fastidiously washing its paws.

Simon looked. 'Cute, but not mine,' he said. 'Anyway, forget the cat, sit down.'

'I wasn't snooping, really I wasn't, and...'

'Please, Evie, sit down.'

She sat.

'I came back because I'd forgotten something.'

'I thought you were an intruder.'

'And I thought I was being burgled.'

'Given that you'd just left me outside your flat, surely you might have reasoned it was me. You are a detective after all.'

'Fair point. Anyway,' he said, moving across towards his desk, 'I came back to collect a folder; can't believe I left without it.'

'You obviously need a secretary or something, your mail…'

Simon's eyes widened. 'You've been reading my mail?'

'Certainly not,' she exclaimed. 'It was the cat.'

'The cat was reading my mail?'

Evie's eyebrows shot heavenwards. 'No, obviously not. The cat knocked the letters off your desk when the phone rang. I was only trying to help.'

They both glanced at the phone to see the message-light flashing.

'It was a woman. She sounded scared, something about it happening again.'

Simon gave her a piercing stare.

'I couldn't help overhearing it,' she wailed, as Simon pressed play and Mrs Ferris's voice once more filled the room.

'What's happening again?' asked Evie.

'Honest answer. Nothing,' said Simon. 'The woman has a vivid imagination. I've spoken to the police about her. She's a serial reporter of fictitious crimes. Sad really, just lonely, I suppose.'

'And you're sure about that, are you?'

'Well, she lives alone.'

'I mean about the crimes being fictitious.'

'The police wouldn't lie.'

'That's a moot point these days,' said Evie. 'No, I meant are you sure it's a fictitious crime *this* time? She sounded anxious, scared even.'

Simon played the message again. He looked at Evie. 'You're right, she does.'

'So, what are you going to do?'

'Visit her again, I suppose.'

'You don't sound very enthusiastic.'

'I've got so much on at the moment. I seem to be chasing my own shadow.'

'And attacking friends with large sticks.'

'I did no such thing.'

Evie's gaze shifted to the settee.

'It's an ordinary walking stick.'

'Trouble with your knees? I never...'

'I keep it by the front door for, well, for emergencies.'

'I see.' Evie cleared her throat. 'Sarah was telling me you work alone.'

'I do now.'

'So, not always, then.'

'No, not always—I used to work with Adam, my brother, but he buggered off.'

'Did you threaten him with a heavy wooden implement too?'

'Most amusing.'

'When did he "bugger off"?'

'Oh, a long time ago.'

'Weeks, months?'

'Years. In 2000, to be exact.'

'And you've worked alone since then?' she exclaimed.

'Yes.'

'Bloody hell, no wonder you look exhausted.'

'Thanks.'

'So, why did he go?'

Simon shrugged. 'I've no idea.'

'He must have given you a reason.'

'You'd have thought, wouldn't you? But I just don't know. I think he had a breakdown of sorts. He was in Leeds, working on a case, can't remember what. He rang to say he'd had enough. When I asked him what he'd had enough of, he said he was tired of finding people who didn't want to be found, tired of looking into the lives of unhappy people and disillusioned with the entire human race.'

'So, where is he now?'

'Last I heard he was in Ireland, living what he called *the simple life*.'

'And is he happy?'

'Haven't a clue, we don't communicate.'

'That's very sad.'

He shrugged again.

'Look, tell me to butt out, but Sarah also mentioned...'

'Am I the sole topic of conversation between you and Sarah?'

'You wish.'

Simon grinned.

'Anyway, she mentioned once, *in passing*, that you needed help and I wondered if you were actively looking, you know, for an assistant or something.'

'What, you?'

'There's no need to look so incredulous. I was a very good PA, a quick, independent worker and entirely trustworthy.'

'I don't doubt that for a second, but Adam and I were a good team, we complemented each other.' He looked down at his hands and swallowed. 'You'd have liked him.'

'I'm sure I would. I certainly like you,' said Evie, a blush rising in her cheeks the moment the words left her lips.

'Ooh, I say, steady on.'

'I've no idea why though.' Glancing again at his desk, Evie remarked, 'You could certainly do with someone to sort that lot out. God knows how you find anything.'

Simon's eyes crinkled, as a broad grin spread across his face.

'What?'

'That's what Adam used to say. His desk was always immaculate. Every pen, pencil, notepad and file had its place.'

'Sensible bloke.'

'Evie?'

'Yes?'

'I could be about to make the biggest mistake of my life, but how about joining me next Friday?'

'To visit Mrs Ferris?'

'To see how you get on.'

'You mean with a view to hiring me?'

'It's a possibility. Obviously, you'll need time to think abo…'

'Yes, yes, yes.' She punched the air. 'Oh, this is so exciting.'

'It's not like in books or on TV, you know. It's mostly mundane stuff.' Simon snatched open his desk drawer and removed a manila folder. 'Not unlike this case, in fact.'

Evie cocked her head to one side.

'It's the results of boring surveillance. Endless hours sat in the car, eating crap food and trying not to nod off. Anyway, sorry, but I really must dash.'

The cat jumped down and followed them down the hallway.

'And you can scarper too,' said Simon, giving the cat a gentle nudge towards the front door.

Chapter 4
Scotland, Strontian, April 23rd-May 1st 2013

Paul and Julia arrived at Euston Station thirty minutes before the departure of the sleeper train and were directed to Platform 14. Julia's eyes widened. 'Look at it, Paul, it's beautiful.'

Paul straightened his glasses. 'According to this information leaflet, it's the longest passenger train in the UK. It has sixteen carriages. And, wow, now this *is* impressive, it...'

Julia's eyes glazed over as Paul continued to share statistics gleaned from the leaflet.

A smartly-dressed steward was standing outside each of these carriages. Paul showed their tickets to the first steward they came to. 'You need to be in the Fort William section, sir. Fourth carriage along.'

Once inside, Paul presented their tickets to another steward who examined them, smiled, nodded and handed them back. 'Welcome aboard. Please, come this way.'

As they followed him down the walkway that ran alongside the cabins, Julia squeezed Paul's hand and whispered, 'I'm so excited. I've always wanted to travel on a sleeper train.'

'Here we are, sir, madam, your cabin. If you need anything, just let me know.'

'Thank you,' said Paul, holding the door open. 'After you, Julia.'

She entered the cabin, did a 360 degree turn and exclaimed, 'I love it. Bags top bunk.'

'What are you, twelve?'

They checked into *Kilcamb Lodge* at 11.30 the following morning. After lunch, armed with a map of the local area, they set off along the A861 in a north-westerly direction, away from the loch.

'Where are we going?'

'To visit the Strontian Parish Church. The receptionist assured me it wasn't far along here. She reckoned it was a fifteen to twenty-minute walk.'

'A church?'

'The picture looks quite nice.' He handed her a leaflet. 'Look.'

Julia gave the leaflet a cursory glance. 'It's not very big.'

'I shouldn't think it needs to be, given the size of the local population.'

'True. Oh, come on, Paul, give me a hint. Why are you suddenly so interested in this little church in the middle of nowhere?'

'You'll see.'

Julia gave a deep sigh. 'Fine. I can see by your face you're not going to tell me. So, against all odds, I shall remain patient.'

'Bloody hell, there must be something in the water up here.'

Julia glanced around. She grabbed Paul's arm. 'Listen.'

'What?'

'Just listen.'

They stood, eyes closed and listened.

'I can't hear anything.'

'I know; brilliant, isn't it?'

Paul shuddered. 'I think it's spooky. Anyway,' he said, consulting the map. 'We need to turn right just along here and the church should be a little further along on the right hand side.'

'There it is,' exclaimed Julia, moments later.

Paul sped up. 'Come on.'

Julia strode along the stone pathway towards the church entrance. 'I bet this church has oak pews inside rather than awful rows of chairs. There's just something about pews, don't you agree?' She turned and looked behind her. 'Paul, where the hell are you? Paul.'

'Over here.'

'Oh, very helpful. Where?'

Paul popped out from behind an ancient yew tree, whipped his glasses off and waved them above his head. 'Here.'

Weaving her way carefully through the gravestones, she said, 'What *are* you doing?'

'Looking at gravestones.'

'I can see that. But why?'

Eyes dancing with excitement, Paul said, 'Mum—new identity—come on, Julia, think.'

Julia looked at the gravestones and banged the heel of her palm against her forehead. 'Oh, I get it,' she exclaimed. 'She needed to locate a dead individual who was born on or around the same time as she was. Then she could use that name to obtain a birth certificate and start a new life.'

'That's it,' said Paul. 'Mum was born in 1973, so…'

'So, we need to look for gravestones marking the death of someone who was born what, between 1970 and 1975, and died soon after?'

Paul nodded.

'Right, I'll look over there,' said Julia.

Crouched down, peering at yet another lichen-covered headstone, Julia was beginning to lose heart. At the sound of a snapping twig, she looked up.

'Any luck?' said Paul.

'It's so depressing. Look at this one; *Our beloved angel taken in his sleep aged 4 months*. And over there, an entire family wiped out,' she said. 'Some of these headstones are over a hundred years old and they died so young. I actually felt quite cheered when I found one marking the death of a ninety-year-old man.'

'I know, but have you found any useful ones, if you get my drift.'

'No, you?'

'No.'

'OK, so, which part of the cemetery have you covered?'

Paul swept his arm in a broad arc, 'From over there, by the yew tree, to that wall. You?'

'Just this segment but, in my defence, there are lots of graves.'

'I'm going to try behind the church, OK?'

Julia nodded. 'I'll press on then.' She hesitated and added, 'What if we don't find any?'

Paul shrugged. 'There are other churches.'

'Great,' mumbled Julia, as Paul wandered off.

Moments later a cry went up. 'Julia, Julia, quick.'

Julia dashed along the pathway to the back of the church, where Paul was waving frantically. 'Over here. I've found three,' he exclaimed.

Julia knelt beside him.

'This one's the grave of Bridget Gilmore, just fifteen when she died.'

They stared at the gravestone. It was engraved 16.06.1970—09.12.1985. There was a brief dedication beneath the dates that read; *Filled with despair, now reunited with her father* and, beneath that, an angel carved into the stone.

'Committed suicide?'

'That's how I interpreted it,' said Paul. He glanced at Julia's handbag. 'We need to write these names down.'

'No problem,' she said, as she rummaged through her bag's contents. 'I put your notebook in here somewhere— ah, here it is.' She scribbled down the name and dates. 'Where are the others?'

Paul pointed off to the left. 'Just over there.'

Sitting on a rickety bench a little while later, Julia said, 'OK, so, we have three names. What do we do now?'

'We need to search the current National Database and, if we find any of these names, we'll need to see if we can find out where they live.'

'Putting aside the fact that I'm not sure how we'd go about that, there's another problem.'

'Which is?'

'While I agree with the premise that your mum took on a new identity,' said Julia. 'How do we know she found it here, in this particular graveyard?'

'We don't. It's just that Strontian is the last place she was seen and this is the nearest graveyard.'

Back at the hotel, Julia consulted the note book and read out the names.

'If it's any of those my bet's on Morag,' said Paul.

'Because she was just a baby?'

Paul nodded. 'The thing is, you know, what you said about not knowing if Mum used that particular graveyard —well, I agree and so…'

'We're going to look round other graveyards?'

Paul again nodded.

Julia sighed. 'Fine. Presumably there's only a few.'

'There are nine more, actually.'

'Nine!'

'I know, unbelievable, isn't it? They're all much further away though. Four about twenty-five minutes by car. Four, just over an hour with two of them involving a ferry and one, again involving a ferry, over two hours away.'

'I'd hardly call that last one 'local', in fact I'm not sure I'd consider the ones over an hour away local either, especially if you need to get on a ferry to reach them.'

'I agree, and so I thought we'd start with the closest ones. The receptionist is organising a hire car for us. It'll be available tomorrow.'

Chapter 5
Yorkshire, Friday 5th April (18 days earlier) 2013

Evie surveyed her appearance, posed with her hand on her hips, sighed and stripped off again. She picked through the pile of discarded clothing scattered across her bed, before finally deciding on a pair of black trousers and a simple white blouse. As she was buttoning up the blouse, Sarah knocked on the door and poked her head round. 'Simon's here.'

Evie took one last glance in the mirror, realised that she was dressed in the outfit she'd put on fifteen minutes earlier, giggled, donned a pair of dark glasses and grabbed her bag. 'Just coming.'

Sarah looked her up and down. 'Most appropriate, for a spy.'

Evie whipped off her glasses and looked down at herself. 'I was aiming for smart, yet casual.'

'Hurry up, Evie,' called Simon, 'or we'll be late.'

'Coming,' she yelled, as she shoved her glasses back on.

Driving along the A684, Simon said, 'Did you feel the sun was particularly bright this morning?'

Evie pushed the sunglasses up onto her head. 'Too much?'

Simon smiled.

'I wasn't sure what to wear.'

'There isn't a dress code for private detectives, you know.'

'No, right, of course not, sorry.'

Simon smiled again and, keeping his eyes on the road, patted her knee before returning his hand to the steering wheel. 'Nervous?'

'Not really, no. Should I be? Is there something you haven't told me?'

'There's a folder on the back seat. Can you reach over?'

'I see it.' She twisted round and stretched her arm towards the file. 'Got it.'

'Before you look, I need to say something,' he said, glancing across at her.

Evie turned her huge green eyes towards him and fluttered her eyelashes.

'You can cut that out for a start,' he said, returning his attention to the road. 'Those techniques won't work with me.'

'Techniques?'

'You know perfectly well what I mean.'

'Fine. So, what do you need to say?'

'I've been thinking...'

'Oh, no, don't tell me you've had second thoughts.'

'I know we get on well together...'

'You *have* changed your mind.'

'Will you please *listen*,' he exclaimed.

'Sorry. Carry on.'

'Thank you. As I was saying, we get on well, although God knows why, but socialising together and working together are two very different things and—Evie, I can sense you're about to interrupt again.'

'I was not,' she said, clamping her lips together.

'For instance, it's important for each of us to listen to what the other is saying without constantly interrupting. We...'

'You're absol—sorry.'

'We need to work as a team.'

'I can work in a team.'

'I'm sure you can, but remember, you're coming along today to observe, leave the talking to me.'

'Absolutely, yes, no problem. My lips are sealed.'

'Good. Right, everything you need to know about the case is in that file.'

'Right chief.' She settled back into the seat, put her head down and skimmed through Simon's concise notes.

She closed the file as they drove under the A1(M). 'So, Joan Ferris, widow, contacted the police on several occasions, informing them that someone had been in her home and stolen several items.'

Simon nodded. 'Yes, but the items taken were worthless cat ornaments. The police went to her house following the first two reports, but found no evidence. No fingerprints, no footprints, nothing.'

'And so they what, closed the case?'

'In their opinion there wasn't a case to close.'

'How did she find out about you?'

'A local reporter pointed her in my direction.'

'And you haven't found anything either?'

'Her cat ornaments are arranged on windowsills and all around the fire on the hearth. She polishes the bloody things every day.'

'I hope you didn't suggest she'd simply forgotten where she'd put them.'

'It seemed the most likely explanation.'

'You poor deluded fool,' said Evie.

'She did rather turn on me. Anyway, we're here. Bring the file.'

'Yes, sir.'

Simon stopped before mounting the steps to the front door. 'Remember what I said. Leave the talking to me.'

Evie saluted.

He rang the bell.

Evie straightened her hair, adjusted her collar and tucked her blouse into her trousers.

Simon nudged her. 'Stop bloody jigging about,' he hissed.

'Sorry,' she mumbled.

A tall, elegant lady with imposing bone structure opened the door. 'Oh, Mr Trent, thank you for coming,' she said, peering over her glasses.

'I'd like to introduce my new assistant, Miss Morgan.'

Joan extended her heavily-ringed hand. 'A pleasure to make your acquaintance, my dear.'

Evie took the proffered hand and gave a small curtsey.

Simon bit his lower lip. 'Miss Morgan is learning the trade, Mrs Ferris, but if you have any concerns about her becoming involved then…'

Joan waved her hand. 'Don't be silly, Mr Trent, I'm sure she'll be a great asset to you, now, come in, do.'

She led them along a wide hallway into her living room. 'There they are,' she said, sweeping her arm to encompass the entire room, 'or rather, there they are not.'

Evie walked into the room. She counted twenty small cats on the windowsill, a similar number on the hearth, a few on an occasional table and an eye-watering number peering into the room from a glass-fronted cabinet. 'You obviously like cats.'

'I like their independence, young lady. A trait to be much admired, in my opinion.'

'Do you have a cat yourself?'

'Monty. He's out at the moment.'

'How many…'

Simon bent down and whispered in Evie's ear. 'What part of *let me do the talking* did you not understand?'

'Mr Trent, I may be old, but I'm not deaf,' said Joan. 'Now then, dear, you were saying?'

'How many ornaments have been taken altogether?'

'Now, let me think—it must be at least a dozen, yes, at least. I can't understand it, really I can't.' She closed her eyes momentarily and sighed. 'My sister thinks I'm going loopy, Mr Trent.' She turned to Evie. 'I'm not, you know. Those ornaments *have* been taken.'

'I understand these thefts occur when you're out of the house.'

'Yes, that is quite correct, Miss Morgan. I take tea three afternoons a week with the charming Mrs Richards. We go to Angelo's, a little bistro in town, not far for either us to walk and so most convenient. That's when it happens, you see, and it implies that I'm being watched, don't you think?'

'Does Monty have a particular place where he sleeps?' said Evie.

'I beg your pardon?'

'Your cat, Monty…'

'Yes, I know who Monty is, dear,' said Joan. 'I'm just a little confused as to why you're interested in where he sleeps.'

'Because my little sister, Charlotte, has a cat too, and…'

'I'm sure Mrs Ferris isn't interested in…'

Joan held up her hand. 'Mr Trent, do let the poor girl finish her sentence. It's very rude to interrupt.'

Evie averted her eyes from Simon as she bit into her thumb.

'My apologies. Carry on, Miss Morgan.'

Clearing her throat, Evie continued. 'Yes, well the thing is, it's weird, but one day Mandy, she's my sister's Nanny, came across a pile of Charlotte's soft toys in the cat's basket.'

Joan smiled sweetly. 'How interesting,' she said, with little conviction.

'But don't you see,' said Evie. 'The cat was stealing them from Charlotte's room, and I wondered…'

Joan's eyes widened. 'Oh, I see. You think Monty's been stealing my ornaments.'

'It's a possibility.'

Joan stood and beckoned to Evie. 'Oh, gracious me, come on. He has a basket in the laundry room where it's always warm. He's got a touch of arthritis these days, poor old thing.'

In the laundry room, Evie pulled back the old towels lining Monty's basket and there, tucked away underneath, were the missing ornaments.

Joan clutched at her pearl necklace. 'Oh, dear, how embarrassing,' she gasped. 'All those phone calls to the police, they thought I was a deranged old biddy and I got rather cross with them. Oh, dear, I feel such a silly.'

'Don't worry, Mrs Ferris,' said Simon, 'leave the police to me. The important thing is, the mystery's been solved.'

'And I'm not going loopy.'

'No, Mrs Ferris, you're not going loopy,' said Evie.

Joan gave Evie a warm smile. 'Thank you, dear. Now then, Mr Trent, I need to settle up. How much do I owe you?'

Simon consulted his notebook, but when he looked up he found Evie's eyes fixed on him, her expression stern. He slammed the book closed. 'No charge, Mrs Ferris, this...'

'I wouldn't dream of...'

'Not another word on the matter,' he said. 'It's been a valuable training exercise for Miss Morgan, allowing her to demonstrate her skill in detecting feline felons.'

Evie stuck her tongue out at Simon just as Joan turned to pat her on the arm. Sucking her tongue back in, Evie adopted an expression of angelic innocence.

'I can't tell you how pleased I am that you managed to solve the mystery,' said Joan. 'And your response to Mr Trent's teasing was fully justified. Such a satisfying gesture to stick one's tongue out.'

Evie howled with laughter and hugged Joan.

'Gracious child.' Disentangling herself, she held onto Evie's hands and smiled. 'I do hope you'll enjoy working with Mr Trent, dear. Just remember, don't be shy, stand your ground and don't let him ignore you.'

Back at the flat, Simon threw his jacket across the kitchen table and called out, 'Do you want a coffee?'

'Lovely, thanks—when do you want me to make a start on your filing?'

'Monday?'

'Is it just the two filing cabinets?'

'Sorry, what was that?' said Simon, sticking his head through the kitchen hatch. 'The kettle's on, couldn't quite hear you.'

'I was asking if it was just the two cabinets?'

'Ah, right. No, it's just the one. The grey one was Adam's, you won't need to touch that because...'

'It's perfectly organised.'

Simon grinned. 'Exactly right. Whereas mine...'

'Isn't.'

'Quite.'

'No problem,' said Evie.

'Here we are,' said Simon, placing two mugs on the coffee table.

'Mrs Ferris was nice, wasn't she?' said Evie.

Simon nodded.

'I know I was only supposed to be observing.'

'It was a good job you were there,' said Simon, a wry smile playing at the corners of his mouth. 'That was my first feline-related crime.'

'Oh, ha, ha—alright, Mr Wonderful, what sort of crimes do you normally work on?'

'All sorts.'

'Give me an example,' said Evie, taking a swig of coffee. 'What was that thing you were working on last week?'

Simon sighed. 'Depressing one; a bloke who suspected his wife of bonking his brother.'

'Shit, really?—And was she?'

'Yes,' said Simon, 'energetically and frequently.'

Evie, having just taken another sip of coffee, swallowed and gasped simultaneously with the unavoidable and unbecoming loss of coffee from her nostrils.

'You alright?'

Coughing and spluttering, Evie managed to assure Simon that she was fine. 'It was the energetically bit that got me,' she snorted. 'That and the fact that it was,' she bit into her hand and suppressed another giggle. 'And the fact that it was frequent. Sorry, it's not funny, not really.' She raised her mug towards her mouth. 'Carry on, I'm alright now.'

'Right. Well, I also investigate stalkers; they're mostly sad lonely sods, but you have to be careful, some are seriously deranged. Then there are the people suspected of benefit fraud; you'd be amazed at what lengths people go to in order to claim a disabled parking permit.'

'Do you ever get asked to find missing persons?'

Simon nodded. 'Had one the other month actually.'

'And did you find them?'

'I did, but...' he sighed. 'But that was Adam's speciality.'

Chapter 6

Yorkshire, Sunday 28th April (lunch at *Honeypot Cottage*)
2013

Evie, in T-shirt and pyjama bottoms, was in the kitchen ironing her Indian-cotton, multicoloured skirt.

From the hallway, Sarah called, 'Evie, Simon's here.'

'I'm nearly ready,' she yelled.

Simon wandered into the kitchen and looked Evie up and down. 'I didn't realise it was to be an informal affair. Shall I go and change?'

'Very funny.' She snatched her skirt from the board and switched off the iron. 'Two minutes,' she said, dashing past Simon. 'Be a dear and put the ironing board away for me.'

Sarah watched as Simon struggled with the board. 'Do you want me to do it?'

'I refuse to be defeated by a bloody ironing board.' He gave the board a final shove before kicking the cupboard door shut. 'There we are, easy,' he declared.

The door immediately sprang back open. He skipped to the right as the board fell towards him. 'Shit, bloody thing's got a mind of its own.'

Sarah failed to stifle a laugh.

Muttering, Simon squared his shoulders and approached the ironing board again. 'This is war.'

Evie appeared at the door, tapping her foot. 'Come on, Simon, this is no time for fun and games.'

'See you later, Sarah, and good luck with this confounded contraption,' he said, thrusting the board towards her.

At the end of the road, Simon said, 'So, are you going to give me a clue?'

'Sorry?'

'A clue to where we're going?'

'Oh, right, yes, sorry. The cottage is in Ripon, in Skeldale Close…'

'I know it,' said Simon. 'Under the Ripon bypass and turn left; very secluded round there. I assume it backs onto the River Skell.'

Evie nodded. 'That's the one.'

Alex threw open the front door. 'Evie, thanks for coming.' He looked behind him, bent down to kiss Evie on her cheek, lowered his voice and blurted. 'Try not to look too shocked when you see who I'm with now.'

A woman appeared from the kitchen, wiping her hands on a tea towel.

'Darling, look, it's Evie,' said Alex, straightening up and sweeping back his hair.

Evie started and reached for Simon's arm.

'Evie, how lovely,' said the woman. 'Gracious, you look just like your mother.' She extended her hand towards Simon. 'And you must be the boyfriend.'

'Hardly,' said Simon, glancing at Evie's hand, now clamped on his arm.

'Simon, this is Martha,' said Alex. 'Martha, this is Simon, Evie's um…?'

'Friend and business partner,' said Simon, shaking Martha's hand, 'pleased to meet you.'

'And what business is that?' asked Martha.

Alex threw his arms wide. 'You'll never guess.'

Martha sighed.

'He's an actual bona fide private investigator,' declared Alex.

'How exciting,' said Martha. Shifting her gaze towards Evie, she added, 'So what's your role in the enterprise—not just making the tea, I hope?'

'Yes, that's right,' said Evie, as her eyes flicked from Alex to Martha.

'Evie, that's not true at all,' exclaimed Simon.

'What isn't?'

'You don't just make the tea.'

Evie frowned. 'What?'

Martha narrowed her eyes. 'Alex,' she growled.

'What, my precious?'

'Don't you 'what' me; you didn't warn her, did you?'

Alex turned doleful eyes towards her.

'Oh, for goodness sake,' exclaimed Martha, taking Evie's hand. 'Come with me to the kitchen.'

'I bought flowers, but I've left them in the sink back at the flat.'

'Oh, Evie, don't worry about that—come on.'

Evie allowed herself to be led away. At the kitchen door, Martha whirled round. 'Gerry will be here soon. I suppose you haven't told him either.'

Alex shook his head. 'I wasn't sure how to.'

'Honestly, you're hopeless,' said Martha. 'I'll talk to Evie, you sort out the drinks and while you're doing that you can explain everything to Simon—the poor man looks totally baffled.'

Evie sat on a stool at the central breakfast-island while Martha bustled around adding final touches to salads and dips. 'I don't know what to say really,' she said, pouring wine and handing a glass to Evie. 'It must seem odd, me being with Alex.'

Evie concentrated on her wine.

'I don't know if your mother told you, but we met Alex at Cambridge.'

'I think she mentioned it.'

'And did she tell you about me and Alex?'

Evie shook her head.

'I'm not surprised,' said Martha. 'I was besotted with him, you see. Your mother told me to be careful; said he'd love me and leave me.' Martha gave a nervous laugh. 'And she was right, of course. Alex and I were together for a few months, happy, or so I thought, but once he got that offer from MIT he was off without a backward glance.' She sipped her wine as she concentrated on a recalcitrant tomato. 'This knife needs sharpening.'

'Give it here, you just need to be firm,' said Evie, as she sliced the tomato into quarters. 'But you're back together now?'

Martha shrugged. 'Yes, I still can't believe it.' She placed the quartered tomato in a neat pattern in the centre of the salad. 'I hadn't thought about him for years, so when I saw him again, at your mother's funeral, it was quite a shock.'

'But he was working at the University with Mum and Dad; surely you must have met up with him before?'

Martha shook her head. 'No, I knew he was working there, your mother told me, but I never contacted him.'

'But why not?'

'Too embarrassed,' said Martha, clearing her throat. 'You see, when he told me back then that he was going to America, I'm afraid I made a complete and utter fool of myself. I begged him not to go, I was hysterical. Sobbing, shouting, the full works.'

'I shouldn't think Alex would even remember that,' blurted Evie. She gasped and covered her mouth. 'Oh, sorry, I didn't mean, Christ, that sounded…'

Martha threw back her head and whooped. 'No, you're absolutely right, Evie, he didn't. He and I spoke at the funeral and he told me all about his ten years in America and how brilliant it'd been. Said I'd been an idiot not to go with him and…'

'He'd asked you to join him?'

Martha nodded. 'Sort of.'

'Sort of?'

'You know, an offer given in a half-hearted manner. I knew he didn't mean it. Anyway, Jean's dad, your grandad, of course, had just been diagnosed with dementia, she needed all the support she could get, I couldn't just abandon her.'

'So, you gave up the love of your life to help Mum. That was an amazing thing to do. I, well, I didn't know.'

Martha lowered her eyes. 'Not such an amazing thing to do, Evie, I'm not a saint. I stayed because it was the easiest option. I could see that, mentally, Alex had already left me. His mind was on the opportunities ahead. I would have been neglected within weeks, days even.'

Evie took a gulp of wine. 'Knowing Alex,' she said, 'You may be right.'

'Anyway, we talked for ages at the funeral and we just seemed to slip into a companionable relationship. We started meeting once a week for lunch.'

Evie blushed. 'But ever since Mum's funeral Alex has, well he's...'

'Dated young, blonde, ditsy women,' said Martha.

Evie's blush deepened.

'Whereas I'm old, grey and serious.'

'I wouldn't say you're old.'

'Just grey and serious.'

Evie grimaced. 'No, I didn't mean that either, I meant...'

'That I'm not in my twenties. It's alright, Evie,' said Martha, with a warm smile. 'I'll actually be fifty-three this year.'

'That's how old Mum would be.'

Martha reached across and patted Evie's arm. 'I know.'

Evie took another gulp of wine.

'At our lunches, he'd spend the entire time telling me about whatever new girlfriend he was with. Saying how wonderful everything was, but I wasn't convinced he was happy, not really; he seemed lost. My heart ached for him.'

'I'm afraid I lost patience with him years ago,' said Evie. 'He was old enough to be their fathers.'

'A slight exaggeration.'

'Possibly, but even so...'

'He even suggested that I should get myself a young man. I mean, can you imagine?'

'But you were looking after your mum, weren't you?'

Martha nodded. 'Your mum was marvellous, a great support to me. It was so awful, her dying like that in a stupid car accident.' She swallowed. 'Anyway, after her death I struggled on as my mum's sole carer. Nearly nine years, but I don't think that ever once impinged on Alex's consciousness.'

'Didn't that make you cross?'

'You'd have thought so, but no,' said Martha, emptying a large bag of plain crisps into a ceramic bowl. 'I enjoyed the time with him. I looked forward to seeing him each week. It was a couple of hours of escapism, free from responsibility. It was liberating.'

Evie smiled. 'Yes, I can understand that.'

'And then, last year, just before Christmas, my mother died and, I know it's a terrible thing to say, but I felt relief. At last, I was free.'

'It's isn't a terrible thing to say, not at all,' said Evie.

'Alex and I spent Christmas and New Year together and, clichéd as I know this sounds, we kissed at the stroke of midnight and that was it. We've been together ever since.'

'Sarah said you had a man in your life now.'

'Oh, yes, you're living with Sarah Watson these days. Lovely girl, astute and hard-working.' Martha's eyes twinkled. 'What made her think I had a man in my life?'

Evie's face flushed. 'I don't want to get her into trouble; she didn't mean...'

'She's not in trouble,' she said, 'I'm just intrigued.'

'Something to do with a new hairstyle and shoes,' said Evie, burying her face in her wine glass.

Adopting an austere expression, Martha remarked, 'As I said, a very astute young lady, that Sarah Watson.'

Evie snorted.

The kitchen door burst open and Gerry strode in. Taking in the sight of Evie and Martha collapsed over the kitchen counter in fits of laughter, he staggered backwards and exclaimed, 'Well, I never.'

Evie spun round on her stool and raised her glass. 'Hi, Dad. Look who...'

'Hi, love,' he replied, before turning his attention to Martha. 'I thought Alex was winding me up. Martha Green, as I live and breathe, how lovely to see you again. It's been years; well, I suppose it's been...'

Dabbing at her eyes with a paper towel, Martha swallowed. 'Oh, Gerry, hi there, it's so lovely to see you too. And yes, it has been ages. It's been nine years, Gerry. We haven't seen each other since Jean's funeral.'

Gerry nodded. 'I was sorry to hear about your mother.'

'It was a quiet funeral. Just family.'

'No, no, I quite understand.'

'Has Alex sorted you out with a drink?'

'No, not yet. When he said who he was with, well, I...'

'Wine?'

'Smashing,' he said, accepting a glass.

'Where's Charlotte?' asked Evie.

'In the garden with Alex and Simon.'

Martha smiled. 'Shall we go and join them?'

A flurry of blonde curls was ducking and darting between trees and bushes, avoiding the clutches of Simon, while Alex leaned back against a tree trunk gasping for breath. 'Oh, to be young again.'

'Come on, you two,' exclaimed Evie. 'Surely you're not going to let a child defeat you.'

'Can't catch me, can't catch me,' cried Charlotte, darting left and then right. 'Hurray, I win, I win.' She jumped in the air, flung her arms above her head and promptly fell backwards into a flower bed, giggling.

'Food's served.'

Alex hauled Charlotte up and attempted to remove twigs and leaves from her curls as they made their way towards the patio.

'Come on, you two,' said Martha. 'I've set your place next to Uncle Alex, Charlotte, alright?'

'And can Evie sit next to me, too?' said Charlotte.

'Check the nameplate next to yours,' said Martha. 'What does it say?'

Charlotte picked up the card. 'Evie Morgan. Brilliant!'

Alex settled Charlotte into her seat and leaned down to whisper in Evie's ear, 'She's saved me from myself, Evie. Martha's a bloody saint. Loves me for all my faults and foibles. I can't believe it, especially when I think about what I've put her through.'

Evie smiled up at Alex. 'Well, abandoning her for the bright lights of America was selfish, but I suppose you were only young and so...'

A shadow passed across Alex's face as he stared off into the distance. His eyes closed and he swallowed.

Charlotte grabbed her napkin and shook it open, nudging Alex's arm in the process. Blinking, Alex refocused on what Evie was saying.

'...there we are, the important thing is the here and now and I really hope you'll both be happy.' Flapping her napkin across her lap, Evie added in a quiet voice, 'She's certainly more suitable.'

Alex cleared his throat. 'As in not a bimbo.'

'You said it, Alex, you said it.' She leaned across to Charlotte. 'Shall I tuck your napkin in for you?'

Charlotte sent a frosty gaze towards Evie. 'I'm eleven years and eight months old. I'm not a baby.'

'Quite right, silly of me. On your lap, then.'

Simon and Evie arrived back at Simon's flat to find a large padded envelope on the hall floor. Evie picked it up and examined it. 'Where's this come from? There isn't a delivery on a Sunday.'

'It'll be my PO Box mail. Alan, he works at the post office, collects it, bundles it together and drops it off as and when,' explained Simon, as he hung his jacket up. 'Would you mind making a start on opening it? I'm desperate for the loo.'

Evie ripped open the envelope and removed a bundle of letters. She tucked the envelope under her arm and was about to sort through the letters when a high-pitched scream came from the bathroom. Dropping everything, she dashed out of the living room to find Simon, in the middle of the hallway, clawing at his back as he attempted to disentangle himself from a purring cat.'

'Oh, look at that, how adorable.'

'Adorable my arse, bloody thing jumped in through the window.'

Evie reached up. 'Here, let me. Did the nasty man startle you?'

Rubbing at his neck, Simon growled as the cat scuttled off towards the living room. 'Oh, no you don't,' he said, as he followed the cat. 'Evie, be a treasure and get some wine. There should be some in the fridge—come on shitface, here puss, puss.'

Evie entered the living room with two glasses of wine and smiled at the sight of Simon sitting on the settee, with the cat curled up on a cushion next to him, one paw dangling over the edge. She handed him his glass. 'He's so sweet.'

'Yes, well, I suppose he has a certain charm.' He took a sip of wine. 'I was wondering—is there a particular reason why my mail is currently festooned across the floor?'

'I thought you were being attacked.'

He stroked the cat. 'What, by this?'

'No, you cried out and I—oh, never mind.' She plonked her glass on the table, scooped up the mail and began sorting through it.

'Anything interesting?'

Evie rubbed her forehead.

'What's the matter?'

She studied the small white envelope she was holding. 'It's, well, it's addressed to Adam Trent.'

Simon put his glass down and took the envelope.

Evie reached for her own glass and took a mouthful. She watched Simon; his face was expressionless.

He sat, drawing his hand with a gentle firmness over the cat's back, as he read the letter. The purr of the cat was the only sound penetrating the stillness of the room. After a few moments he stopped stroking the cat and sighed.

'Well?' she said.

Simon took a deep breath. 'It's from someone called Paul Sharp. He's asking Adam if he'd be prepared to reopen his investigation into the disappearance of a woman called Alice Sharp.' He looked up. 'She's his mother, disappeared in 1992, when Paul was a baby.'

'But that's...' Evie started counting on her fingers.

'Twenty-one years ago.'

'Didn't Adam ever find her, then?'

'According to this letter, Adam found her in Strontian, Scotland, but by the time Paul's father arrived, she'd disappeared again.'

'Do you remember the case?'

'Vaguely. But I only started working with Adam in 1991.'

He glanced down at the letter again. 'It says here that he and Julia, that's his girlfriend, are off to Strontian...'

'Well, she's hardly going to have gone back there,' exclaimed Evie.

'No, he says he's following up on Adam's suggestion that his mother may have adopted a new identity.'

'So, what are you going to do?'

'Find Adam's file on the case.' He pulled open the third drawer of Adam's cabinet and searched through the files. 'That's odd. It's not here.'

'I thought you said he was a meticulous filer.'

'He was.' He slammed the drawer shut and yanked open the top one. After a few moments of searching, he announced that it wasn't there either. Evie made her way over and shoved Simon out of the way. 'Let me look. Presumably he filed his notes under Sharp.'

Simon raised his eyebrows. 'Obviously. Except he didn't, it's not there.'

'What about under 'Alice'?'

'Looked.'

'OK, let's think—what about the woman's maiden name, what was that?'

Simon gave her a pitying look. 'I'd need the bloody file to tell you that.'

'Well, that's easily solved. You just need to ring Adam.'

Simon frowned.

'What?'

'I told you, we don't communicate.'

'But surely…'

'I don't even know where he is, Evie.'

'You said he was in Ireland.'

'Ireland's a big place.'

'But you're a private investigator, couldn't you…?'

'Just let it go, Evie,' said Simon.

'So, what *are* we going to do?'

'I don't know. Let me think about it.'

Chapter 7
London, Bexleyheath, May 2013

Over breakfast, the day after his return from Scotland, Paul sat with his father in the kitchen.

'Right. So, let me get this straight,' said James. 'You believe your mother trawled round graveyards in the dead of night...'

'I don't recall suggesting she went in the dead of night, Dad.'

'Nevertheless, you believe she trawled round graveyards until she found the name of a dead baby that she could steal. Is that what you're saying?'

'I am.'

'And you think that's a realistic scenario, do you?'

'I do. The problem is working out which name she stole, and...'

'If indeed she stole *any* name.'

'OK, *if* she stole a name, the problem is working out which one. Then, there's the small matter of finding her.'

'You're wasting your time. Even if you decide on one of those names, how many did you find again?'

'Fourteen, but only eight were young children or babies.'

'And how exactly are you going to trace them? The census data from the seventies is private and it will remain so until 2070.'

'I *know*, Dad, I told you. That's why I wrote to Adam Trent, asking for his help.'

'It was a long time ago, Paul. He's probably retired and, even if he hasn't, what makes you think he'll agree to help? I had to call the search off back then because, well...'

'Because Mum emptied the savings account and you couldn't afford for him to carry on. I know, Dad, it's in the file.'

'That money was for your college fees,' said James. 'Still, I suppose I should be grateful, she did pay it back—eventually.'

Paul started. 'What? When?'

'On your sixteenth birthday.'

'Why didn't you tell me?'

'You didn't know she'd taken it in the first place, and so...'

'Oh, right, I see, and it didn't enter your head that I might have a bloody right to know.'

'How would it have helped?'

'It would have shown that she cared about me, for one thing.'

'Well, she didn't include an address for you to contact her so, as I said, what was the point?'

'Couldn't you trace where the money came from?'

'It was cash, Paul. It arrived by private courier.'

Paul removed his glasses and wiped the lenses on his T-shirt. 'Dad?'

'What?'

'Assuming Adam Trent is still in business and assuming he agrees to reopen the case, would you be able to help, you know, with some money.'

'Sorry, I'm not going down that road again.'

'I'm just asking for some financial help. I'll pay you back.'

'I don't doubt that,' said James, 'but the answer's still no.'

'Why?'

'Because I don't want you to get hurt.'

'What makes you think I'm going to be hurt?'

James closed his eyes and sighed deeply. 'It's complicated.'

'Oh, for God's sake, Dad, *it's complicated*? Is that the best you can come up with?'

James shrugged.

'You know something, don't you? Jesus, you know why she left—and you can stop shaking your head, I don't believe you. I deserve to know.'

'Paul, I, I can't, I'm sorry.'

Paul pushed his chair back and stormed out.

'Where are you going now?' demanded James.

'Out,' yelled Paul, as he slammed the front door.

James remained seated at the kitchen table, listening to the reverberation of the front door as it echoed around the house. Barbara wandered in. 'I take it that was Paul leaving?'

James nodded.

'Have you two had a row?'

'Not as such.'

Barbara sat next to James and took his hand into hers.

'I gave him the file last month,' said James.

'All of it?'

'I removed the letter.'

'You knew this day would come. At least he's being open with you.'

James looked deep into Barbara's eyes. 'He thinks I know why she left.'

'Well, you do.'

'I know what she said in the letter, Barbara. I just don't understand why she fell apart when she did. After all, she'd seemed happy with me. She knew I'd protect her. I don't know what to do? Should I tell Paul?'

'That's not really my decision to make, is it?'

'No, I suppose not,' said James, a frown creasing his brow. 'Barbara, I've been thinking, during those early months, after Paul's birth, she spoke to you more than me. Did she give you any clue, any clue at all, about why she had to leave?'

Barbara closed her eyes.

'Barbara?'

'Oh, James, she was just so confused, so damaged by the whole experience. She tried to love Paul, she really did.'

Paul pressed the bell and held it down until the door was snatched open

'What the hell...? Paul, whatever is it, lad?'

'I'm sorry, Mr Forrest. Is Julia in?'

'Yes, lad. Come in, come in.' He strode to the bottom of the stairs. 'Julia,' he yelled. 'Paul's here. Hurry up, he's in a bit of a state.'

Paul wiped at his eyes as Julia came pelting down the stairs.

'Paul?'

'It's Dad. He refuses to help.'

'I'll sort out some tea.'

'Thanks, Dad—come on, Paul.' She took his hand and led him upstairs. 'Sit down and tell me what happened.'

'He just doesn't get it, Julia. He refuses point blank to help.'

'Well, that's not entirely true, is it? He let you see the file.'

'He did, but I'm not convinced he showed me everything.'

'What do you mean?'

'He's knows something, Julia, I'm certain of it. He knows why Mum left, but he denies it, he says, *it's complicated*, for God's sake!'

'Oh, come on, Paul, you sound like a petulant child. We've found all those names and...'

'And that's the other thing. He thinks that exercise was a complete waste of time.'

Julia took a deep breath. 'Yes, and you and I both know he could be right. Still, we can make a start, apply for copies of the birth certificates. That will give us the parents' names and then...'

'And then that's basically it,' said Paul. 'As Dad so helpfully pointed out, the data is protected until 2070.'

There was a gentle tap at the door. 'Julia, it's me. I've brought you both some tea.'

'Come in, Mum, it's quite safe.'

'Yes, well, I knew that. I just didn't want to—anyway, here you are.' She placed the tray on Julia's desk. 'I made the ginger snaps last night.'

Julia screwed her face up.

'You may not like them, madam, but Paul does.'

'Thank you, Mrs Forrest.'

'You're welcome.' At the door, she turned. 'I don't mean to pry,' she said, 'but Julia's told us what you're trying to do, and we fully understand.' She pulled her cardigan a little tighter. 'I expect your father's finding all this rather difficult.'

'He's certainly not prepared to help in any way.'

'Oh dear, I'm sorry to hear that. Now, if you need financial support…'

'Oh, Mrs Forrest, I couldn't poss…'

She held her hand up. 'Nonsense, you're almost family. George and I will do what we can—enjoy the biscuits,' she said, pulling the door to behind her.

'Right, let's see what we need to do to access those records,' said Julia, reaching for her laptop.

Paul slumped back, selected a ginger snap and closed his eyes to the sound of Julia tapping away on her keyboard.

After a ten-minute search through several links, Julia looked up from her laptop. 'Paul, there were six ginger snaps on that plate,' she exclaimed.

'And each one was delicious—so, what have you found?'

'Nothing that's going to cheer you up, I'm afraid. It seems that in order to search recent census data you need to be an 'approved researcher', whatever that means.'

'Fucking brilliant.'

Chapter 8
Yorkshire, May 2013

Having decided to leave well alone, Simon found himself dialling Paul's number.

'Mr Paul Sharp?'

'Yes.'

'This is Simon Trent, Adam Trent's partner.'

'Jesus, what? Bloody hell, hi there. Adam got my letter then?'

'Yes and no.'

'Excuse me?'

'*I* got your letter, Mr Sharp. My brother no longer works here.'

'Oh, right, so does that mean you can't help me?'

'Not necessarily.'

Paul took the phone away from his ear and clutched it to his chest.

'Mr Sharp, are you still there?'

Simon waited and called out again, louder. 'Hello, are you still there?'

'Sorry, hello. Yes, I'm here.'

'Good. Right, well my main problem is the file covering your mother's case. It seems to be missing.'

'I've got all, well *some*, of my Dad's notes and stuff from back then if that helps,' said Paul.

'Does that include correspondence from my brother?'

'Yes.'

'Excellent, maybe we can work with that. Are you able to come to my office? It's in Northallerton.'

'Absolutely. Oh, I can't believe it. I can't thank you enough, really, I can't. Julia and I managed to get hold of masses of names when we were up in Scotland, and...'

'Mr Sharp, I can't promise that I'll be able to find your mother. After all, we're talking about an event that occurred over twenty years ago.'

'Anything you can do, anything. I'd really appreciate it.'

'As long as we're all clear on that matter.'

'We are.'

'Right then, it's the sixth today so, how about in a couple of weeks? Monday the twentieth of May, at 2pm, are you free?'

'Yes, yes, thank you, that's fantastic.'

'And could you bring a photograph of your mother?'

'I can, but it was taken over twenty years ago.'

'That doesn't matter, it may help. I'll text the address to you.'

'Thank you again, Mr Trent.'

'Oh, before you go,' said Simon, 'what was your mother's maiden name?'

'Gray, with an 'a'.'

'One or two slices of toast?'

'Two please,' groaned Sarah. 'Where did the weekend go?'

'The usual place, Saturday followed Friday, and then...'

'Just hand me that coffee.'

Evie set Sarah's mug down and gave a small curtsey.

'Sorry,' mumbled Sarah. 'I hate Mondays.'

'Will you remember to have a word with that colleague of yours, what's his name?'

Lathering a mountain of butter and Marmite on her toast, Sarah said, 'Brian Metcalf. Are you absolutely sure about this?'

'You said he was a fount of knowledge.'

'He is. I told you, he's obsessed.'

'Brilliant. Shall I...? Hang on, that's my phone—hi, Simon.'

72

'Evie,' he said. 'I've just spoken to Paul Sharp and…'

'So, we're taking the case, then?'

Sarah jigged up and down. 'Ooh, exciting, what case?'

'Stop it!'

'What?'

'Not you, I was talking to Sarah.'

'This is confidential stuff, Evie.'

'I *know* that. My lips are sealed.'

Sarah pouted. Evie thumped her.

'I haven't made any promises. I've simply agreed to talk to him. He's coming to see me, sorry, us, in a couple of weeks so, can you pop up later to…?'

'I might have an appointment.'

'You *might* have an appointment?'

'I won't know for certain until…' Evie glanced at Sarah.

'I'll ring him now,' said Sarah.

'…Sarah's ringing him now.'

'Ringing who?'

'A colleague. He's an expert on crime.'

'Committing or solving?'

'Most amusing—hang on, what?'

'Nothing,' said Simon.

'No, I'm talking to Sarah.'

'He'll see you at 10:30 this morning,' said Sarah.

'Did you hear that, Simon?'

'Yes, 10:30. So, when will you be back?'

'Oh, before lunch, I should think.'

Sarah sniggered. 'You wish; it's not beyond the bounds of possibility you'll be there all day and all night.'

'What was that? What did Sarah say? Something about all night?'

Evie again thumped Sarah. 'Ignore her, it's her attempt at humour. I'll ring you when I get back from the meeting.'

Full of vigour and enthusiasm, Evie met Brian Metcalf in his tiny office in the bowels of the library. Six hours later, laden with notes, books and bulging files, she staggered back to the flat and collapsed onto her bed. Sarah returned an hour later to find her still lying there. 'Productive meeting?'

Evie pushed herself up into a sitting position. 'He's very keen, isn't he?'

'I did try to warn you.'

Evie swung her legs over the side and rubbed her neck. 'He talked for two hours. Then he took me to the canteen for lunch, where he continued to talk. We went back down to his office where he carried on for another *three* hours.' She nodded towards her desk. 'That lot should keep me busy for years.'

'Have you been up to Simon yet?'

'No, I rang him at lunchtime and told him I may be some time.'

'Do you fancy a coffee?'

'Oh, yes please.'

Sarah joined Evie on the bed and handed her a mug. 'Here you go.'

Evie took a sip. 'Lovely, lovely.'

'Is that an old writing slope I espy on your desk?'

Evie nodded. 'It belonged to Mum.'

'My mum's got a similar one. I love them.'

'This one has a secret compartment under the pen tray.'

'It'll have other ones too.'

'I don't think so.'

'I beg to differ. I bet it has.'

'Really?'

'Mum said some of the compartments are more secret than others.'

'How intriguing,' said Evie, handing her mug to Sarah and hauling herself over to her desk. 'Show me.'

'OK, let's see,' said Sarah, exchanging mug for slope. 'Right, here's the so-called secret tray compartment.' She ran her fingers along the sides and back of the newly-exposed section, muttering and mumbling under her breath as she did so. 'Ah, here's something. Have a feel.'

Evie did as she was told.

'Do you feel that little depression?'

Evie nodded

'Give it a firm press.'

'Like this?—Oh, wow,' she exclaimed, as a little drawer shot out from the back panel.

'Anything exciting?'

'Aside from the fact that I didn't know it was there, no, it's empty.'

Sarah grinned. 'Now, remove the drawer and run your fingers along the exposed sides and back.'

'There's another depression.'

'Press it.'

Evie looked up at Sarah. 'Nothing.'

'Didn't you hear that click?' asked Sarah.

'I heard something.'

'Lift up the writing slope and look at the depth of the compartment inside and then look at the outside of the box, from the side.'

Evie looked.

'What do you notice?'

'They're different.'

'Which implies…?'

'There's another compartment underneath?'

'Precisely,' said Sarah. 'Run your hands gently just along the edge, *under* the box.'

'Which edge?'

'Both.'

Evie started. 'Bloody hell, I can feel a button thingy.'

'Can you grab it with your fingertips?'

'Just about.'

'Give it a yank.'

Evie pulled the button and a drawer, the same width as the writing slope, popped out from the base.

'Told you,' exclaimed Sarah. 'Some compartments are more secret than others. Anything exciting in that one?'

Evie pulled the drawer fully open. 'Letters, tied up with a blue ribbon,' she exclaimed. She removed one of the bundles and her eyes filled with tears. 'They're addressed to Mum.'

'Oh, Evie, how romantic. I expect they're from your dad, you know, when they first started dating.'

Evie nodded. 'Yes, I expect so,' she said, replacing them and slamming the drawer shut. She picked up her mug and took another sip.

Sarah picked up her own mug and took a sip.

They peered at each other over the rims.

'Right, I'll let you get on.'

'Thanks for showing me the compartments and everything.'

Sarah stood. 'Have you finished your coffee?'

Evie nodded.

'Give it here, then.'

The moment Sarah closed the door, Evie repeated the sequence of presses and pulls to open the bottom drawer of her mother's writing slope. She untied the blue ribbon and looked again at the address on the top envelope. She frowned and checked the addresses on the others. Three simply bore the name, *Jean,* in purple ink, the rest were addressed c/o a property in Bootham. She glanced at her mother's photograph. 'I don't understand, Mum,' she said. 'Why have these letters been sent care off Birch House, Grosvenor Terrace, Bootham? We've never lived in Bootham.'

Taking a deep breath, Evie slid the single sheet from the top envelope. It was dated August, 2002.

My beloved,

It's killing me not being able to call you but you're absolutely right, the risk would be too great. I miss being able to hold your hand, to smell your hair. I think of you every day, every minute really. And then, when I see you and we have to pretend—it tears me apart.

I've managed to book a room for next weekend. You said you might be able to get away. It's where we went last time. Our idyll.

Not wanting to be over-dramatic but just so you know, my heart beats faster and my soul feels lighter as our time together draws nearer. Please, please say you can make it.

Love you xx

The letter dropped from Evie's hand. She leaned back and closed her eyes. Her breathing was ragged. She removed another and another, reading them with growing fascination before laying them down in sequential order on the floor. She started at the sound of her mobile vibrating across her desk. It was Simon. She swallowed and picked up. 'Hi there,' she said brightly.

'Hi there, yourself,' said Simon. 'Where are you?'

'In my room.'

'Is everything alright?'

'What? Yes, why shouldn't it be? What do you mean?'

'I thought you were supposed to be coming up to discuss the Alice Sharp case?'

'Shit, I forgot.'

'You forgot? Are you sure you're alright?'

'Yes,' she exclaimed. 'No. Oh, I don't know.'

'I'm coming down.'

Sarah answered the door. 'Oh, hi there, Simon. Sorry about Evie being so late, it wasn't...'

'Excuse me,' he said, pushing past. 'I need to see Evie.'

'She's in...'

Simon dashed down the corridor and threw open Evie's door.

'… her room,' said Sarah, shutting the front door.

'Oh, Simon,' wailed Evie, thrusting an envelope towards Simon. 'Read this.'

'It's addressed to your mum.'

'I *know*. Read it.'

He read it.

'Well?'

'I'm assuming it's not from your dad.'

'Oh, brilliant. I can see why you're a private eye— obviously it's not from Dad, look at the address for a start.'

'Not yours?'

'No! We've lived in Fulford Park since I was a baby.'

'And I assume you've no idea who lives at Birch House.'

Evie raised her eyes to the ceiling.

Simon glanced at the letters laid out at Evie's feet. 'More of the same?'

Evie nodded.

'What do you want me to say?'

'Tell me straight. How would you interpret it?'

'Speaking dispassionately, as a private investigator, I'd say these letters imply an extramarital affair. It's not unusual for lovers to communicate via a third party.'

'I, I agree but, Jesus, Simon, my mother; bonking some other bloke. Do you think Dad knew?'

'I couldn't say, Evie.'

'No, of course you couldn't, stupid question.' She stood. 'I need a drink, join me?'

'Never say no to a drink. What have you got?'

She shrugged. 'No idea. I think there's some wine in the fridge, there usually is.'

'Do you want me…?'

'No, I'll get it.'

'Have you looked at the others?' said Evie.

'No, I wasn't sure if you'd want me to.'

78

She held up a bottle of Sauvignon Blanc. 'This is all there was, OK?'

'Fine. Glasses?'

'Shit.'

'Sit down, I'll get them.'

Evie looked up as Simon returned. 'The first one's dated the seventeenth of August, 2002 and the last is dated the twenty-first of May, 2004. That's two weeks before she died, Simon.'

Simon poured the wine and handed Evie a glass. She gulped down most of it and Simon topped it up. 'You alright?'

'I feel strangely detached, as if it were a case we're investigating.' She took another swig of wine. 'We can, can't we?'

'What?'

'Investigate, you know even though we've taken on the Sharp case.'

'Do you want to?'

Evie nodded.

'Then yes, we can.'

'So, what do we do first?'

'We need to find out who lives at Birch House in Bootham for a start. I take it none of the letters are helpfully signed with the full name of the gentleman concerned.'

'You take correctly.'

'Worth a try,' said Simon, with a grin. 'Can I use your laptop?'

'Help yourself.'

He took a sip of wine and began tapping at the keys. After a moment he said, 'Now that's interesting.'

'What?'

He turned the screen to face Evie. 'Look who lives in Birch House.'

'Martha Green,' exclaimed Evie, taking a gulp of wine.

'Thus explaining why the letters were sent there.'

'Because Martha was Mum's friend.'

Simon nodded.

'So, this bloke, whoever he is, writes to Mum c/o Martha, who then hands the letters on to Mum.' Evie ran her hand through her hair. 'So, that means Martha knew Mum was having an affair. Do you think she also knew the bloke?'

Simon shrugged. 'Difficult to say really.'

Evie frowned. 'A few of the letters did just have Mum's name on the envelope though, implying...'

'That the gentleman in question hand-delivered them to Martha.'

'So, that means Martha must know his identity.'

'Possibly,' said Simon. 'Or it could mean he was in the area and slipped them through the letterbox while Martha was out.'

'Still...'

'There's no point speculating, Evie, let's move on. Where did you find the letters and was there anything else?'

Evie sighed. 'The letters were hidden in a secret drawer in my mum's writing slope. I only discovered it when Sarah popped in to see how I was after my meeting with Brian Metcalf.'

'Who?'

'Her colleague at the library who, oh, it doesn't matter now. What am I going to do, Simon?'

'Does the drawer come right out?'

'What?'

'The secret drawer, can you remove it?'

'I've no idea. Hang on.' Evie heaved herself up and went over to her desk. 'I wonder how Mum replied to the letters.'

'Depends,' said Simon. 'If the bloke was married, he probably had a similar arrangement at his end. If he wasn't married...'

'Mum would have written directly to him.' Evie grabbed hold of the drawer and yanked. She turned to face Simon with the drawer hanging down from her hand. 'Yes, it comes out.'

'So I see. Look underneath.'

She turned it upside down. 'There's something stuck to the underside.'

'Thought there might be. What is it?'

She peeled away the yellowing Sellotape. 'It's a leaflet advertising B&Bs in North Wales. It's from 2002.' She opened it up. 'One's been highlighted. A Country House B&B, it's in, um, Treeview?'

'How's that spelt?'

'T, R, E, F, R, I, W.'

'Let's see.' He bent over the laptop and began typing again. 'Trefriw, here we are. It's a small village on the B5106, not far from...'

Evie started. 'What road did you say?'

'The B5106.'

'That's the road where the accident occurred, Simon.' She took a deep breath, 'She was going to meet her lover.'

'It looks like it.'

'Oh, God,' she said, taking a few steps backwards and collapsing onto her bed. 'This is awful.'

'Look, are you absolutely sure you want to carry on with this?'

'No—yes—oh, I don't know. What do you think?'

'It's not for me to say, Evie.'

She pushed herself upright, leaned back against the headboard and reached for her glass. 'He must have been someone special. I know she loved Dad, really, she did, and yet this affair was going on for at least three years. I just don't understand.'

'Our meeting with Paul Sharp isn't for a fortnight. We've got plenty of time to make a start.'

'He doesn't come across as a Casanova type. In some of his letters he expresses concern for Charlotte's welfare and that, to me at least, implies an essentially good man.' She rolled off the bed to kneel amidst the pile of letters. 'And in at least one of them he accepts that Mum loves Dad. Hold on, I'll find it.' She selected one, dismissed it, looked again and dismissed that one too. 'Can't find it. Anyway, he said something like, *I know I can't have all of you, I accept that and respect you immensely for it...* or words to that effect. And in another he says something about wishing he'd listened to her and how different things could have been. As I read through them I actually began to feel sorry for the poor man.'

'I could see if I can book us into this Country House, what was it called?'

Evie glanced at the leaflet and frowned. 'Um, Er Stabel. Spelt; Y, R, one word, then, Y, S, T, A, B, L.'

'That's *Yr Ystabl*. If your mother and this gentleman friend...'

'*Gentleman friend*,' Evie exclaimed, 'have you slipped back into the nineteenth century?'

'Well, what do you suggest I call him?'

Evie swallowed. 'Sorry, you're being tactful, most unlike you.' She ducked to avoid a swipe that didn't come.

'As I was saying, if the pair of them stayed there regularly, the owners might remember them,' said Simon, as he punched in the B&B's number. 'Failing that, we can think about talking to Martha Green. OK?'

'Fine,' said Evie, reaching for the wine bottle and replenishing their glasses.

'Yes hello, I'm hoping you have two rooms available for a short stay before the twentieth of this month.'—'Oh, excellent, yes, my name's Simon Trent.'—'My card number; hold on.' He extracted his card and read out the number. 'That's great, thank you.'

'All booked,' said Simon. 'Alright?'

'It's hard to take in. Mum and Dad were, well, they seemed so happy,' said Evie, rubbing her forehead. 'Dad made two albums, one for me and one for Charlotte, with pictures of Mum from when they first met.' She staggered towards the bookcase. 'It's here somewhere—can't miss it, it's yellow with butterflies—shit, where the fuck is it?'

Simon steered her back towards the bed. 'Sit down; I'll look.' He topped up her wine glass and set the empty bottle on the floor. 'Drink this.'

Evie sat and sipped. 'I'm sure it's on the bottom shelf, I just...'

Simon held up a blue album covered with butterflies. 'Is this the yellow album you mean?'

'Ah, yes, that's the one,' said Evie, with a sheepish grin.

'So, I take it Charlotte has the yellow one.'

'Yes, alright, don't rub it in.' She patted the bed. 'Come on, bring your wine and I'll show you.'

Evie set her glass down on the bedside cabinet and opened the album. 'Here she is with Dad in 1985. They do look happy, don't they? She'd just started at York University as a lecturer. Dad had been there forever, he'd done his undergraduate and postgraduate studies there and then stayed on.'

'A bit different to my parents,' said Simon. 'Mum was a secretary and Dad worked in a factory. Adam and I were the first in the family to go to university.'

Evie smiled as she continued to turn the pages of the album. 'Oh, look, here's me and Mum at *Piglet Land.*' She peered at the date. 'In 1997, so I would have been about ten. I loved it there. Alex used to take us.'

'Your dad not keen on pigs, then?'

'What? No, I mean yes, he loves pigs, well, love is a bit strong, I suppose...'

Simon raised his eyes.

'Oh, I see, why Alex and not Dad—sorry,' she hiccupped, 'Dad was working in Africa.'

'Africa! What was he doing there?'

'Something to do with his research on the seventeenth century African slave trade,' said Evie. 'He was out there for three years—not permanently, he popped back home every few months—Mum stayed here.' She continued to flick through the album. She burst out laughing. 'Oh, look at this one,' she exclaimed.

Simon looked. 'What the...?'

'York University's Halloween do in 2001, doesn't Mum look amazing? She makes a surprisingly good witch. And look at Dad. He looks terrifying.'

Simon pointed at a masked figure. 'And judging by the overflowing locks of hair obscuring the eyes, I'd say that was Alex.'

Evie nodded. 'And that hideous gremlin-like figure he's holding is baby Charlotte.'

'And you are?'

Evie pointed. 'There!'

'That's never you. You look horrific.'

'Why thank you, kind sir.'

'Getting back to the matter in hand,' said Simon, 'we need a photo of your mum to show to the owners of the B&B. Are there any photographs of your mum taken between 2002 and 2004?'

'Dad put a load at the back,' said Evie, flicking through the pages.

'May I?'

Evie stroked the cover of the album before handing it to Simon. 'Need the loo. Back in a minute.'

Simon leaned back against the bed and opened the album. He examined each photograph with care.

He was still looking through the album when Evie returned. 'Sorry I took so long. I decided we could do with a coffee.'

'What?'

'I made coffee. Is that alright?'

'Yes, yes, fine.'

'So, did you find a suitable picture of Mum?'

'There are several possibilities—actually, do you mind bringing the whole album?'

'Why?'

'No particular reason,' said Simon, 'I just thought it'd be easier.'

Evie frowned. 'OK.'

Chapter 9

Loading their bags, Simon remarked, 'It's about a three and a half hour journey if we use mostly motorways.'

Evie groaned. 'Not too keen on motorways.'

'Me neither. So, I thought we'd go on a more scenic route and stop on the way for lunch. Is that alright with you?'

Evie nodded.

'Did you bring the photo album?'

'In my rucksack.'

'All set?'

'I think so, yes.'

'Welcome to *Yr Ystabl*, have you booked?'

'Yes,' said Simon. 'Simon Trent.'

'Ah yes. I'm not sure if I explained when I spoke with you, but we only have one single room available, all the others are double.' She handed over two keys. 'The rooms are through the stained glass door. Room 2 is the single, Room 3 the double, I hope that's alright. They both have en-suite facilities, their own entrance and terrace.' She looked down at their luggage. 'Is that everything?'

Simon nodded.

She turned the registration book towards them and rang the desk bell.

A man who could have been a prop for the Welsh rugby team, appeared from a back room and bowed. 'You rang, m'lady?' he said, in a deep husky voice.

Evie gave a nervous giggle.

'Oh, don't encourage him, for goodness sake. This is my husband, William. He'll show you to your rooms.' She butted William with her hip. 'Rooms 2 and 3,' she said. 'Hop to it.'

William backed out from behind reception, pulling at his forelock. Evie hooted with laughter as he began to make heavy weather of lifting their bags.

'William, will you stop messing about.'

'Very heavy bags these are, Branwen, my love.'

'Oh, give over.'

William winked at Evie and swung both bags across his shoulders with ease. 'This way.'

'Do the owners live nearby?' said Simon, as they followed William through the glass door.

'You're speaking to one,' said William. 'We finally took the place over from Branwen's parents in 2011. We've only recently finished all the refurbishment.'

Evie shot a glance towards Simon.

'Oh, dear,' said William, 'is there a problem? We've tried to keep all the original features, and...'

'No, no,' said Evie. 'It all looks fantastic, it's just we were hoping to speak to the people who ran the place in 2002.'

'To your wife's parents, it would seem,' added Simon.

'Oh, that won't be a problem,' said William. 'Branwen's parents still live in the village, opposite the post office, in the house where Dafydd, that's Branwen's dad, was born.'

'Would they mind if we asked them a few questions?'

'If it's about the history of this place, then I...'

'No, about my mum. Some questions about my mum, she often stayed here.'

'Right, I see,' said William, not seeing at all. 'I hope she gave you a good report of the place.'

'Absolutely,' said Simon. 'She said it was idyllic. Thoroughly recommended it, hence our presence here.'

'I hope you won't be disappointed. As for Dafydd, he'd be only too happy to talk to you. But I warn you, he does ramble on, it drives me nuts,' he said, glancing over his shoulder. 'Don't tell the wife I said that, Branwen may be small, but she's feisty.'

'We won't breathe a word,' said Evie.

He unlocked both rooms. 'Who's going where?'

'I'll take the single,' said Evie.

'It looks like I'm in the double, then,' said Simon.

'Right you are. Rucksack yours, Miss?'

Evie nodded.

'Any problems just ring through to reception. I'll let Dafydd know you'd like a word. He and Nerys take breakfast here every morning at 9:30, so you'll meet them then.'

The information leaflet in their rooms informed them that breakfast was a flexible affair, starting at 8:30 and running through to 10:30. Simon knocked on Evie's door at 9:15. 'Ready?'

'As I'll ever be.'

'Did you decide on a photograph?'

She patted her handbag. 'In here.'

'It'll be fine,' said Simon, taking her hand as they walked towards the main building.

Stepping through an archway from the reception area, they entered the dining room. The walls were painted white. The floor was covered in reclaimed oak with a white on green paint effect. The tables were light oak, as were the chairs, and each table sported a simple white linen runner with a small vase of wild flowers. Sunlight streamed in through two long, rectangular windows overlooking the garden.

Simon was pouring more coffee for Evie when a rotund, jovial man with a Father Christmas beard, approached their table. 'Dafydd Jones at you service. William said you wanted a word.' He pulled up a chair and plonked himself next to Evie. 'Nerys will be along in a bit, she's just fetching the register for 2002.' He dragged his chair closer. 'I understand that's when your mum stayed here.'

'Yes, that's right, and…'

'Nerys and I had some good times running this place back then, I can tell you.' He touched the corner of his nose. 'A lot of shenanigans went on, if you know what I mean.'

The colour drained from Evie's face.

Dafydd blundered on. 'Mind you, I expect it's the same these days. Human nature, can't change it, can you?'

A diminutive woman marched across the dining room. 'I do apologise,' she said, holding out her hand towards Evie. 'Nerys Jones. You must be Evie Morgan and,' she held her hand out towards Simon, 'you must be Simon Trent. Please excuse my husband.' She grabbed the back of his collar. 'Let these people finish their breakfast in peace, Dafydd.'

'It's alright, your husband was...' began Simon.

'Nonsense, cariad. You finish your breakfast. We can have a chat in *Y lolfa haul* when you're ready.'

'Sorry?' said Evie.

'The sun lounge, just through there,' she said, pointing towards the sign on a second stained-glass door.

Branwen set a tray with a coffee pot and cups on an oak table between two leather settees in the lounge. 'I've opened the windows. But, if you're cold just close them.'

'No, it's fine,' said Evie.

'We like to make the most of the sun when it shows its face,' said Dafydd.

'Yes, I've heard it tends to rain a lot,' said Simon.

'You could say that. Buckets it down here, it does.'

'You won't be disturbed,' said Branwen, 'our other guests have gone out for the day.'

Nerys dumped her carpet bag under the coffee table, collapsed back into a settee and patted the cushion. 'Come and sit next to me, Evie. The boys can sit opposite.'

'Come on, lad,' said Dafydd. 'I won't bite.'

'Now then,' said Nerys, 'William tells me you wanted to ask us about your mam. Is that right?'

'Yes, but it's all rather awkward,' said Evie.

Nerys smiled sweetly. 'We ran this hotel for twenty-five years, Evie, and we've seen some things, things that, well, no matter. The point is, you can ask us anything.'

Evie removed the photograph from her bag and handed it to Nerys. 'This is her.'

'Gracious me, you look just like her.'

Evie cleared her throat. 'She um, well it seems she stayed here with—oh dear.'

'Coffee, Mrs Jones?' said Simon, handing her a cup.

'Thank you—look, I think I know what you're trying to say,' said Nerys, handing the photograph to Dafydd and picking up an exquisite silver coffee spoon from the tray.

'You recognise her then?' said Simon.

Nerys closed her eyes for a moment before spooning two sugars into her coffee and stirring. 'Oh, yes, I…'

'It's that poor woman,' said Dafydd, as he too accepted a cup from Simon. 'Thanks—she came with that tall chap.' He winked at Simon. 'Obviously her…'

'Dafydd,' exclaimed Nerys, throwing her husband a warning glance. 'She was Evie's mam.'

'Oh, right. Yes, I see, sorry, cariad.'

Evie's eyes widened.

Simon handed her a coffee.

'Thanks,' she mumbled. 'She was killed in a car accident on the B5106.'

Nerys toyed with the coffee spoon, turning it over and examining it. She sighed before placing it with inordinate care onto her saucer. 'It was just up the road. A terrible thing. I'm so sorry.'

'I was seventeen, but my sister was only three. She didn't really understand,' said Evie, 'but I've always wondered what my mother was doing on a back-road in North Wales.'

Dafydd and Nerys exchanged a look.

Evie sent a pleading glance towards Simon.

'That's why we're here,' said Simon. 'Evie found some letters addressed to her mother.'

'They were in a secret compartment in her writing slope,' said Evie. 'My friend Sarah found them. I never even knew the drawer existed. She thought they were the love letters sent to my mum from Dad, but they weren't. I could see that straight away. The address wasn't our address for a start and it certainly wasn't Dad's handwriting. It was a shock; I mean you hear about that sort of thing...'

Dafydd snorted.

Nerys threw him her warning glance; a glance not to be ignored.

'...but you don't expect it to be happening right under your nose. I don't even know if Dad knows. He's never said anything—not the sort of thing you discuss over the evening meal with your children though, is it?' Evie's eyes filled with tears.

Simon jumped up and rushed to her side.

Nerys busied herself with refilling everyone's coffee cups.

Evie fumbled in her bag for a tissue, wiped her eyes and took a sip of the fresh coffee. She set her cup down with care and gave Nerys a weak smile. 'Thank you.'

'Croeso, cariad.'

'Where exactly did the accident happen?' said Evie, her voice hoarse.

'About two miles away, near Dolgarrog, just outside our friend Dei's farm,' said Nerys, taking hold of Evie's hand. 'Dei was driving his tractor late that night and your mam's car came around the bend, straight into his trailer, terrible. There was nothing he could do. Your mam died instantly.'

'A tragedy it was,' said Dafydd.

'Dei's wife used to work in reception back then and when she arrived the next morning she was telling us about it when your mam's, um...'

'Lover,' said Evie, with another weak smile.

'Yes, quite. Anyway,' continued Nerys, 'Sioned, Dei's wife, was telling us about it when he came down to reception.'

'He was in a terrible state. Ashen he was,' said Dafydd, 'saying she'd gone.'

'And then Sioned, all puffed up and full of herself, piped up and told him straight out that she was dead,' said Nerys. 'I swear I nearly floored the woman.'

'So, what, what did he do?' said Evie.

Nerys glanced at Dafydd.

Dafydd shrugged.

'Please, I need to know,' said Evie.

'He turned on his heels, cariad. Went back to their room, packed his bag and checked out,' said Dafydd.

'We never saw him again,' said Nerys.

'He had his own car with him, then?' said Simon.

Nerys nodded.

'Can you remember what name they used?' said Evie.

'I can remember your mother's name—or rather, the name she used when she stayed here,' said Nerys. 'It was Martha, Martha Green.'

Evie's eyes widened. 'Martha!' she exclaimed.

Nerys patted Evie's hand. 'It's alright. We found out, about a week after the accident I think it was, that her real name was Jean Morgan; she'd been identified from her driving licence originally and then, well then your...'

'My father came to identify the body?'

'Yes, cariad.'

'The report was in our local paper,' said Dafydd. 'The village was twittering about the affair for...'

'Dafydd,' exclaimed Nerys.

'I'm just saying.'

'I know what you're *just* saying, but...'

'It's alright, Mrs Jones, I can imagine. Did my father come here, you know, to ask questions?'

Nerys picked up her coffee spoon and again began to twirl it around, sunlight glinting off its polished surface. 'No, he never did, and I've always wondered about that. It seemed strange.'

'Did he know she'd been staying here?' said Simon.

'Oh, yes,' said Nerys. 'The police told him.'

'But you never spoke to him?' said Simon.

Nerys shook her head.

'We saw him though,' said Dafydd.

Evie frowned.

'He sat on the wall opposite the main entrance,' said Dafydd. 'Thought he was going to come in, I did. He'd get up, take a few steps towards the door and then go back and sit on the wall. I was going to go out and have a word, but…'

'I told him to leave the poor man alone,' said Nerys.

'So, do you think he knew she'd been with another man?'

'I think so, yes.'

Evie turned to Simon. 'He's never said a word. Do you think he knew who she was seeing?'

'It's possible,' said Simon.

Sounds of laughter drifted in through the open windows. Nerys sipped her coffee. 'We'd suspected they weren't married right from the start,' said Nerys.

Dafydd tapped the side of his nose. 'You get a feel for it after a while,' he said.

'I suppose arriving in separate vehicles is a bit of a giveaway,' said Evie, a hint of hysteria in her voice.

'I just can't remember the man's name,' said Nerys, 'well, apart from his surname, Green.' She stared off into the distance. 'Now what was his first name, it's sitting on my tongue, what *was* it?'

'So, could we have a look at the registers?' asked Simon.

'The registers, yes, yes, of course.' Nerys reached down and dragged her carpet bag out from under the coffee table.

'I've brought the ones covering the years from 2002 to 2004. Those are the years William told me you were interested in.' She placed them on the table and selected the one dated 2004. 'This is the one you need. The accident was in June.'

Evie took the register and held it to her chest. She closed her eyes and took a deep breath. 'Right, let's see.'

As Evie began to turn the pages, Nerys glanced towards her husband. 'Dafydd, can you remember the man's name?'

'Sorry, cariad.'

Evie emitted a gasp. 'This could be them,' she said. 'A Mr and Mrs B. Green. Booked and paid in advance. Eighteenth to the twentieth of June.'

'Bruce, no, Brian, no,' Nerys screwed her eyes shut. 'Barry, that's it! His name was Barry. At least, that what he said his name was.'

'Can you remember what he looked like?' asked Simon.

'Oh, dear, men are so much more difficult to describe somehow. Dafydd, how would you describe him?'

'Let me think,' said Dafydd, scratching his head.

'This is all for show,' said Nerys. 'He never forgets a face. Forgets the names of the simplest of items he does, but never a face. He just wants to milk the moment. Come on, Dafydd, this is serious.'

'Sorry, you're absolutely right, cariad. Now then, I remember he was a good-looking chap. Tall, as I said, at least six-foot, a gangly type, all limbs, if you know what I mean. And his hair, do you remember his hair, Nerys?'

'Oh, yes,' she exclaimed. 'It was forever falling over his eyes, used to drive me mad.'

'Probably not much help,' said Dafydd.

Simon set his coffee cup down. 'Evie, would you mind fetching your photo album.'

'What for?'

'Humour me.'

'Fine.'

Simon watched Evie as she made her way across the room. At the door, she turned. 'I love this door, the way the sunlight plays on the stained glass, so beautiful.'

Simon nodded and smiled.

As the door clicked shut, Nerys patted Simon's knee. 'It must have been a shock for her.'

Simon nodded. 'I think it's hit her quite hard.'

'Of course it has, poor girl. Her mother having an affair, not an easy thing to deal with, I quite understand. But, if it's any consolation, they did seem to be very much in love. Although I think he was the one most smitten.'

'But it all came to nothing in the end. Hen biti,' mumbled Dafydd.

'Hen bitty?'

'Hen biti, a terrible pity,' said Nerys. 'And it was. They seemed well suited somehow. You know, sometimes you can look at a couple and...'

At the sound of the door opening, all heads turned.

'Here it is,' announced Evie.

Simon stood and took the album. He flicked through until he found a photograph showing Jean, Gerry and Alex sitting at a large, round table. Without saying a word, he handed the album to Nerys.

Nerys looked at the photograph and gasped.

'What?' said Evie.

Nerys pointed to Alex. 'That's him. That's Barry.' She passed the album to Dafydd.

'Well, blow me down. She's right, that's him alright.'

'It can't be,' exclaimed Evie, 'that's Uncle Alex.'

'Your uncle?' exclaimed Nerys.

'Not an *actual* uncle, but as good as. I've known him since I was about seven. Are you *absolutely* sure?'

'Positive, cariad,' said Dafydd.

'But, but...' She sent Simon a withering look. 'Have you known all along?'

Simon took the album from Dafydd. He pointed to the group picture. 'It was when I was looking through the album. I was drawn to this photograph. Look at Alex, look at his body language. Do you see how he's positioned himself, turned towards your mum? And his expression, his eyes are fixed on Jean and they're shining,' said Simon. 'The moment I saw that, I knew he loved her. As to whether he was the lover, well, I couldn't be certain, until now that is.'

Chapter 10
Yorkshire, May 12th 2013

They arrived back in Northallerton late on Sunday night. Evie declined Simon's offer of a nightcap. 'I think I'll just get to bed,' she said. 'I still can't take it in, my mum and Alex. I mean, what the hell am I going to do? Should I say anything to Dad, or to Alex, and what about Martha? Presumably she's known all along and now she's Alex's bloody girlfriend. God, it beggars belief. Should I just let it go? I should probably let it go. Raking up the past won't change anything, will it? Oh, I don't bloody know.'

'Did you want me to answer any of those questions, or…?'

She took her rucksack from him. 'No, sorry. I'm rambling, there's no rush. I'll think about it.'

'Are you sure you're alright?'

Evie nodded.

'Why don't you come up tomorrow and I'll cook you lunch.'

'Oh, I don't know, Simon.'

'I'll do your favourite.'

'Mushroom risotto?'

'I was thinking more along the lines of beans on toast.'

'Sounds delightful.'

'Great, see you tomorrow, then.'

He bent to kiss her cheek just as she looked up.

Their lips met as the front door was thrown open.

'Ooh, I say, sorry. It's you. You're back.'

'There's no fooling you, is there?' said Simon.

'It's just I wasn't expecting you back until tomorrow. Is everything alright? Are you coming in, Simon?'

'No I won't, thanks. It's been a— well, anyway, I think Evie wants to get to bed. So, I'll love and leave you both. Goodnight.'

Sarah dragged Evie into the flat. 'Come on in, give me your rucksack, sit down, you look like you could do with a drink, or three.'

'No, really, I should…'

'Sorry, can't hear you,' said Sarah, pushing Evie into the living room. 'Now sit down. I'm desperate to hear what's been going on between you two.'

'Nothing's been going on.'

'Oh, right. So, I just imagined that passionate kiss, did I?'

'It wasn't a passionate kiss, it was just…'

'Whatever—white wine alright with you?'

Evie nodded as she sank into the sofa. 'Thanks.'

Sarah returned to the living room clutching a half-full bottle of Chablis and two glasses. 'Go on, tell me all.'

'You can wipe that expression off your face, it was nothing like that.'

'Weekend away, furtive kiss on the doorstep, come on.'

'It wasn't a furtive kiss. It was just an accidental coming together of lips.'

'Hah, good one; must remember that line,' hooted Sarah, pouring the wine. 'Cheers.'

'Cheers.'

'So, ignoring the *accidental coming together of lips*, you seem, well, you seem sad.'

'Oh, Sarah, I'm so confused.'

'I told you ages ago that he fancied you. He's a good bloke, and…'

'It's not that.'

'What then?'

Evie cleared her throat. 'Well, it all started…'

'So, I was right, you and Simon *are* an item. I knew it.'

'Sarah,' exclaimed Evie, 'will you just *listen*.'

'Sorry.'

'You remember those letters in Mum's writing slope.'

'The love letters from your dad to…'

Evie shook her head. 'Not from Dad.'

98

'What? Hell, you mean, shit, really? So, who? Oh, is that why you and Simon were in Wales?'

'Sarah, I'm trying to tell you.'

'Yes, right sorry, go ahead.'

Evie set her glass down with care. She took hold of a cushion and hugged it to her chest as she explained the events of the last couple of days, with Sarah's eyes growing wider at each new revelation.

'Well, bugger me.'

'Would *you* say anything?'

'Who to?'

'To *your* dad, you know, if you'd found out something like that.'

'I honestly don't know,' said Sarah. 'I suppose you have to ask yourself what would be achieved by opening up that particular can.'

'Nothing, I suppose, it's just, oh, I don't know,' said Evie. 'I've always considered Alex to be a decent bloke, and yet...'

'He's still the same Alex, you know,' said Sarah. 'He hasn't changed one iota.'

'No, but my view of him has.'

'That maybe so, but from what you've told me it seems he loved your mum and your mum presumably loved him. The fact that she drove away in the dead of night suggests to me that she'd decided to call it off, and...'

Evie started. 'Do you think so? I hadn't thought of that.'

Sarah shrugged. 'It's possible,' she said. 'And, if you're going to talk to anyone about this, then I suggest it should be Alex. After all, he's remained a good friend since your mum died, hasn't he?'

Evie nodded. 'He was brilliant actually, especially with Charlotte.'

'Well, there you are. Talk to him. You certainly can't keep it bottled up inside, otherwise it'll eat away at your soul and destroy it.'

'Bloody hell, Sarah; have you had a visit from the Jehovah's Witnesses while I was in Wales?'

'You know what I mean.'

'I'll think about it,' said Evie, with little conviction. 'Anyway, there's nothing I can do immediately, we've got a meeting with a new client next week and…oh, shit, bugger, damn.'

Sarah's eyes widened again.

Evie threw the cushion at her. 'I'm not supposed to talk about current cases.'

'It's that case Simon rang you about the other day, isn't it?'

Evie retrieved her wine glass, took a sip, hic-cupped and adopted an innocent expression.

'Hah! It is, isn't it? Come on, tell me. I won't breathe a word.'

'I'm not supposed to say anything, Sarah, it's confidential. I told you.'

Sarah looked around the room, leaned backwards, picked up a table lamp and scrutinized it.

Evie drained her glass and frowned. 'What *are* you doing?'

'Checking for bugs.'

Evie's wine slid down her chin. She clamped her mouth shut, but it continued to dribble out from the sides. Sarah, giggling, snatched a tissue from a box on the coffee table and thrust it towards Evie. 'Here.'

As she dabbed at the sides of her mouth, the wine found its way out through her nose. Coughing and spluttering, she gave up and threw the tissue aside.

'So, come on, give me a clue.'

'Is there any more wine in that bottle?'

Sarah topped up their glasses. 'I'm listening.'

'It's fascinating. It's a case Simon's brother was…'

'His who? What?'

'Simon's brother, Adam, he was…'

'I didn't know he had a brother.'

'Well, nor did I until the other day. Anyway, they had a falling out and he left.'

'I wonder why he's never mentioned it before.'

Evie shrugged. 'It all happened a long time ago; anyway, the point is, we've been asked to reopen this old case that Adam was working on. It was never resolved you see.'

'About what?'

'I can't say, really I can't.'

'Who's asked you to reopen the case?'

'I can't say.'

Sarah growled. 'OK, so, when was the case closed?'

Evie smiled. 'Now that I *can* tell you, the file was closed in 1992.'

'You're joking. That's, well, that's…'

'Twenty-one years ago, I know.'

Chapter 11
Yorkshire, Monday May 20th 2013

Paul and Julia stood on the doorstep looking at each other. 'Well, are you going to ring the bell, or what?'

Paul took a deep breath and raised his arm just as the door was flung open. 'Oh, hi there, can I help?'

'We're looking for Mr Trent.'

'Ah,' said Sarah. 'Are you here for a meeting?'

'Yes, that's right,' said Paul, craning his neck. 'Is he in?'

'Wrong flat,' said Sarah, nodding her head towards the steps. 'He's up there, top flat.'

'Oh, right, thanks. Sorry to disturb you.'

'No problem. I was just on my way back to work.'

'Up those steps, you say?'

Sarah nodded as she pulled her door shut.

Julia took Paul's hand. 'Are you ready for this?'

'I think so.'

At Simon's door, Paul's breathing was rapid and his face pale. He took another deep breath and rang the bell. 'Here we go.'

Evie opened the door and extended her hand. 'Paul Sharp?'

Paul nodded as he took her hand.

'Evie Morgan, Simon's assistant—and you must be Julia. Come in, come in, Simon's in the living room. Would you both like a drink, tea, coffee?'

'Coffee please,' said Julia. 'Paul?'

'What?'

'Do you want a coffee?'

'Oh, right, yes. Yes, that would be lovely.'

'I'll take you through.'

Simon stood as they entered the living room. 'Good of you both to come all this way,' he said. 'Has Evie offered you a drink?'

Evie raised her eyes and Julia smiled. 'Yes, Mr Trent, she has.'

'It's Simon. Well, come and sit down. How was the journey?'

'Fine,' said Paul. 'Look, I can't tell you how grateful I am. I just want to know, well, I just want to know *why*, I suppose.'

'I'm sure you do, Mr Sharp...'

'It's Paul.'

'Right, Paul, but don't forget what I said. I can't promise anything. It was...'

'A long time ago, yes, I know.'

'And, as I mentioned on the phone,' continued Simon, 'the file has been lost. It wasn't filed under Sharp, Alice or Gray so I'm completely in the dark. Did you remember to bring your father's notes?'

Paul nodded as he rummaged in his briefcase and, hands shaking, thrust a blue file towards Simon. 'Here. This is what my father gave me. And this one contains a photograph of Mum and the list of names that Julia and I found when we were in Strontian.'

'I wasn't sure about the milk or sugar requirements, so I've gone all posh, made the coffee in the cafetière and included a milk jug and sugar bowl,' declared Evie, bustling in and plonking a tray on the coffee table.

Paul shifted about on the settee and rubbed his forehead. Julia reached for his hand, gave it a squeeze and whispered, 'Alright?'

He gave a small nod.

'I didn't know I possessed a sugar bowl,' remarked Simon, winking at Paul and Julia.

Evie emitted a small shriek. 'Oh, God, what is it, then?'

Simon peered at the bowl. 'Do you know what, I think that's the cat bowl.'

Julia sniggered.

'No, it isn't,' cried Evie, throwing Simon a death glare. 'Don't listen to him. He hasn't even got a cat.'

Julia nudged Paul and flicked her eyes towards the hatch. Evie whirled round to see the cat nonchalantly washing its paws. 'Shit. That's not his cat; honestly, we don't know who it belongs to.'

'I do feed him though.'

'Oh, hell,' said Evie, snatching up the sugar bowl.

'I use an old saucer.'

Evie thumped him.

A chuckle escaped from Paul's lips.

'Right, having sorted that dilemma out, let's move on to your problem,' said Simon, setting the files down. 'Why don't you take me through what you know?'

'And do you mind if I take notes?' asked Evie.

'No, that's fine,' said Paul.

'Whenever you're ready,' said Simon.

Paul took another deep breath and explained the circumstances of Alice Sharp's disappearance, and how Adam had located her in Scotland. 'I suppose it was all a bit much for such a young woman, she was only eighteen when she had me, you see.'

'You say Adam sent your father, James, is it?'

Paul nodded.

'You say he sent James a summary in which he outlined the possibility that Alice may have adopted a new identity?'

Paul nodded. 'Yes, his summary letter's in the blue file. That letter is the reason that we, Julia and I, went up to Scotland,' he said, giving Julia a smile.

'We visited several graveyards. Paul thought...'

'That his mother had taken on one of the names, yes, I understand,' said Simon, opening Paul's green folder and taking out the photograph. 'She looks happy here.'

'It was taken soon after I was born.' Paul's eyes followed the photograph as Simon handed it across to Evie. 'You'll look after it, won't you?'

'Of course we will,' said Evie.

Simon then removed a single sheet of A4 from the green folder and glanced down the list of fourteen names. 'And these are the names you obtained from the local graveyards?'

Paul nodded. 'There was one within walking distance from *Kilcamb Lodge*, where we stayed; others were up to an hour or more away by car, some involved a ferry trip as well. I've noted the distances down next to the names.'

Simon nodded. 'Ah, yes, so I see.'

'The thing is, we realise that if Paul's mum did steal someone else's identity, and we don't know for sure that she did, but if she did, it *might* be one of those names on the list, but it might not,' said Julia.

'That's not a problem,' said Simon. 'I have a contact in the records office and she's always happy to help.'

Evie shot Simon a questioning glance. 'You never said.'

'We go back years. Anyway, Paul, since I'm unable to locate Adam's old case notes, some background information about your mum's early life might be helpful.'

'I only know what Dad told me.'

'That's alright,' said Simon.

'Does anyone want more coffee?' asked Evie.

'Oh, yes please,' said Paul.

Julia?'

She shook her head.

Simon held out his mug. 'Thanks.'

'So, what sort of things do you want to know?' said Paul.

'How about starting at the beginning. For example, do you know where they first met?'

Paul smiled. 'Oh, yes, that I *do* know. They met in Plymouth. Dad was a lecturer at the art college and Mum worked in the college café.'

'And when was this?'

'In 1989, Mum was sixteen.'

'So, she was still living at home.'

'Sort of, she and Janet lived with their grandparents.'

'Janet?'

'Mum's older sister.'

'And they both lived with the grandparents?' said Evie, pouring out the fresh coffee.

Paul nodded. 'Aunt Janet moved there in 1985 to study at the art college.' He held out his hand to accept his cup from Evie. 'Thanks.'

'Which grandparents?' asked Simon.

'Sorry?'

'Maternal or pater...?'

'Oh, right, sorry,' said Paul. 'Maternal grandparents. Anyway, after college, Janet was able to rent a small art studio in Plymouth. She stayed living with her grandparents and then Mum joined her in 1989.'

About to hand Simon his coffee, Evie frowned. She turned to Paul. 'So, are your mum's parents dead, then?'

'Oh, no, they're both still alive.'

'Is that coffee for me?' asked Simon.

'What?'

'The coffee, in your hand, is...?'

'Oh, yes. Here you are,' said Evie, turning once again to face Paul. 'So, sorry? Why were the girls living with their grandparents?'

'I'm not really sure. According to Dad, they couldn't get away from home soon enough.'

'And why was that?'

Paul shrugged. 'Dad told me they both hated their father.'

Evie looked up from her note book. 'Hence why Janet and Alice chose to live with their mother's parents, I assume.'

'Possibly,' said Paul. 'I've never really thought about it. I assumed it was simply because they lived in Devon.'

'He certainly seems to be a nasty piece of work,' said Julia. 'Tell them what he did to your dad.'

'I'm only going on what Barbara told me, so...'

'Sorry to interrupt, Paul,' said Simon. 'But who's Barbara?'

'Barbara Philips. Dad hired her in May 1991, soon after I was born, to help Mum. And then, when Mum ran away, she stayed on.'

'So, just to be clear,' said Evie, gesticulating with her pen. 'Are you saying that Barbara is still living with your father?'

'Yes, but it's not like it sounds,' said Paul. 'Dad told me that he and Barbara only became close *after* Mum ran away.'

Julia added. 'My mum says it was bound to happen. She said that the news of Alice leaving unsettled the whole community. She told me that James and Barbara were in a state of shock and, according to my mum, James came to depend on Barbara more and more. She's convinced that, without Barbara, James would simply have given up. It was Barbara who got him through the trauma and by doing so they inevitably became close.' Julia turned to Paul and smiled. 'She's a smashing woman, isn't she, Paul?'

Paul smiled back. 'She certainly is; she's treated me as her own and she and Dad are good together.'

'Right,' said Simon. 'That aside, what was it that Barbara told you about your grandfather?'

'She said that Jack, Mum's dad, turned up at Plymouth College one day and accosted Dad.'

'And when was this?'

'1990 sometime, the year before Mum and Dad got married.'

'Sorry to interrupt again,' said Evie. 'But how did Barbara know about the threat? You said she wasn't hired until 1991.'

'Dad must have told her about it.'

'And do you know what form this threat took?' asked Simon.

Paul took a sip of coffee. 'Barbara told me that he'd accused Dad of cradle-snatching. She said Jack punched him, gave him a black eye.'

'Did your father report the incident?'

Paul shook his head. 'No. According to Barbara, he didn't even tell Mum that Jack had turned up at the college.'

'So, how did he explain his damaged eye?' asked Evie.

Paul shrugged. 'Probably told Mum he'd walked into a lamp post while he was day dreaming about their future together. I don't know, is it important?'

'Probably not,' said Evie.

'I know Mum was only sixteen when she and Dad met, but she was eighteen when they married, and Dad's only ten years older. Hardly cradle-snatching.'

'It was, according to your granddad,' said Julia.

'I take it your father doesn't keep in touch with Alice's parents, then.'

Paul shook his head.

Julia took hold of Paul's hand. 'Paul's never met his mum's parents and his dad's parents died before he was born, so my grandparents have sort of adopted him. They call him their bonus grandson.'

'Oh, what a lovely expression,' said Evie.

'You said Barbara was employed to help your mum after you were born,' said Simon. 'Do you know why that was necessary?'

'Barbara told me Mum suffered from postpartum depression. She suggested that it may have been the reason why Mum left, you know, because she feared harming me.'

Evie gave Paul a warm smile. 'Your mum probably thought she was doing the best thing.'

'Maybe, but why hasn't she bothered to get in touch since?'

'This may be a stupid question,' said Evie, 'but I assume your mum knows you live in London now.'

'Not stupid at all. Dad told me he'd wanted a fresh start for them both and so he'd applied for a job at the Camberwell Art College. They moved to Bexleyheath in March 1991 and that's where I was born, so yes, she knows. Dad and Barbara and I still live there.'

Julia squeezed Paul's hand, looked up and locked eyes with Simon. 'So, where do we go from here?'

'I'd like to have a chat with your grandparents,' said Simon. 'Do you know their address?'

'Only since Dad gave me that file,' said Paul. 'Adam spoke to them soon after Dad hired him; reading his comments, I got the impression that Jack did all the talking and wasn't particularly cooperative.'

'Weren't you tempted to contact them once your dad gave you the file?' asked Evie.

Paul shook his head. 'Not after what Barbara told me, no.'

'And what about Janet, do you have any contact with her?'

'She sends me birthday and Christmas cards, but that's it.'

'That's rather sad,' mumbled Evie.

'Anyway, when Dad realised Mum had run off he assumed she'd gone to her sister in Plymouth, so he rang Janet. He only…'

'Sorry to interrupt,' said Evie. 'But does that mean your father has Janet's number?'

Paul shrugged. 'I don't think so, no, not anymore, and, well, I'd rather you didn't bother my dad about all this. I mean, he knows I've contacted you; it's not a secret, it's just that...'

'It's alright, don't worry; I'll soon be able to get hold of your aunt's number,' said Simon.

'More of your contacts?' said Evie.

'Let's just say it won't be a problem and leave it that,' said Simon with a wry grin. 'And was your mum with Janet?'

'No.'

'And Janet had no idea where her sister might have gone?'

Paul frowned. 'Well, no, I assume that's why Dad contacted Adam.'

'Didn't he contact the police?' asked Evie.

'Oh, yes, sorry. He reported her missing as soon as he'd spoken to Janet.'

'And?'

'Nothing. Barbara said they questioned Dad, but when no dead body was found they left him alone and that was that. They circulated her details. There was no response and no sightings and after a few months her disappearance was put on file. The police told Dad she was an adult and had the right to leave.'

'Look, I'll be frank with you, Paul, the likelihood of us finding your mother is remote, and even if we do, it's not beyond the bounds of possibility that she won't want to meet you.'

'I know that, so I've written her a letter.' Paul reached down into his bag and handed a sealed envelope to Simon. 'If you do manage to find her and she doesn't want to see me, would you give her this?'

Simon nodded. 'Of course,' he said. 'Right, so unless there's anything else, I think...'

'Not wanting to be grubby,' said Julia, 'but can you tell us how much this is likely to cost?'

Simon slid a folded sheet of paper across the table.

Paul picked it up and gasped. 'Gosh, right...'

'My contact in records works quickly. Don't worry.'

'I really appreciate you taking this on.'

'Remember, I can't promise anything. Safe journey back. We'll be in touch.'

The moment Paul and Julia left, Evie frowned. 'I wonder why Alice and Janet wanted to get away from their parents.'

Simon handed Evie the blue file. 'See if you find Jack Gray's address,' he said, as he scrolled down his phone.

'Who are you ringing?'

'The address, Evie.'

'Right, sorry.'

'I'm going to see if'—'Oh, good afternoon, could I speak to Sergeant John Harris please?'—'Simon Trent.'—'Yes, I'll hold.'—'Hi there, John, it's me...'—'Yes, you're absolutely right, I need a favour.'—'I know, sorry. I just need any information you might have on a bloke called Jack Gray.'—'His address? Yes, hang on.'

Simon waved his hand and hissed. 'Evie, the address?'

Evie stuck her tongue out and handed a scrap of paper to Simon.

Simon rattled the address off to John. 'He's the father of Alice Sharp. She married Dr James Sharp in 1991 and went missing from her home in Bexleyheath in 1992.'—'Because her son has now hired me to look for her.'—'That's brilliant, thanks. I owe you.'

'Well?' asked Evie.

'He'll text me.'

'Another one of your contacts, I assume?'

Simon nodded. 'A mate from the Met. He's Angela's husband, as it happens.'

'And who is Angela?'

'My contact in the records office.'

Chapter 12
London, Tuesday 21st May 2013

Amy and Jack Gray lived in a neat, three-bed terrace house on the Cromwell Road in Muswell Hill. The front door was opened by a small woman in a floral housecoat. A faint smell of mothballs drifted into the street.

'Mrs Gray?'

'Yes, that's right.'

'My name is Simon Trent, and this…'

The colour drained from her face as she grabbed for the door jamb.

Evie rushed forward. 'Mrs Gray, are you alright? Come on, you need to sit down.'

Mrs Gray leaned on Evie as they made their way down the corridor.

'This way,' mumbled Mrs Gray, pointing towards a door on the left.

'Simon, go and put the kettle on.'

Evie settled Mrs Gray into an armchair and patted her hand. 'Tea won't be long. Do you take sugar?'

She shook her head.

'I'll just let Simon know. Will you be alright if I leave you for a moment?'

'I'm fine.'

'I'll be back in a tick,' said Evie, making her way towards the door. 'Oh, no need, look, Simon's here with your tea now.'

'Forgot to ask about sugar.'

'No, she doesn't.'

'Good, because I couldn't find any,' said Simon, handing the cup to Mrs Gray.

'Thank you, young man. I'm sorry about that, it was just the shock, hearing that name again, after all these years.'

'Is your tea alright?'

'Lovely, you make a good cup of tea. Thank you.'

'I do apologise. I didn't mean to startle you. Perhaps I should have rung…'

'No, no, it's fine, *I'm* fine, no need to worry,' she said, leaning towards the coffee table, hand shaking.

'Here, let me take that,' said Evie.

'I didn't catch your name, dear.'

'I'm Evie, Evie Morgan. I work with Mr Trent.'

'Have you, oh, gracious me, have you found my Alice?'

'Well, no…'

'No,' she exclaimed. 'So, why are you here, then?'

'We've been asked to reopen the case.'

'Who by?'

'I'm not at liberty to say, sorry.'

'Oh dear, oh dear.' She fumbled in her pinafore pocket and removed a crumpled tissue. 'Have you spoken to Janet? She hasn't said anything to me. I don't understand. She would have said. Oh dear.'

A heavy, 1930s mahogany mantle clock struck three. Mrs Gray started. 'Is that the time? You have to go. I can't talk to you. You have to go. Now, before, before…'

The front door slammed. 'Here I am, Mrs Gray. Celebration time. Not only have I managed to lay my hands on a Hozelock hose reel at a bargain price, but I've also been able to purchase a beautiful mattock. Not so cheap I'll admit, but the craftsmanship; well, it's worth every penny. Put that kettle on while I stow them safely away in my shed, there's a good girl.'

Mrs Gray pushed herself upright and with impressive speed for one who, just a short while ago, had seemed near to collapse, hastened towards the door. 'Kettle's just boiled, Jack,' she called. She turned towards Simon and Evie, raised her finger to her lips and pulled the door shut behind her.

Simon tiptoed towards the door and pressed his ear against the wall. Evie shuffled up beside him. 'Can you make out what's happening?' she whispered.

Simon shook his head.

'What are we going to do now?'

'Tricky one.'

'Oh, very helpful.'

'It seems Jack's home.'

Evie raised her eyebrows.

'It also appears that Mrs Gray doesn't want him to know we're here.'

'Brilliant deductive work. So, what do we do? Make a dash for the front door while they're in the kitchen?'

'It's as good a plan as any,' he said, grasping the door handle.

Heavy footsteps approached. 'Well, something's going on,' boomed a male voice. 'Who's here?'

'Nobody, just...'

The living room door burst open.

Simon and Evie jumped backwards.

'It seems we have guests, Amy.' He clicked his heels. 'Jack Gray. And you are?'

Simon thrust his arm forward. 'Simon Trent. Pleased to meet you.' He nodded towards Evie. 'And this...'

'Trent, did you say, Trent?'

'I did.'

Jack frowned. 'That name rings a bell.'

'Yes, I expect it does,' said Simon. 'Anyway,' he nodded towards Evie again. 'This is my assistant, Miss Evie Morgan.'

'Assistant, is she? And what precisely does she *assist* you in?'

'She assists me in my work.'

'And that would be?'

'Well, currently we're involved in locating a missing person.'

'How fascinating. Who's missing?

'Your daughter, Alice.'

'What? My daughter; you're not serious, she's been—ah, that's it,' exclaimed Jack, prodding Simon in the chest. 'You're related to that obnoxious Adam Trent.'

'He's my brother.'

Jack swung around. 'Amy,' he bellowed. 'Amy.'

Amy appeared silently by his side.

'What's this all about?' he demanded.

'I don't know, Jack, really I don't.'

'Mr Gray, we've just been explaining to your wife that we've been asked to reopen the case.'

'By whom?'

'Well, again, as my assistant and I explained to your wife, we're not at liberty to say.'

'Is that a fact?'

'It is.'

Jack took a deep breath and glanced over Simon's shoulder. 'Just one tea cup, Amy? Didn't you offer our guests any?'

Evie swallowed. 'No, no, that's fine, we'd best be on our way now, don't you think, Simon?'

'Nonsense, Mrs Gray makes magnificent cupcakes,' he said, looking Evie up and down. 'You're not on some fancy diet I hope. Can't be doing with all that nonsense.' He patted his large, but firm, belly. 'A few extra calories never did me any harm, as you can see. Solid as a rock this is, all muscle.'

'I eat cake, if that's what you mean,' said Evie.

'Splendid. Off you go then, Amy dear. Put the kettle on,' said Jack. 'And let's see what this is all about, shall we?'

'I'll help you, Mrs Gray,' said Evie.

'Most kind, most kind. I do find carrying trays rather troublesome these days. Because of my knees, of all things, you wouldn't think that problem knees would affect one's ability to carry a tray, but it does, it most certainly does.'

With a smile thrown in Simon's direction, Evie followed Amy through to the kitchen.

'Would you pop the kettle on, dear? I just need to visit the bathroom.'

After locking herself in the downstairs toilet, Mrs Gray fumbled in her pinafore pocket for her phone.

'Janet, oh, Janet,' she whispered.

'Mum, what is it, what's happened?'

'They turned up this afternoon and then Jack came home and…'

'Mum, who turned up?'

'A sweet girl, very well-mannered she is. Evie, I think she said her name was, yes that's right, Evie, Evie Morgan.'

'I've never heard of her, Mum. You said *they*, who else is there?'

'It's Adam Trent's brother, Simon.'

'No!'

'Yes, Janet. What are we going to do?'

'I'm coming over, Mum.'

Janet screwed her eyes shut. 'Fuck, fuck, fuck.' Taking a deep breath, she scrolled down her contacts list. 'Come on, come on, answer, please answer.'—'Ah. Hi there. Good, it's me,' she said.

'Hello there, me, how are you?'

'I'll get straight to the point, Mum's…'

'Oh, God! Is she alright? What's happened?'

'She's fine. Well, as fine as she ever is, no, the thing is, oh, bloody hell, this isn't easy.'

'Is this your idea of getting straight to the point, sister dear?'

'Fine. Simon Trent and his assistant, some woman called Evie Morgan, are talking to Dad as we speak,' she blurted.

The faint sound of Imelda May's singing drifted down the line.

'Did you hear what I said?'

'Yes, I heard. But how…?'

'I don't know. I should imagine Paul contacted them. Does it matter?'

'No, I suppose not.'

'I think he should be told, don't you?'

'Who should be told what?'

'Oh, for God's sake, don't be obtuse. Paul, Paul should be told. He's a big boy now.'

'Just give me a moment, Janet.'

'Right, yes, fine.'

'I need to think—I'll ring you back.'

'But what shall I say?—Hello, hello, hello.' Janet stared at her phone's home screen. 'Shit.'

'Ah, Miss Morgan, tea at last,' said Jack. 'I thought you'd both popped across to India to pick the leaves.'

'Here we are,' said Amy, as she entered. 'Cakes.'

'Well, don't just stand there, my love, hand them round.'

Simon jumped up. 'Here, let me take those. You sit down and relax, you look worn out.'

'Most considerate. Thank you, young man.'

'I've explained everything to Mr Trent here,' said Jack, as he selected the largest cake. He glanced towards Evie, who was poised with an open notebook balanced on her lap. His eyes narrowed.

'You don't mind if I take a few notes, do you?'

'No, why should I? It's all quite simple, boring and mundane stuff.' He took a bite of cake and swallowed. 'Alice and I had a disagreement. We argued. She buggered off to Plymouth to live with the grandparents, happens all the time to lots of families. I explained it all to that Adam chap when he came sniffing round all those years ago.'

'Yes, I understand it happened with both your daughters,' said Simon.

'And your point is?' said Jack, stuffing the remainder of the cake into his mouth.

'No point,' said Simon. 'I'm merely stating a fact.'

117

Amy cleared her throat. 'Yes, our Janet's very talented. She wanted to go to college, but well, Jack couldn't really see the point, couldn't see any future for her.'

'Wanted to be an artist, of all things,' said Jack, brushing crumbs from his front. 'I told her she could do that in her spare time, nothing wrong with a woman doing a few pictures as a hobby.'

'I understand she studied at Plymouth Art College, is that correct?'

'What of it?'

'Nothing, it's just that, generally, art colleges don't accept people unless they show promise,' said Simon.

Amy bent her head forward and gave a nervous laugh.

'She was always a bolshie little madam, that one. She turned my little Alice against me and that's a fact. Kept on and on at her, she did. Saying how wonderful life was near the sea. It broke her mother's heart when our Alice left home as well,' said Jack, reaching for another cake. 'Thinks she's something special does our Janet, just because she's sold a few paintings.'

'Jack, she's done very well for herself,' said Amy, glancing up. 'She has her own studio in Avenue Mews. She exhibits her work around the world, you know.' She pointed towards a seascape hanging above the mantle. 'Our Janet painted that one for me.'

'Chocolate box stuff if you ask me.'

'It's the view from my parents' house,' added Amy.

'And that's another thing. That house should have come to Amy, but no. They left it to their precious grandchildren.'

'I didn't mind.'

'Well, I bloody did. That house was worth a lot of money, but Janet sold it without a by-your-leave and we never saw a penny, not a single, bloody penny. She used the proceeds to rent that poncey studio up the road. Bloody waste.'

'And what about Alice?' asked Simon.

'What about her?' said Jack.

'Did Janet share the proceeds with her sister?'

'I don't see what that's got to do with you, *Mister* Trent, but as it happens, she didn't. The selfish cow kept it all for herself.'

'Jack,' exclaimed Amy.

'What? It's a fact, so there's no point pretending otherwise.'

'My father died in 1989, Mr Trent, not long after Alice moved down to live with them. So, it was a blessing in a way, you know, the girls being down there; they were a comfort to my mum,' croaked Amy. Blinking back tears, she turned on Jack. 'When Mum died in '98, Alice had been missing for six years, so how could Janet share the proceeds, Jack, how?'

Jack stiffened, leaned forward and grasped the arms of his chair.

Amy flinched.

Simon cleared his throat. 'I understand Alice was working as a waitress at the art college when she met Dr Sharp.'

'*Dr* bloody Sharp, don't make me laugh, he's just a jumped up arty-farty lecturer type.'

'He has a PhD,' said Simon.

'Well, bully for him.'

'We've been told that you and he had a disagreement.'

'So, you've spoken to the toffee-nosed, pretentious arse, have you?'

'Mr Gray, you clearly remember the incident. I simply thought you might want to relay your version of the event, but if not...'

'I gave him a piece of my mind, if that's what you mean. Alice was only sixteen when he took up with her. Two years later, she's his bloody wife. He was old enough to be her bloody father.'

'Well, not quite,' said Simon.

'Got children of your own, have you?'

'No, but...'

'You're not in a position to comment, then, are you?'

'Have you any idea why she didn't come back here when she left her husband?' said Simon.

'No, I bloody haven't.'

'You said Janet turned Alice against you, do you think...?'

'That the dear, wonderful, self-righteous prig, Dr Sharp, did the same,' growled Jack, 'I'm certain he did.'

'So why didn't she go back to be with her grandparents?'

'Remember, it was just Mum by then, Mr Trent,' said Amy, almost whispering. 'Perhaps she didn't want to burden...'

'She and Janet didn't worry about descending on the old dears when it suited them, so I doubt very much if her concern for your mother even entered her head,' said Jack.

'And you've no idea where she might have gone?'

'What a bloody stupid question. If I knew where she'd gone, she wouldn't be missing, would she?'

'He's only doing his job,' muttered Amy.

'You're wasting your time. I'm sure she's fine,' said Jack. 'We'd have heard if she'd been murdered.'

Amy gasped. 'Don't, Jack. I can't bear it.'

'Oh, give over, woman,' said Jack, 'no doubt she and the wonderful Dr Sharp had a row, and we both know what Alice does when arguments surface, don't we? She buggers off. She'll have moved in with some other sucker.'

Evie glanced across at Amy. 'It must be hard, not seeing your grandson.'

'Yes, well, there we are. Help yourself to cake, dear,' said Amy, 'before my Jack finishes them off.'

'And that's another bloody thing,' snarled Jack. 'We didn't even know we had a grandson until your brother came sniffing round,'

'And who's fault was that?' mumbled Amy.

'What did you say?'

'Nothing, dear.'

'You bloody said something.'

Evie looked Jack directly in the eye. 'She said it was an insult.'

Jack returned Evie's gaze. He narrowed his eyes. 'Too bloody right, it was an insult,' he said. 'Still, all the same, aren't they? Full of shit, literally, as babies, and full of shit, metaphorically, when they grow up,' said Jack, with an uproarious laugh.

At the sound of the doorbell, Amy jumped to her feet. Her knee caught the side of the table, sending the tray, the plate and her cup sliding towards the edge. Simon grabbed the tray, Evie caught the plate, but Amy's half-empty cup slid to the floor.

'That'll stain, that will,' snapped Jack.

The doorbell rang out again.

'Shall I get that?' asked Simon.

'No, you stay where you are,' said Jack.

'I'll get a cloth,' said Evie.

'How's your knee, Mrs Gray?'

'I'll live, Mr Trent, but thank you for asking, most considerate of you.'

Evie, cloth in hand, side-stepped Jack as he stormed out of the living room. 'I'll soon have this sorted,' said Evie, now on her hands and knees at Amy's feet. 'My grandmother told me never to rub at a stain, simply blot it with an absorbent cloth.' She looked up. 'There we are, Mrs Gray, look, all gone.'

'Oh, thank you, my dear.'

Jack strode back in and gave his wife a penetrating stare. 'Well, look who I found loitering on the doorstep. Our Janet.'

Amy bit her lip and closed her eyes.

'Oh, I'm sorry, I didn't realise you had visitors.'

'Did you not? Quite a coincidence you turning up now then, isn't it?' said Jack.

Simon extended his hand. 'Simon Trent, and this is my assistant, Evie Morgan.'

From her crouched position, Evie gave a little wave.

'How interesting. Are you by chance related to Adam Trent?' said Janet, shaking Simon's hand.

'What do you think?' said Jack.

'Well, I don't know, do I, Daddy dear, that's why I asked.'

'I'm Adam's brother,' said Simon, 'Evie and I are here to...'

'We've covered all that, thank you, Mr Trent.'

'Sorry? You're here to do what, exactly?' said Janet.

'To investigate your sister's disappearance.'

'We *have* been through all this before,' said Janet.

'He's perfectly aware of that,' snapped Jack. 'But it seems someone, Alice's son presumably, has asked him to reopen the case.'

'Has he?' said Janet.

'I'm sorry, but...'

'He's not at liberty to say,' parroted Jack.

Amy began to shed silent tears and Janet rushed to her mother's side. 'Come on, Mum, let's get you upstairs for a lie down.'

Amy leaned into her daughter's arms and sobbed.

Janet sent Simon a withering look. 'Dragging up the past like this has upset my mother all over again. We don't know anything more today than we did the day she disappeared, so why don't you just bugger off and leave us alone.'

'This is my house, Janet. I decide who goes and who stays.'

'It's not a problem,' said Simon. 'We really should be on our way now.'

'I'm taking Mum upstairs. Good-bye to the pair of you.'

'You've been very helpful,' said Simon to Amy's retreating figure.

'I hope Mrs Gray feels better soon,' said Evie.

Jack opened the front door. 'She'll be fine. She's always been hysterical.' He twirled his forefinger near his temple. 'She told me years ago that Alice had contacted her. All in her head, as far as I'm concerned. Alice hasn't written or phoned since the day she left this house, and that's that.'

'Well, that was all very awkward,' said Evie, as they drove away. 'What's going on?'

'Good question.'

'Have you got a good answer?'

'Not as yet.'

'So, what do we do now?'

'Perhaps we should give Dr Sharp a ring, see if he'll talk to us about his confrontation with Jack Gray.'

'I thought Paul asked us not to bother his father.'

'You're quite right, he did,' he said, as he turned left towards the A1. 'Who'd have thought? It seems it's a good job that I've got you as an assistant after all,' he added, with a broad grin.

'You can go off people, you know.'

'You love me really,' said Simon.

'Debatable.'

'Anyway, let's hope Angela's had some luck with the names that Paul and Julia dug up.'

Evie groaned.

'Sorry, that was unintentional.'

'Odd, wasn't it? Janet turning up like that,' said Evie.

'Wasn't it just? We certainly need to have a word with *her*, preferably on her own, and as soon as possible. Did you note where her studio was?'

'I did. It's in Avenue Mews.'

'Such an excellent assistant.'

Evie whacked his knee with her notebook.

Chapter 13
Yorkshire, Tuesday May 21st (evening)

When Simon and Evie drew up outside the flat, Sarah came rushing out. 'Why didn't you answer your phone? Everyone's been ringing and ringing.'

Evie frowned as she retrieved her mobile and noted fourteen missed calls. 'I had it on silent,' she mumbled.

'It's Charlotte,' said Sarah. 'She's in hospital.'

Evie gasped.

'What's happened?' asked Simon.

'An accident, at school, something to do with a climbing frame; anyway, she lost consciousness briefly, but she's alright now, well, as alright as you'd expect given...'

'Which hospital, Sarah?'

'York Hospital, on the Wigginton Road.'

Simon gunned the engine and drove off. Evie leaned back in the passenger seat, pale-faced and silent.

Simon's knuckles were white as he steered the car on to the main road. 'We'll be there in three quarters of an hour, less if the traffic stays like this. She'll be fine, don't worry, she's in the best place.'

They rushed into the ward to find Charlotte sitting up in the bed playing snap with Mandy. 'I fell off the climbing frame,' she declared with pride.

'So I heard,' said Evie.

Mandy tut-tutted. 'Out of my sight and the child behaves with reckless abandon.'

'I did not,' cried Charlotte, slapping down a card. 'Betty Price pushed me.'

'Now, now, poppet,' said Mandy.

'She did so—snap!—I win again.'

Gerry turned from the window, his face drawn.

'Dad?'

'She's alright, Evie. She gave us all a fright, but well, as you can see, she's fine now.'

'Very resilient things, children,' said Simon.

'Do you want to play with me?'

'I'll beat you,' said Simon.

'No you won't.'

'Oh, yes I will.'

Evie burst into tears.

'You can play too,' said Charlotte.

Evie smiled and sniffed. 'I should hope so, you know how I *love* playing snap.'

'Fibber, you hate it.' She grinned at Simon. 'I always beat her.'

'You do not,' said Evie.

'I do so.'

'Come on then, deal and we'll see,' said Simon.

'Before you get beaten…'

'Dad! Don't encourage her.'

'Before you start, Evie, could you come with me for a moment?'

'Why, where, what's wrong?'

'Nothing's wrong, I just thought we could all do with a coffee and I can't carry four.'

'Oh, right—Simon, do you want a coffee?'

'I'd kill for one.'

'Mandy?'

She nodded.

'Right then—don't worry, you little terror,' said Evie, 'I'll be back in a tick, and then we'll see who's champ.'

Charlotte smiled at Simon. 'It's me. I'm the champ.'

Walking along, arms linked, Evie said, 'I'm so sorry I missed your calls, Dad. I had the phone on silent because…'

'It's fine,' he said, chewing his lip.

Evie stopped and took hold of his hand. 'What is it, Dad? Something's wrong, I can tell.'

125

'Let's sit down a moment,' he said, guiding Evie towards a row of orange plastic chairs lining the wall. 'Not the most comfort...'

'What is it? Is something wrong with Charlotte?'

Gerry swallowed. He closed his eyes as he shook his head. 'Sit down, darling.'

Evie sat. 'Dad, you're frightening me.'

'It seems that, well...' he took a breath. 'It seems that,' he exhaled. 'How can I put this...?'

'Succinctly.'

Gerry brushed a few strands of hair from Evie's eyes. 'It seems I'm not Charlotte's father,' he blurted.

'I'm sorry?'

'You heard.'

'I heard, but I don't understand, how...?'

'I was just browsing, God knows why, I'm no scientist.' He took another breath, deeper this time. 'Anyway, in a box at the top of her chart was her blood group and, and...'

'And what?'

'She's blood group O, Evie.'

'So? Lots of people are. It's the most common blood group.'

'I'm AB.'

Evie stared at her father.

'That means I'm...'

'I *know* what it means, Dad.' She took a deep breath. 'So, who is?'

'Who is what?'

'Who's her father, for God's sake?'

Gerry shrugged.

Evie screwed her eyes shut tight and rocked backwards and forwards. She clutched at her stomach.

'It makes no difference you know; she's still my little girl, no matter what.'

Evie's eyes snapped open. 'Oh, Dad.'

Gerry sighed. 'We were happy, your mother and I, I don't want you to think otherwise...'

'But?'

Gerry shrugged again. 'We'd been married for seventeen years and we'd got into a kind of companionable relationship. I took her for granted; I was a fool.' He rubbed at his forehead. 'Then, I had that time away in Africa. When I got back, I realised that we were in danger of falling apart. We, well, we had a happy reunion the weekend of my return, and I'd always assumed Charlotte was the result of that marvellous night when we'd reconnected.'

'But she wasn't?'

'It would seem not,' said Gerry. 'The thing is, I'd suspected there was someone else for some time.'

'Did you ever ask her?'

'No, of course not. I was too scared to hear the answer.'

'So, how did you know?'

'I found out by accident. She said she was at a conference, I needed to speak to her, can't remember why now. I know it was soon after my return from Africa though. Anyway, when I tried her mobile there was no response, so I rang the hotel where she said she was staying and...'

'She wasn't there.'

'No, she wasn't there.'

'Oh, Dad,' repeated Evie.

'Anyway, I didn't ask, so we'll never know.' He closed his eyes momentarily. 'I know Charlotte was born early but it never entered my head that she wasn't mine. What do I say to her? She'll need to know at some point, I suppose. There are medical implications if nothing else.'

'Dad, I...'

'There you are,' exclaimed Simon, striding towards them. 'What's the problem? The long walk too much for you both? We're gasping back there you know.' He raised his eyebrows. 'And you were right, Charlotte's a mean snap player, we must have played…'

Evie rushed into Simon's arms.

'Oh, I say, steady on. A nurse has just been in and she said Charlotte's made a remarkable recovery,' he said, patting Evie's back. 'She'll be able to go home tomorrow and convalesce until the end of the week. Charlotte's thrilled. It didn't take her long to clock the fact that next week is half term, so she's going to get a two-week break from school.'

'Simon, coffee, yes sorry. It's all been rather traumatic,' said Gerry.

'You get back to Charlotte, Gerry,' said Simon. 'Evie and I will get the coffees. OK, Evie?'

Evie nodded mutely.

Walking towards the café area, Evie turned to Simon. 'He knows.'

'Sorry, who knows what?'

'Dad, he knows about Mum's affair.'

'Since when?'

'Since he discovered Charlotte's blood group.'

Simon stopped in his tracks. 'Sorry, maybe I'm being particularly dim here, but what exactly are you talking about?'

'Charlotte's blood group, Simon, she's blood group O.'

Simon frowned.

'Dad is AB.'

'Ah, right.'

'So, you know what that means then?'

'Yes, Evie, I know what that means; it means Gerry can't be Charlotte's father.'

Evie stared intently at Simon and widened her eyes.

'Oh, right, yes, God, I see,' he gasped. 'Alex.'

'I don't know why I didn't see it before.'

'See what?'

'The discrepancy, Simon, the discrepancy. Charlotte was born in August 2001.'

'Yes, so?'

'So, that means she was conceived in November.'

'Again, so?'

'Dad was out in Africa, Simon. I *told* you.'

'You did. You also told me he came back to England every few months.'

'But he wasn't around in November 2000. He didn't finally get home until the week before Christmas,' wailed Evie. 'Oh, what the hell am I going to do?'

Evie felt a gentle tap on her shoulder. 'Miss, are you in the queue here, or what?'

She turned to see an old man, bent double. 'I'm so sorry, please, after you.'

He gave a curt nod and hobbled towards the counter. 'My usual, Mavis, there's a love.'

Having furnished the old man with a sausage roll, Mavis turned to Simon. 'Same time every evening, poor old soul, his wife's in ward 19; been there for months she has. Still, there we are, we all need to carry on. So, what can I get you?'

'Four coffees, please.'

'Do you think Alex knows?' whispered Evie.

'What, that Charlotte could be his?'

'Yes,' she hissed, 'unless you're suggesting Mum had multiple affairs.'

'I wasn't suggesting that for—sorry, thanks; how much?'

'Eight pounds, please.'

'Here,' said Simon, handing Mavis a ten-pound note. 'Put the change in the society tin. 'Come on, Evie, let's get back. We'll think about what to do later.'

At the same time as Simon and Evie were making their way back to the ward with the coffees, a man was reversing into his driveway. Rain was drumming on the roof as he switched off the engine. The wipers clunked into their rest position and he sat for a moment, watching the rivulets of rain pour down the windscreen until his view was obscured. He leaned over to the back seat and grabbed his coat. With a sigh, he forced the door open against the buffeting wind and made a dash for the front door, the razor-sharp, salty rain stinging his face.

Once inside, he shook his coat and kicked the door shut. 'My God, I'm bloody drenched, just look at me, the proverbial drowned rat.' He hung his coat up and, laughing, called out. 'Hello? Come out, come out, wherever you are.'

Silence.

'Where are you?'

He strode into the kitchen, the living room, the study. They were all empty. He dashed upstairs calling her name, but he knew; he knew she was gone. He stood at the top of the stairs and took several deep breaths before trudging back downstairs. Slumped on the bottom step, he retrieved his mobile from his trouser pocket and phoned. It went straight to voicemail. He left a message. Hands shaking, he scrolled through his contacts and rang Janet.

Chapter 14
Yorkshire, 22nd-23rd May 2013

Evie rang Alex the following afternoon. 'Hi there. I take it you've heard about Charlotte?'

'No, what?'

'She was in hospital…'

'In hospital? Jesus! What happened? Is she alright?'

'Don't panic. She's fine now. She fell off a climbing frame at school yesterday. They kept her in overnight, you know, just to be sure. Anyway, she's home now, got the rest of the week off school.'

'Bloody hell, Evie. You gave me a scare,' he exclaimed. 'Still, you say she's home now, yes?'

'Yes.'

'And I bet the little minx is loving every minute of that; everyone at her beck and call.'

'Quite, and the school holiday starts on the twenty-seventh, so…'

'So, she gets an extra week of holiday; excellent timing. That's my girl.'

Evie gave a small gasp. 'Yes, as you say, excellent timing. Anyway, that wasn't really why I was ringing.'

'Oh, so why?'

'Simon and I, you remember Simon?'

'Of course I remember Simon, Evie,' he said. 'I'm not in my dotage yet.'

'No, right.'

'So, apart from informing me about Charlotte and checking on my brain's capacity to recall simple facts, what…?'

'Simon and I were wondering if you and Martha fancy coming over for a meal at his flat.'

'You mean come to Northallerton?'

'Yes, to Northallerton, you don't have to sound like I'm suggesting a visit to the slums.'

'Evie, I wasn't suggesting anything of the sort, for goodness sake. An evening with you would be great and anyway, you know me, never say no to a free meal. Will Gerry be there?'

'No, we, well I, need to talk to you and Martha about something in private.'

'Sounds ominous, am I in trouble?'

'We thought tomorrow, at eight o'clock. Are you free?'

'Tomorrow? *Thursday*, you mean?'

'Yes, Alex. Today is Wednesday and, as far as I'm aware, Thursday generally follows…'

'And yesterday was Tuesday, yes, I fully grasp the concept, Evie, it's just a little odd.'

'Odd?'

'Yes, odd; convention dictates that dinner parties are normally held on a Friday or a Saturday evening.'

'It isn't a dinner party, Alex, it's just a bloody meal.'

'Evie, what's going on?'

'Nothing's *going on*. Look, are you free, or not?'

'You didn't answer my question.'

'What question?'

'Am I in trouble?'

'You normally are.'

'Oh, very amusing. Come on, Evie, something's afoot, I can…'

'For God's sake, Alex, can you come or not?'

'Who could refuse such a gracious invitation? Eight o'clock tomorrow, *Thursday* at the flat, I look forward to it —I think.'

Evie clattered around the kitchen table, banging spoons and forks down, pushing placemats around and sighing, while Simon stirred the Bolognese sauce.

'Evie, what exactly are you doing?'

'I can't decide where we should sit.'

'There's only four of us, how many variations can there be?'

'Should I be sitting next to him or opposite him? And if I sit opposite, should we be at either end or across from each other? What do you think?'

Simon abandoned the sauce, poured a glass of wine and handed it to Evie. 'Here, drink this and relax.'

She took a gulp. 'Am I doing the right thing?'

'I'm not sure you've got much choice,' said Simon.

'Dad didn't seem remotely surprised that Charlotte wasn't his.' She took a gulp of wine. 'Do you think he already suspects that it's Alex?'

'Evie, I don't know.'

'No, of course you don't; stupid thing to ask—how the hell am I going to broach the subject with him? I mean I can't just launch right in and say, '*Oh, by the way, Alex, I know about your affair with Mum, and guess what? Dad's just found out that he isn't Charlotte's biological father, so, it must be you*', can I?'

'Well no, but…'

The front door bell rang out. Simon glanced at his watch. 'That'll be them. Do you want me to answer it?'

Evie downed the rest of her glass and dragged her hand across her mouth. 'No, I'll get it.' At the kitchen door, she turned. 'Thanks for doing this.'

The bell rang out again.

'Go on, otherwise they'll wonder what we're up to.'

Evie stuck her tongue out.

'We come bearing red wine and sparkling apple juice for Martha. She drew the short straw.'

'Thanks. Come on through. Simon's just finishing off the sauce.'

Alex smiled at Evie and whispered, 'He cooks as well. He's a keeper.'

'Oh, give it a rest, Alex, for God's sake,' she hissed.

'Just ignore him, Evie,' said Martha, handing Evie a bunch of flowers. 'Look, I didn't leave them in the sink.'

'Hah! Lovely, thank you.'

'Nice to see you again,' said Simon, wiping his hands. 'What would you like to drink?'

'What have you got?'

'Most things,' said Simon. 'Evie, could you keep an eye on the sauce? I'll take our guests through to peruse the drinks cabinet.'

Alex rubbed his hands. 'Splendid, a drinks cabinet, lead on.'

'Don't worry about me, I'm on apple juice,' said Martha. 'I'll help Evie.'

'No, no, that's fine,' said Evie, wiping her palms down the sides of her skirt.

'Well, at least point me in the direction of the vases and I'll arrange these flowers for you.'

'So, let's see,' said Simon, 'I have, gin, whisky, martini…'

'Oh, what a cute cat,' exclaimed Alex, striding towards Simon's desk where the cat sat washing his paws.

'It's not mine; hard to believe, given the amount of time he seems to spend here—so, what would you like?'

'A dry martini, please,' said Alex, stroking the cat before picking it up. Glancing down at the desk as he did so, he gasped. 'Good grief, what are you doing with this?'

'The cat? I told you…'

'No, this,' said Alex, as he put the cat down and picked up a photograph. 'The cat was sitting on it.'

Simon handed Alex his drink and took the photograph. 'That's not supposed to be lying about.'

'I don't understand. Why have you got a photograph of Elspeth?'

'Elspeth?'

'The delightful brunette in that photo, Simon,' said Alex, taking a swig of his drink. 'A much underrated hair colour in my opinion. You can forget your blondes. Now, Elspeth...'

'Who's Elspeth?' said Evie, marching into the living room.

'Yes, who's Elspeth?' repeated Martha.

'I thought you two were watching the sauce.'

'We were. It's done, I've turned the gas off. So, come on, who's Elspeth?'

Simon held up Alice Sharp's photograph. 'This is.'

'But, that's...' began Evie.

'It seems Alex knows her,' said Simon, with a brief, but emphatic shake of his head, aimed at Evie.

Evie clamped her lips shut.

'Would you like ice with your apple juice, Martha? asked Simon, tongs poised above the ice bucket.

'Lovely, thank you.'

'Yes, I knew Elspeth years ago.' He glanced towards Martha. 'Long before you and I got together, my love.' He closed his eyes for a moment. 'Well, when I say 'knew' that's not strictly true, I *met* her on several occasions.'

'Oh, where?' asked Simon, dropping a couple of ice cubes into Martha's glass.

'It was at the Mansion House, in Leeds. During my first conference with York University, soon after I returned from MIT, it must have been in '94 or '95, I suppose. She was the event organiser, very efficient she was, and very attractive, as you can see.'

Evie's eyes widened. 'Does she still work there?'

Alex shrugged. 'No idea. All I know is I didn't see her the last time we held a conference there.'

'And when was that?' asked Simon.

'Around 2000 I think,' replied Alex, taking a swig of his Martini.

'2000?'

'I think so,' said Alex, with a frown. 'Yes, that's right. We've organised our own in-house conferences since then

—budget cuts—short-sighted policy if you ask me. Meeting and talking to colleagues out of your everyday working environment can be stimulating. Still, far be it for me…'

'I don't suppose you recall her surname?'

'Her surname? You've got her photograph, for God's sake, don't you know?' Alex narrowed his eyes. 'Hang on. Is this why you've invited us here, to talk about Elspeth? And, for the record, no, I don't know her surname.'

'No, Alex, that wasn't why we invited you,' said Evie.

'Why then?'

'You might as well tell him,' said Simon.

Alex's eye's sparkled. 'Ooh, I say.'

Evie glowered at him. 'Oh, for God's sake, Alex, grow up.'

'Evie and I spent an interesting weekend in North Wales, Alex, and…'

Martha stiffened.

'Did you indeed,' said Alex, winking at Simon.

'We stayed at *Yr Ystabl*,' blurted Evie. 'It's in a little place called Trefriw. Perhaps you've heard of it.'

Alex knocked back his martini and peered into his empty glass, his hair flopping across his eyes.

'Yes, we had a lovely chat with the owners, didn't we, Simon? And the weirdest thing; they remembered a woman staying there who looked just like Mum, isn't that right, Simon?'

Simon nodded. 'And this woman, the one who looked like Evie's mum, stayed there with some chap who bore a striking similarity to you, Alex.

'And this couple registered as Mr and Mrs; oh, now, what did they say their name was, Simon?'

'Green, Barry Green and…'

'Yes, that's it, Barry Green. And here's another weird thing,' said Evie, glaring at Martha, 'the woman gave her name as Martha Green.' She gave Alex a penetrating look. 'Such an odd coincidence, don't you think, Alex?'

Alex, pale-faced, staggered to the settee and slumped down.

Martha remained standing, apple juice untouched, concentrating on a small patch of carpet beneath her feet.

'Then, of course, there was that terrible accident. It seems that Martha Green collided with a tractor on the very same road where Mum was killed, the B5106, and...'

A gasp escaped from Martha's lips.

Alex held up his arms. 'Alright, that's enough. You obviously know the truth, so what can I say?'

'I don't know, Alex. What *can* you say?'

'Do you think I could have another?' he said, handing Simon his empty glass.

'The same again?'

Alex nodded.

'Evie?'

'I left my wine in the kitchen.'

Alex began to push himself up from the settee.

'Oh, no you don't,' said Evie, pushing him back down. 'Start explaining.'

'We tried so hard not to,' said Alex. 'Your mum loved Gerry, but she also loved me. It was torture, Evie.'

'My heart bleeds.'

'We had a huge argument that night. It was all too much for her, the lies, the deception, she couldn't bear the thought of hurting Gerry and that's why she was ending it. That's why she drove off. She was in a terrible state. I tried to stop her, but well, I didn't and then, well, you know what happened.'

'I know you buggered off the moment you heard.'

'Jesus, Evie, what else could I do? If I'd stayed your dad would have found out and how would that have helped? It would have been the last thing Jean wanted. In her mind, she was doing the right thing. She was leaving me.'

'How long?' said Evie.

Simon handed them their drinks.

Alex took a gulp. 'How long what?'

'How long had it been going on?'

'Um...'

'Months, years? It's not a difficult question, Alex. How long?'

'I'd loved her for years, Evie, long before she married Gerry, and...'

'You what?'

'I met Jean at Cambridge, Evie; but, you knew that, didn't you?'

'What exactly are you saying, Alex?'

'Oh, for God's sake, Evie. We were lovers at Cambridge.'

Evie, her face tortured with confusion, turned towards Martha. 'But you told me it was you and Alex who were lovers.'

'I know, Evie, I know. I'd fancied him from the moment I first set eyes on him.' She glanced across at Alex. 'Sadly, he only had eyes for Jean.'

Alex nodded. 'We were besotted with each other. We had it all worked out and then, when I got the chance to go to MIT, I assumed Jean would come with me, but she wouldn't, no, that's not fair, she couldn't.'

'Why couldn't she?'

'Her dad had just been diagnosed with dementia. He was only fifty-six. She asked me to stay in the UK, but I couldn't...'

'You mean, you wouldn't,' said Martha.

Alex bowed his head. 'It was too good an opportunity; they had plenty of other people lined up for the position. If I'd shown even a glimmer of hesitation they'd have offered it to someone else.'

'And then, while you were away, she met Dad.'

'I don't blame her...'

'That's bloody big of you,' spat Evie.

Alex shrugged.

'And then you came back to England, got a job at York University, the same University where she and Dad worked, and...'

'That wasn't planned, Evie, I swear to you, it was just as much a shock to me as it was to Jean.'

'And what, your eyes met over a crowded conference hall and the flames were re-ignited?'

'Something like that, yes.'

'And then you cynically used Martha to act as a go between.'

'No,' exclaimed Martha. 'It wasn't like that at all. Jean came to see me soon after Alex joined the University staff. You mustn't think badly of her, really you mustn't. She'd loved Alex, that's true, she had done since Cambridge.' Martha swallowed. 'But when he left for America she thought that was it. She thought she'd never see him again. She started lecturing at York and got on with her life. When she met lovely, kind Gerry she fell in love with him. She was happy. Truly happy. Meeting Alex again threw her world into complete turmoil.'

'And yet she still started the affair; an affair that you conspired in. You helped them, Martha, you helped them deceive Dad.'

Martha bowed her head. 'I know, but oh, Evie, they were my dearest friends. Nothing I could have said would have stopped them. Alex especially.' She raised her head and locked eyes with Evie. 'I could tell that he loved her still, he loved her with all his heart, Evie.'

'What, and now he loves you? Really? After all these years, give me a break,' said Evie.

Martha blinked back tears and lowered her head again.

'Enough, Evie,' exclaimed Alex, reaching for Martha's hand. 'I know you're angry with me, but don't you dare speak to Martha like that. She was a good, supportive friend to Jean and she's been a good supportive friend to me, especially after Jean died. I'm only sorry it took me so long to realise what I was missing.'

Martha looked up and smiled

'And Charlotte, Alex, what about Charlotte?' said Evie.

'Sorry, what about her?'

'Oh, don't give me the old Mr Innocence look.'

Alex turned to Simon. 'Do you know what she's talking about?'

'I do.'

'Well?'

Evie downed her wine, grabbed the bottle from the table and refilled her glass. 'Think about it, Alex.'

'Think about what?'

'The timings, Alex, the timings.'

'I'm sorry, Evie, the timings of what exactly?'

'Are you being deliberately obtuse? When did you came back from America, Alex?'

'In 1994.'

'And you and Mum started your affair when?'

'It was a few years later.'

'They *did* try to be just friends, Evie, but…'

'It's alright, Martha. I just need to get these dates clear. So, Alex, your affair with Mum started around 1997, is that right?'

'About then, yes.'

'When Dad was abroad.'

'In Africa, yes.'

'And you, me and Mum used to go around like a happy little family.'

'Well, yes, I suppose. Look, where's all this leading? Charlotte wasn't even around then.'

'Exactly!'

'What's that supposed to mean?'

'Charlotte was born in 2001, Alex.'

'Yes, thank you, Evie, I know when she was born.'

'In August.'

'Yes, and?' he demanded.

'Well, correct me if I'm wrong, but that means she was conceived in November 2000.'

'So?'

'Dad was in Africa, Alex. He didn't get back home until December 2000. A few days before Christmas.'

Martha gasped. 'No!'

'Has the penny dropped yet, Alex?' demanded Evie.

'This is madness. Charlotte came early, that's what Jean told me,' said Alex.

'Well, she would say that, wouldn't she?'

'Jesus, Evie, are you saying what I think you're saying?'

'Put it like this, Alex, Dad isn't Charlotte's biological father.'

'But he's never said.'

'He's only just found out.'

'How?'

'Their blood groups. At the hospital, Alex. Dad found out that Charlotte is group O. Dad is group AB.'

'Ah.'

'Ah—ah? Is that all you've got to say—fuck you, Alex.'

'What do you want me to say, Evie?' He turned to Simon. 'I had no idea, really I didn't. God, what a mess.'

Chapter 15

The Bolognese sauce, cold and congealed, remained on the hob. The candles guttered and spat. The cat sat, statue-like, staring towards the front door.

Simon poured Evie another wine.

Mutely, she accepted.

'It looks like we'll be eating spaghetti Bolognese for a few days,' said Simon.

'What?'

'Given that nothing was eaten, I was just saying...'

'Yes, right, the Bolognese,' said Evie, taking a gulp of wine. 'It's a good job we both like it.'

'Yes.'

'Poor Dad.'

'I know.'

'And Charlotte; who's going to tell Charlotte?'

'Look, I don't wish to belittle your situation, but there's nothing much that can be done immediately, so I think we should concentrate our efforts on Paul Sharp's case. What do you think?'

Evie peered up at Simon. 'What?'

'This Elspeth thing—the fact that Alex...'

'Alex,' spat Evie.

'Yes, quite, but the thing is, don't you see? He's given us a lead.'

Evie blinked away tears and wiped her nose. 'A lead?'

'Into the Alice Sharp case.'

'Right.' Evie sat up straight. 'Oh, right, yes, bloody hell, he did, didn't he? So, what do we do?'

'Well, we could try contacting the Mansion House in Leeds.'

'Absolutely, yes, right,' said Evie, catapulting herself towards Simon's desk. She opened his laptop and began a frantic search. 'Here we are, Mansion House Hotel, and they have a twenty-four-hour contact service,' she said, turning the laptop to face Simon. 'Here's their number.'

Simon downed the remains of his whisky and dialled.

'It's Martha I feel sorry for, she...'

Simon held up his hand. 'Hello, is that the Mansion House Hotel?'

'It is. How may I help you?'

'I'd like to speak to the manager.'

'I'll put you through now. May I ask what it's in connection with?'

'It's personal.'

'Hold the line.'

Covering the mouthpiece, Simon mumbled, 'They're putting me through now.'

'What are you going...?'

Simon held his hand up again. 'Good evening. I'm sorry to bother you at this late hour.'

'Not at all. How may I be of assistance?'

'My name is Simon, Simon Trent.'

'Good evening, Mr Trent, Mrs Georgina Richardson speaking, Manager of the Mansion House. Now then, my receptionist said you wanted to speak to me about a personal matter.'

'It's a shot in the dark really. I'm ringing on behalf of my sister. She's trying to get in touch with a friend of hers. They lost touch oh, must be about twelve or thirteen years ago now. The thing is, my sister isn't very well and she keeps asking for someone called Elspeth. She's certain that Elspeth worked at The Mansion House in the '90s but she simply cannot recall her surname. I don't suppose you...'

'Elspeth, oh, yes. Elspeth Mitchell, she was marvellous; not only did she organise conferences, but she also worked in accounts. An excellent, hard-working and efficient woman. I was extremely sorry to lose her. I even offered her a pay rise, but to no avail.'

'Mitchell, yes, that sounds familiar. I'm sure I recall my sister mentioning that name in the past,' said Simon, winking at Evie. 'But, you're saying she no longer works there.'

'No, I'm sorry, but your sister was right about the timing, Mr Trent. Elspeth was with us for eight years. She left in 2000.'

'I don't suppose you know where she went after she left your employ?' asked Simon.

'No, sorry, not a clue. I do know she had an admirer, well, she had many admirers to be honest, but there was one who I think was the main contender, as it were.'

'Oh, and who was that?'

'Again, not a clue. Elspeth never revealed his name. All very cloak and dagger.'

'But you met him?'

'Well, not as such, no. But I did see him on occasion, waiting in his car at the end of Elspeth's shifts. A good looking chap. Dark hair. Late thirties or early forties, I'd say.'

'I don't suppose you can remember anything about the car?'

'Not wishing to perpetuate sexist ideas about woman and cars, Mr Trent, but I'm afraid all I remember is that it was blue.'

'Well, thank you for your help.'

'I haven't been much help at all, sorry. I hope you find her. And if you do, please remember me to her. She did say she'd keep in touch but, well, there you are, I expect life got in the way, as is often the case—what?—I'm on the phone here—right, fine—look, Mr Trent, I'm sorry…'

'You're needed, no problem, thank you again. Goodbye'

Evie stared at Simon. 'Well?'

'Elspeth Mitchell, Evie; ring any bells with you?'

Evie frowned.

'Paul and Julia's list from...'

'From the graveyards, oh, yes, of course. I think that was one of the names on the list, but you sent it to that friend of yours, didn't you?'

'To Angela, yes, I did, but I kept a copy.'

'And where did you put it?'

'I filed it.'

'I'm impressed,' said Evie, making her way towards the cabinet. 'Under 'Sharp', I assume.'

Simon nodded.

'Got it.'

'And is the name Elspeth Mitchell there?'

Evie scanned the list. 'Yes, it's here,' she exclaimed. 'Elspeth Mitchell, born on August the ninth, 1970 and died on October the twelfth, 1972, buried in the Acharacle Parish Church graveyard, twelve miles from Strontian.'

'Bingo,' said Simon, pressing the call button. 'Hi, there, Angela, Simon here.'—'Sorry, is it that late?'—'No, I'm not hassling. I'm just ringing to tell you I've found out the name Alice Sharp is using.'—'No, it was serendipity as opposed to excellent detective skills on my part; anyway, she's using the name Elspeth Mitchell and it seems she had an admirer.'—'No idea; all I can tell you is that he drove a blue car.'—'Hah, yes, I know.'—'Right, brilliant. I look forward to your phone call in the near future.'—'Well, as soon as possible really.'—'That would be great. You're a star.'

The following evening, Sarah opened the door to a frazzled-looking woman clutching a briefcase. 'I'm sorry to bother you, but I'm looking for Simon, Simon Trent?'

'He's in the upstairs flat, you just need to...'

'No, I know that, I've already been up there, but there's no answer. It's very important. I really need to speak to him.'

'Hang on.' Sarah jogged down to Evie's room and banged on the door.

Evie called out. 'It's open.'

Sarah stuck her head round the door. 'Oh, good, you're here. There's a woman at the door looking for you, Simon.' She lowered her voice. 'I think it might be something important. She looks stressed out.'

Simon frowned, and made his way across the room. 'Did you get her name?'

'No, sorry, didn't ask.'

'Angela, what are you doing here?' exclaimed Simon. 'I assumed you'd ring.'

'I was going to but, well, I jumped into the car as soon as I—anyway, the journey wasn't too bad.' She glanced at her watch. 'Eight o'clock, so it's only taken me five hours. I stopped for a snack somewhere, can't remember where, but it was pretty dire. Are you going to let me in?'

'What? Yes, sorry, come in, come in. Evie's here, you haven't met her yet, have you?'

'No,' said Angela, as she followed him down the hallway.

'Here we are,' said Simon, entering Evie's room. 'Angela, this is Evie, Evie, meet Angela, and this is Sarah, Sarah, meet Angela.'

'Hi there,' said Evie. 'Bloody hell, you look exhausted; oh, God, I didn't mean, sorry, that sounded…'

'It's fine, and, as it happens, I am rather tired.'

'Have you just driven all the way up from London?' asked Evie.

Angela nodded.

'Well, I'm not surprised you…'

'So, what's the news, then? Have you tracked down Elspeth Mitchell, aka Alice Sharp?' asked Simon.

'Simon! Give the poor woman a moment to catch her breath.'

146

'Sorry,' said Simon, ushering Angela towards an armchair. 'Here, sit down. Have you arranged anywhere to stay?'

Angela shook her head. 'Not yet.'

'Well, if you don't object to a sofa-bed,' said Evie. 'You can stay here for the night. That would be alright, wouldn't it, Sarah?'

'Absolutely, no problem.'

'Oh, that would be marvellous. Thank you.'

'Would you like a coffee?' asked Evie.

'I don't suppose you've got any wine, have you?'

'We always have wine,' said Sarah. 'I'm afraid it's nothing special, though. I think it's probably something German.'

'Anything,' said Angela, 'as long as it's cold and alcoholic —not that I want to sound desperate.'

'I'll fetch it immediately and then I'll make up the sofa-bed.'

'I don't want to put you to any trouble.'

'It's no trouble at all. I assume you'll need to speak with Simon and Evie in private, so I'll bring the wine through and leave you to it.'

'Perfect,' said Simon, turning to Angela. 'So, come on, why *have* you driven all this way?'

'Because I thought it would be better to speak to you face-to-face.'

'That sounds ominous.'

'It's certainly awkward.'

There was a knock at the door. 'Can someone help me?'

Evie rushed to open the door and relieved Sarah of a bottle of Riesling and three glasses. 'You're a star. Thanks.'

'Is everything alright?' whispered Sarah.

'I'm not sure.'

'Well, good luck.'

'I think we might need it,' said Evie, as she nudged the door shut with her hip.

'This really is very good of you,' said Angela, accepting a glass from Evie.

'Nonsense, it's no trouble. Anyway, Sarah's doing all the work,' she exclaimed, thrusting a glass towards Simon and giving him an encouraging look.

'Thanks,' said Simon.

Evie poured the wine, set the bottle on her desk and turned towards Angela. 'So, you were saying you needed to speak face-to-face.'

Angela took a gulp of wine. 'Right—oh, before I forget; you asked John to see if he could find you any info on Jack Gray, the father of your missing person...'

'I wouldn't be surprised if he had a massive police record,' said Evie.

'You didn't take to him, I assume.'

'Horrid man.'

'Well, sorry to disappoint, but there was nothing, not even an unpaid parking ticket and, trust me, in London that's...'

'Presumably he was interviewed when James Sharp reported his wife missing,' said Simon.

'Obviously, but it was routine stuff. Nothing of any significance came from the interview.'

'I see, well thank John from me, much appreciated.'

'Will do,' said Angela, taking another gulp of wine.

'Anyway, you didn't drive all the way from London to tell me that,' said Simon. 'So, come on, what's going on?'

'I'll get straight to the point, then, shall I?'

'I think that would be best,' said Simon.

'Right. So, the Elspeth Mitchell on the list you sent to me was born on August the ninth, 1970 and died on October the twelfth, 1972. She was buried in the Acharacle Parish Church graveyard, twelve miles from Strontian; correct?'

'Correct.'

'Well, you won't be surprised to hear that I've found another Elspeth Mitchell with the identical birth certificate and the same parents as the dead Elspeth Mitchell, yet miraculously alive and well, living in Heybrook Bay.'

'Where's that?' asked Evie.

'Near Plymouth.'

'On her own?' asked Simon.

'Well, that's the thing, no, she...' Angela took another gulp of wine.

'So, come on, Angela, who's she living with?'

Angela closed her eyes and took a deep breath.

Evie and Simon exchanged confused looks.

Simon shrugged.

'She's living with someone called Adam Trent,' blurted Angela.

'What did you say?'

'I think you heard me, Simon.'

Simon swayed. 'I—hold on, let me get this straight,' he said. 'You're telling me that my brother, Adam, the man who was charged with the responsibility of tracking down Alice Sharp on behalf of her *husband*, is actually shacked up with her? Are you fucking kidding me?'

'Simon, your brother's actions are not Angela's fault,' said Evie.

'You're absolutely right. Sorry, Angela.' He knocked back the contents of his glass, refilled it and took another gulp. 'How long have they been living there?'

'Since 2000. Prior to that Elspeth Mitchell, aka Alice Sharp, was living in Leeds where she worked...'

'At the Mansion House in Roundhay Park, Leeds. Yes, we know,' snapped Simon.

Evie's eyes widened. 'Simon? Wasn't it in 2000 when Adam told you he was going to Ireland?'

'Yes, he bloody did, the bastard. This is unbelievable.' He banged his glass down. 'Fuck him to hell and back.'

'Well, before you do that,' said Evie, 'don't you think we should pay him a visit?'

'Too bloody right. What's the actual address, Angela?'

'It's on Renney Road,' replied Angela, retrieving a folder from her briefcase. 'The details are in there. I've researched the area. There's a small B&B called *The Nobody Inn...*'

'Hah, brilliant name,' said Evie.

Simon threw her a withering glance.

'It's in Down Thomas,' continued Angela, 'a village just up the road from Heybrook Bay, and they have rooms available this weekend.'

'I don't suppose...'

'Yes,' said Angela, their number's in the folder.'

Chapter 16
Devon, Saturday 25th - Sunday 26th May, 2013

Simon staggered through the entrance of *The Nobody Inn* and dropped their bags at reception. Evie rang the bell.

A plump, red-faced woman materialised from behind a curtained-off area. 'Mr Simon Trent?'

Simon nodded. 'I'm sorry we're late. We were supposed to be leaving Northallerton early, but circumstances conspired against us, and then the traffic...'

'Don't give it another thought. It can't be helped. You're here now and that's all that matters.'

Simon bent down to retrieve their bags.

'You leave those be. My Alfred will deal with them,' she said, as she moved out from behind the counter and pushed open a set of double doors opposite the reception desk. 'You sit yourselves down there, my loves. I'll make you a fresh pot of tea. You both look exhausted.'

'That would be smashing, thank you,' said Evie.

They looked round, exchanged a look and burst out laughing.

'Shhh,' giggled Evie, 'she'll hear.'

'Where are we supposed to sit?'

'We just need to move a few cushions.'

'A few!'

Evie pushed several cushions aside and they sank into the soft, deep sofa. The soothing tick of a mantle clock filled the room. Evie smiled as Simon began to sink a little further down, his eyes closed, and his breathing settled into a gentle rhythm.

The double doors burst open and Simon jolted awake.

'Here we are, didn't take long. Kettle was already boiled.'

The double doors swung open again. 'Bags installed as instructed, Beth, my love.'

'You're a dear, Alfred,' said Beth, pouring the tea. 'Will you look at these poor things, exhausted they are. And you'll never guess where they're from. Northallerton, would you believe it?' She handed Evie a cup. 'My Alfred was born there, you know.'

'And what brings you down to these parts?' asked Alfred.

'We've come to surprise my brother, Adam Trent.'

'Well now, there you go, I said, didn't I, Alfred?' said Beth, handing Simon a cup. 'I said to my Alfred, I said you'd be related to Adam.'

'Special occasion, is it?' asked Alfred.

'In a way,' said Simon.

'They haven't seen each other for some time,' said Evie. 'We're especially looking forward to meeting Elspeth.'

'Oh, now, you'll like her, you will. She's a treasure. Helps us with the books, she does. They moved in just after we took over here, didn't they, Alfred? Stayed here for a few weeks while they had some decorating done. You should see their kitchen, it's beautiful, and...'

'No doubt we'll be given the guided tour, tomorrow,' said Simon, his tone icy.

Beth bristled. 'Yes, well, I'm sure you will.'

'You enjoy your tea. Supper's at seven o'clock,' said Alfred, easing Beth towards the door.

Sunday morning, the moment they'd finished breakfast, Evie and Simon set off down Renney Road.

'The house should be on the left just past a turning into Gabber Lane.'

'How far now?'

High hedges loomed above them. 'Difficult to say. It's like driving through a tunnel,' she said brightly.

They flashed past a turning.

'Was that Gabber Lane?'

'I think so.'

Simon slowed down and peered ahead. 'This must be it,' he said, as he flung the car left through a set of ornate wrought-iron gates.

Evie gripped the dashboard as Simon ground to a halt amidst a hail of gravel. Glancing out of the rear window, she said, 'Look at that view, Simon, it's breathtaking.'

Simon slammed the car door and began to make his way up the driveway. 'Yes, lovely.'

Running after him, she managed to grab his arm. 'You can't possibly have taken in anything with such a cursory glance.'

He turned. He looked. 'Well, well, well.'

'What?'

He swept his arm in an arc. 'We've seen that view before.'

'Have we?'

'On a wall, above a fireplace.'

Evie frowned and looked again. 'Oh, yes. The painting by...'

'Janet Gray.'

'A painting of the view from...'

'The grandparent's house.'

'But that means...

'That means...'

'Simon,' exclaimed Evie, 'are you going to let me finish a sentence, or what?'

'Sorry, you were saying?'

'Well, there's no point now, is there?'

'Simon, thank God,' cried a voice from behind them. 'Have you found her?'

Evie turned and saw an older, bearded version of Simon striding towards them. He extended his arm. 'Adam Trent, and you must be Evie Morgan.'

'I am, yes, but how...?'

'Well, Simon?'

'What the hell's going on, Adam?'

'It's complicated.'

'Oh, classic line, well done.'

'Jesus, Simon, have you found her or not?'

'Sorry, am I missing something here,' said Simon. 'If by 'her' you mean Alice, then yes, I've found...'

Adam rushed forward and engulfed Simon. 'Good man; knew you had it in you.' Releasing Simon, he dashed towards the car. 'Elspeth, God, you gave me a fright,' he said, snatching open the door. 'Elspeth?' He whirled round. 'Where is she?'

'Oh, give it a rest, Adam.'

'Simon, don't,' said Evie, her voice stern. 'She's obviously not here.'

Adam ran his hand through his hair. 'Oh, God, God, Elspeth.'

'You're telling me she's run off again?' said Simon.

'I thought that's why you were here. Oh, shit, shit, shit.'

'When did she go missing?' asked Evie.

Adam turned his anguished face towards Evie. 'It's been five days now. There was no note, nothing. I've rung Janet. It's the first thing I did, and she told me you'd been to visit the parents, and...'

'Shall we go inside?' suggested Evie.

'Yes, yes, of course, sorry. Come in, come in.'

'Simon?' said Evie.

'Fine,' said Simon, stomping up the drive.

At this very same moment, some distance away, a woman was sat alone on a bench, staring out to sea. A child's red plastic bucket and spade rested beside her. She balled a damp handkerchief in her hands and shut her eyes. The bright sun burnt through her eyelids, producing an array of multi-coloured patterns in her mind's eye. She closed her eyes tighter.

'Is everything alright, my dear?'

Lifting her hand to block the sun, she opened her eyes. A small, grey-haired lady peered down, her kindly face full of concern.

'Yes, thank you, I'm fine, just a bit of a headache, it'll pass.'

'There's thunder in the air, mark my words,' said the old lady. 'That'll be why you have a headache.'

Still shielding her eyes from the sun, the woman said, 'Do you think? There's not a cloud in the sky.'

'The pressure's falling, dear. Always a sure sign, that is.'

'Right then,' the woman said, standing. 'I'd better get back.'

'On holiday, are you?'

The woman nodded.

'Has your husband taken charge of your little one to give you a break?' said the old lady, smiling. 'That's what my Frank used to do, God rest his soul.'

'My little one?'

'Yes, dear,' said the old lady, glancing at the red plastic bucket glinting in the sunshine. 'Got bored with making sandcastles, did they?'

'Oh, right, yes, I see...'

'My name is Agnes,' said the old lady.

'Lovely to meet you, Agnes, but as...'

'Are you staying locally?'

The woman glanced over her shoulder. 'In the B&B, just across the road there. The yellow one.'

'Mavis's place, how lovely. You'll be looked after there. She and I go back years; she's a good woman, she is. Mind you, I can tell you a thing or...'

'Sorry, but I really should be getting back, especially if, as you say, the weather's about to break.'

'Quite right,' said Agnes, glancing towards the horizon. 'The storm will break soon. Now, you look after yourself. Ask Mavis for a drop of her potion, she makes it herself.

Personally, I swear by it. It'll clear any headache, guaranteed.'

Back in Devon, Adam was setting a tray of coffees down. 'Help yourself to sugar. I assumed you both wanted milk.'

Evie took a mug, handed it to Simon and helped herself to one. 'Thanks.'

Adam and Simon glared at each other, neither spoke.

'This is a lovely place,' said Evie, 'and the view is wonderful. You're very lucky.'

'Yes, Elspeth…'

Simon raised his eyes and harrumphed.

'She's been Elspeth for over twenty years, Simon, and that's how I think of her.'

'Is that a fact?'

'Yes, that's a fact.'

'And whose idea was her change of name? Yours, I assume.'

'Yes, it was my idea. We could hardly be together if she kept her original name, could we?'

'It was your job to *find* her, for God's sake,' snapped Simon. 'Whatever possessed you to…?'

'She possessed me, Simon. We fell in love, simple as that.'

'Oh, give me a break.'

'Putting all that aside for the moment,' said Evie. 'When you spoke to Janet did she have any idea where Alice, sorry, Elspeth, might have gone?'

Adam sighed and again ran his hands through his hair. 'No. I asked her if there was anywhere special they'd gone to in the past. She wasn't very forthcoming, but that's not surprising, I suppose.'

'What's that supposed to mean?' asked Simon.

'They don't like to talk about their past, and Janet can be very secretive. She's kept the whereabouts of her sister from her parents all this time.'

'As have you,' said Simon.

'Yes, as have I, at Elspeth's request, I might add.'

'And James, her husband, the man who *paid* you to find her, what about him?'

'I'd have thought that was obvious, Simon. Don't be deliberately dense.'

'But you *did* tell him where his wife was back in 1992,' said Evie.

'Yes, but that was only after I'd organised her safe passage from Strontian.'

'To the Mansion House in Leeds,' said Simon.

'Yes, a friend of mine owed me a favour. She stayed there until…'

'2000, yes we know,' said Simon. 'And you visited her regularly while lying to me, saying you were working on a case.'

Adam shrugged.

'And then you came here, to live in her grandparents' house,' said Evie,

Adam's eyes widened.

'We recognised the view,' said Evie. 'Mr and Mrs Gray have a painting of it above their fireplace.'

'Do they indeed? Right. Anyway, yes, that's right. Janet inherited the house after their grandmother, Grace, died in 1998. William had died ten years earlier; a coronary, he'd died instantly. A terrible shock.'

'We understood the property had been sold.'

'Jack told you that, did he?'

'Yes,' said Evie. 'He was rather put out that no money had come his way.'

'Janet didn't sell.'

'Obviously not,' said Simon. 'So, how could she afford to move to London?'

'She's a successful artist, Simon, very successful. And when the opportunity of a studio in London came her way, she jumped at it. She transferred the house to Elspeth.'

'That was inordinately generous of her,' said Simon.

'She's an inordinately generous woman,' said Adam.

'Has Elspeth been in touch with Janet?' asked Evie.

'Not since she ran off last week no, not according to Janet.'

'Don't you believe her?' said Evie.

'Not really, no,' said Adam. 'They're very close. Janet sees herself as Elspeth's protector.'

'From what?' asked Simon.

'From events in their past.'

'What events?'

'At the risk of being ridiculed,' said Adam. 'It really is complicated.'

'Shall I make more coffee?' asked Evie.

Coffee mugs replenished, Adam asked, 'So, come on, Evie. Tell me, what did you think of Jack Gray when you met him?'

'Not a lot. I thought he was a bully, full of his own self-importance and obviously of the opinion that a woman's place is in the kitchen. A man of his generation, I suppose. And when Janet turned up, Jesus, it was dreadful. I swear you could feel the air freezing.'

'I can imagine.'

'He told us they hadn't heard from Alice since the day she left their house.'

'Well, *he* certainly hasn't,' said Adam.

Evie frowned. 'So, are you saying Amy's heard from Alice.' She turned to Simon. 'Jack did mutter something about Amy believing Alice had been in touch when we were leaving, didn't he?'

Simon gave Adam an expectant look.

'She did let her mum know she was safe at the beginning; told her not to worry, that sort of thing, but she didn't say much more.'

'And, sorry, but I really can't believe that it was all because of one silly argument that she left,' said Evie.

'No, you're right, it wasn't.'

'So, why then?' asked Simon.

Adam picked his coffee mug up and then set it down again before locking eyes with his brother. 'Because Jack's a nasty piece of work, Adam. A real bastard. He beats Amy, always has. Never where it can be seen, of course, he's not a fool. The children witnessed it all, thought it was normal until they grew up. Then, when they tried to protect their mum, he beat them too.'

'Bloody hell, Adam,' said Simon. 'That's a very serious accusation. Are you sure?'

'Oh, yes, I'm positive.'

'But surely someone must have noticed; the school, their GP, someone,' said Evie.

'If they did, Jack always had a good explanation.'

'I don't understand,' said Evie. 'Why didn't the grandparents do anything after Janet moved in with them?'

'Janet explained to me that she didn't want to burden them and so she made the decision to tell them that it was simply a matter of convenience, to save on accommodation costs, they knew nothing about the beatings.'

'But what about when Alice turned up? She didn't even go to the college, so...'

'They assumed it was because she was missing her sister.'

The distant sound of waves crashing against rocks drifted through the open windows. Simon cleared his throat. 'Does James know about Jack's behaviour towards Amy and the children?'

'He didn't at first. Elspeth told him soon after Paul was born.'

'Because she didn't want Jack to have any contact with Paul?' said Evie.

'Exactly.'

Evie took a gulp of coffee. 'But it simply doesn't make sense. If she'd explained everything to James, then it was all out in the open. Her instinct was to protect Paul from his grandfather, perfectly understandable, so why did she feel the need to run away?'

'That I can't explain,' said Adam. 'Whenever I asked her about it she'd start to shake, so I let it go.'

'And she's never told you, even after all this time?' said Simon.

Adam shook his head. 'What would be the point? It's done now, it can't be undone. The important thing now is to find her. She's alone and vulnerable and I'm terrified, Simon, terrified that she might, she might...'

'Oh, Adam, try not to worry, we'll find her, won't we, Simon?'

'If Adam hasn't any idea where she is, then I don't see...'

'Don't be childish, Simon,' said Evie.

Simon shrugged and glanced around the room. His gaze alighted on a large painting hung above the fireplace. 'One of Janet's?'

Adam nodded. 'One of many portraits of Elspeth that you'll find around the house. Janet says she's an excellent sitter. That's my favourite one. It was painted soon after we moved in.'

Evie stood and wandered over towards the painting. 'It's beautiful, the tones are amazing.' Her eyes flicked to the bottom right corner. 'But it's signed Janet Lee. I thought her name was Gray.'

Adam snorted. 'Not a name she wishes to be associated with, Evie.'

'Ah, no, right and so, Lee is...?'

'Her mother's maiden name.'

'Are you telling me that Alice Sharp used the name Lee when she fled to Scotland and later became Elspeth Mitchell?' groaned Simon.

Adam nodded.

Simon raised his eyes towards the ceiling. 'No wonder I couldn't find the bloody file,' he mumbled.

'I love her, Simon, be it wrong or right, that's the truth. Please find her.' He swallowed, and his eyes filled with tears. He wiped them away with the back of his hand. 'Just find her.'

'Why didn't you tell me?'

'What, that I'd found her, organised her change of name, set her up in Leeds, lied to her husband and subsequently run off with her? Hardly the actions of a professional and I doubt you'd have gone along with it. You'd have felt compelled to inform her husband, as I would have done if the situation had been reversed. I didn't want to put you in that position, simple as that.'

'I can understand that,' said Evie.

'Me too, I suppose,' said Simon, giving his brother a gentle nudge.

Adam nudged back.

'None of us can help who we fall in love with, can we?' remarked Evie.

'Spoken with feeling,' said Adam, glancing from Evie to Simon. 'Is there something I should know?'

'Give it a rest, Adam. We're just good friends.'

'Such a useful expression, I've always found,' said Adam, with a smirk.

'I think Simon and I need to have a chat with Janet,' said Evie.

Adam nodded. 'I agree. Where are you staying?'

'In Down Thomas, in a small B&B.'

'Beth and Alfred's place, we stayed there when…'

'When you first moved in, yes, so they said.'

'I'll meet you there tomorrow morning.'

'You're coming with us?' said Evie.

'I can't just sit here and do nothing, can I?'

Alex and Martha stood outside the flat on Willow Road, unable to look at each other. Martha rummaged through her handbag and extracted her car keys. 'I'll drive you back to Ripon, and then I think it'll be best if I go home.'

Alex nodded.

The drizzle started as they drove through Skipton-on-Swale. Martha switched the wipers to intermittent, their soft, lethargic sweeps the only sound within the car.

Martha pulled into Alex's driveway. She kept the engine ticking over. 'Here we are, then.'

'Yes, here we are.'

Martha glanced at her watch. 'It's a forty-five-minute drive back to York.'

'I'm aware of that.'

'So, I need to get going.'

'Martha, this is ridiculous. Stay.'

'Not tonight, Alex.'

'Will you be alright?'

She rubbed his arm. 'I'll be fine; you?'

He shrugged. 'Probably.'

Alex hauled himself from the car and slammed the door. He gave a weary, half-hearted wave as Martha pulled away.

He stood there, hugging himself as the rain fell. His chest heaved. He turned his face towards the sky and the gentle raindrops ran down his face, mingling with his tears.

With shaking hands, he struggled to unlock the front door. Once inside, he headed straight to his drinks cabinet, snatched up a bottle of whisky and a glass and went to the study. He leaned on the door, bottle hanging down by his right side, glass clutched in his left hand, and heard the gentle click as the door shut. Taking a deep breath, he made his way across the room to his desk. He poured a generous portion of whisky, took a gulp and sat. He opened the top drawer, removed a small wooden box and placed it on the desk. He up-ended his pen-holder. Pens, pencils, paperclips, elastic bands, old and tarnished coins and indeterminate clumps of dust scattered across the desk. Riffling through the mess, he located the tiny key, unlocked the box and removed Jean's letters. Slumped in his chair, he re-read them as he methodically worked his way through the whisky.

On Saturday evening, as Simon and Evie were settling into the B&B in Down Thomas, Alex drove to York.

'Alex, this is an unexpected surprise. Didn't see you at work yesterday, is there a problem?'

'Had a bit of a headache, Gerry. Can I come in?'

'Yes, yes of course, old chap, come in, come in.' He glanced at his watch. 'Excellent. Late enough to offer you a drink,' he added, guiding Alex past a mess of boots, shoes and Wellingtons. 'I'm afraid you've missed Charlotte. She's staying over at a friend's house, a sleepover. A horrendous prospect. Can you imagine? Five excited young girls, all in one room. There won't be much sleeping, that's for sure.'

Making their way towards the living room, Gerry asked, 'So, to what do I owe the pleasure?'

'Do you think we could get a drink down our necks first?'

'Is everything alright?'

'Not really, Gerry, no.'

'Right, so, what can I get you?'

'Any whisky?'

'Can a dragon blow fire?'

'A whisky then.'

'Ice?'

Alex nodded.

Gerry handed Alex his drink. 'Here you are, make yourself comfortable,' he said, pouring his own and bringing the bottle to the table. 'Now, what's this all about?'

Alex stared at the whisky, took a deep breath and raised the glass to his lips. 'Actually, on second thoughts, perhaps not,' he said, setting the glass down onto a coaster that showed a scene of York Minster. He closed his eyes, recalling the day in 1994, soon after he'd returned from America, when he'd bought the set for Gerry and Jean as a Christmas gift.

Gerry sat, shook his head, and banged his ears. 'Sorry, did I hear right? Alex Brown turning down a whisky. It's single malt, you know. None of your...'

'Gerry, I need to talk to you.'

'Sounds serious.'

'It is.'

'Right.'

Alex gave him a weak smile.

'Come on then. What's wrong?'

'It's about Charlotte. Evie told me.'

'Oh, is that all?' said Gerry, taking a swig of whisky. 'She's fine now, no need to worry. One minute, she and Betty are best friends, next minute, mortal enemies with Charlotte claiming that Betty deliberately pushed her. A few days later, best friends again, hence the sleepover. It's at Betty's house. I suppose I should have rung you when it happened, but it hardly...'

'It's not about the fact that you didn't ring, Gerry.'

Gerry frowned. 'I'm not following you.'

'Evie *told* me, Gerry.'

'Yes, so you said. I'm sorry, but you're going to have to be more specific,' said Gerry, tapping his head. 'Ageing brain.'

'She told me about the blood group problem.'

Gerry took another sip of his drink. 'Did she indeed?'

Alex nodded. The ice crackled in his untouched drink.

'And this is the reason for your visit, is it?'

'You're not Charlotte's biological father.'

'I know that, Alex, but I fail to see what it's got to do with you. Unless, well, unless you know something.'

Alex picked up his glass, stared into the amber liquid, gave it a swirl and then, with inordinate care, replaced it onto the coaster.

'*Do* you know something? Did you know she was having an affair? Jesus, Alex, do you know who Charlotte's father is?'

Alex buried his head in his hands. 'Shit, Gerry, look, the thing is…'

'The thing is what, Alex?'

'The thing is, I loved Jean,' he blurted. 'Had done from the moment we met at Cambridge in 1978.'

Gerry sat motionless. 'But you were with Martha at Cambridge, that's what Evie told me the other night.'

'That's what Martha told Evie. It's what she'd wanted back then, but I wasn't with Martha, Gerry, I was with Jean. We were together all the time at Cambridge.'

'Jean told me you were just friends.'

'I know, Gerry, I know. I'm sorry.'

'So, what exactly are you saying?'

'Don't make this more difficult than it already is.'

'Oh, I'm *so* sorry, I wouldn't want to make you feel uncomfortable, perish the bloody thought.'

'Gerry, Jean and I, we…'

Gerry downed his drink, his expression incredulous. 'I refuse to believe it.'

'But it's true.'

'You and Jean? No.'

'I'm sorry, Gerry, but, yes.'

'For how long?'

'Does it matter?'

'Does it matter, does it matter? Of course it bloody matters. How long?'

'Seven years.'

'When?'

'1997 until, well, until the accident.'

Gerry grabbed the bottle and splashed whisky into his glass with such vigour that some spattered onto the polished table. 'Jesus, Alex,' he snatched up his glass, took a gulp and slammed it down. More whisky slopped onto the table. 'Are you saying she was with you at that seedy B&B?'

'It wasn't a seedy...'

'Oh, I do apologise. What was it? A five-star B&B? Well, that's alright then.'

'Gerry, listen to me,' pleaded Alex. 'She, she drove off in the night after she told me it was over, said she couldn't risk hurting you. She loved you, Gerry, really she did.'

'Good of you to let me know,' snapped Gerry. 'So, why the affair?'

'Because she loved me too.'

'Well, lucky old you.'

'I should never have taken that research post in America. I lost her the moment I boarded that plane.'

'You obviously didn't love her enough.'

'You don't know what you've got...'

'Oh, spare me the platitudes.'

'But it's true,' said Alex, his eyes fixed on the last sliver of ice as it melted into his whisky.

Gerry's expression shifted. It became dark, filled with malevolent intent.

Alex repositioned his glass such that its base completely covered the Minster. Keeping his eyes averted from Gerry, he swept invisible dust from his trousers.

Gerry watched him through steely eyes. 'Putting aside the issue of your sordid affair...'

Alex's head snapped up. He held Gerry's gaze. 'It wasn't sordid.'

'If you say so.'

'I do. Jean wasn't like that.'

'Is that a bloody fact? So good of you to point that out.'

'Sorry.'

'So, why now?' demanded Gerry.

'Why now, what?'

'Why are you telling me now?'

'Because of Charlotte; I'm her father,' blurted Alex. 'I didn't know, Gerry, really I didn't. It's as much a shock to me as it must be for you.'

Gerry clenched his fists. His expression darkened further.

'The thing is, what the hell do we do about Charlotte? I mean, she's only eleven.'

'Yes, thank you, Alex, I'm aware of how old she is.'

'Look I...'

Gerry ran his hand through his hair. 'And what the hell do I say to Evie?'

Alex cleared his throat. 'She already knows.'

'She knows I'm not the father, Alex, but she doesn't know who is.'

'Yes she does.'

'For fuck's sake, you've already told her?'

Alex held up his hands. 'I've done no such thing. *She* told *me*.'

Gerry stared blankly at Alex.

'In her new role as a private investigator,' said Alex, explaining about the love letters and her trip to North Wales.

'Oh, brilliant, so Simon knows too,' said Gerry, pouring himself another whisky. He sat in silence sipping his drink. He looked directly at Alex, his eyes thunderous, his jaw set. 'I think you should go now.'

'Yes, yes of course. Gerry, I...'

'Just get the fuck out of my house.'

Alex staggered to his feet. 'I...'

'Go!'

Chapter 18

It was approaching three o'clock that afternoon when Janet stood back from a painting she was working on. Wiping her brush, she viewed the picture from several angles. It was more abstract than her usual style; swirls of yellow, red and blue suggesting the shapes of buildings, rocks and waves. 'That's it, I think,' she declared. 'Not bad, not bad at all.'

The studio door creaked open.

'Hi there, Janet, not disturbing you I hope?'

'Adam, what are you doing here?' she exclaimed.

'I don't know where she is, Janet. She hasn't been in touch since I rang you. That was six days ago. *Six* days. Where the hell *is* she?'

'I'm sure she'll be fine...'

'You sound very certain about that.'

'Look, why don't you come and sit down. I was just about to take a break. Coffee?'

'Where is she, Janet?'

Standing with her back towards him, Janet poured boiling water into mugs. 'I told you. I don't know.'

'I had a visit from Simon yesterday.'

She clutched the kettle handle. 'That didn't take him long.'

'He's good at his job.'

'And what has he discovered?'

'Quite a lot, Janet,' said Adam. 'He's discovered where I live now, obviously; *and,* he's also discovered who lives there with me.'

Janet whirled around.

'Oh, yes, it didn't take him long to find out that Alice had changed her name to *Elspeth Mitchell;* not only that, but he also knows that she and I have been together since she went missing from Strontian, because, as...'

'No,' gasped Janet, her grip on the kettle handle tightening.

'Yes! Because, as I said, he's good at his job. So, you see, he knows you lied to your parents about selling the house and now he's also wondering what else you may have lied about.'

'Well, I've lied about a lot of things, you know that. I had to.' She returned the kettle to the hob and picked up the mugs. 'I've told Mum that she's safe. No more than that. Dad hasn't a clue.'

'I'm aware of that, Janet, but the main concern is where Elspeth is *now*. And, not unreasonably, given the circumstances, Simon was wondering whether you or I had any idea where she might be.'

'I take it you told him we didn't.'

'Well, *I* certainly don't.'

Janet handed him a mug. 'Meaning?'

'It means what it means,' said Adam, his tone unforgiving.

'For God's sake, Adam, I've already told you,' she said, taking a sip of coffee. 'I haven't a clue where she is.'

A voice from the studio door asked, 'And you're absolutely sure about that, are you?'

Janet's head snapped up. A frown crossed her forehead as she took in the appearance of the two people now striding towards her. 'Simon? Evie? What the...?'

'We've come to help,' said Evie.

'Adam, what's going on?'

'We need to find her. You seem convinced she'll be fine, but I'm not so sure. So, if you have any ideas, now's the time to speak, before it's too bloody late,' said Adam, plonking his mug down and advancing on Janet.

Simon clamped his hand onto Adam's shoulder, stopping him in his tracks, while Evie continued across the studio towards Janet, who stood motionless, clutching her mug in both hands.

Evie spoke gently. 'Adam has explained to us about your childhood, Janet. He's told us how you always tried to protect your sister, and...'

Janet glared at Adam.

'...and it's entirely understandable, but Adam's out of his mind with worry. Please, be honest, *have* you heard from her?'

Janet twisted around and placed her mug down with exaggerated gentleness next to the kettle. Hands splayed, she leaned for a moment on the counter. Her back heaved. And then, with slow, deliberate care, she turned to face everyone. She took in a large gulp of air, clutched at the arm of an old, paint-splattered sofa and lowered herself into it before giving Evie a small nod.

Adam lurched forward. Simon tightened his grip on his shoulder. 'Leave it to Evie,' he whispered.

Evie knelt at Janet's feet. 'And did she say where she was?'

Janet grabbed hold of Evie's hand. 'No, she wouldn't tell me. I tried to—I think it's just all got too much for her, and...' Her voice cracked. Tears rolled down her face and her body shuddered as the sobs escaped in strangled bursts.

Simon dug around in his jacket pocket and handed a large white handkerchief across to Evie. She slipped it into Janet's hands. The sobbing gave way to small gasps. Janet took a huge breath, wiped her eyes and blew her nose. 'Sorry.'

Adam's defiant tone softened somewhat, as he took in Janet's appearance. 'I had to tell them about your awful childhood because, well, I had to, to make them understand, you do see that, don't you?'

Janet gave him a weak smile.

Simon cleared his throat. 'Has she rung you?'

'No, *I* rang her immediately after Adam rang me.'

'But, how? Her phone's switched off,' said Adam, 'every time I ring, it goes straight to voicemail.'

Janet chewed her lower lip.

'Janet?' said Simon.

'She has another phone.'

'What *other* phone?' asked Adam, his tone once again unforgiving.

'One I got for her. It only has my number in it.'

'Jesus, bloody shit and hell, Janet, are you saying you know where she is? Because if you do, then fucking TELL us.'

'Alright, Adam there's no need…'

'No need, no need for what, Simon? No need for me to be angry? No need for me to be scared? Don't you all understand? Elspeth's desperate, she's not thinking clearly, she—oh, God, we need to find her.'

Evie took hold of Janet's hand again and said in a calm voice, 'Have you *any* idea where she might have gone?'

Janet shook her head. 'I've been trying to think, really I have. Sometimes painting clears my mind, but nothing's come to me. Nothing.' Her eyes, fixed on Evie, were filled with pain. 'I simply don't know.'

'What about a place you both loved as children,' said Evie, 'sometimes…'

'That's it,' exclaimed Janet, catapulting herself from the sofa and dashing across to her painting. 'Oh, that's it. Look, the colours, the shapes; we had plastic buckets and spades…'

'Plastic buckets,' exclaimed Adam. 'What the…'

'Adam, listen to me,' said Janet. 'I've been an idiot. I don't know why I didn't…'

'Do you know where she is or not?' cried Adam.

'Yes, yes, I think I do.'

'Then, for fuck's sake…'

'Adam!' exclaimed Simon.

He held up his hands. 'Sorry, sorry. Janet, please, anything, anything at all.'

'Oh, Adam, don't apologise, I, I, oh, hell.'

'Janet, where do you think she might be?' asked Simon.

She swallowed. 'I think she might have gone to the B&B we used to go to with Mum when we were little. It was our only time away from Dad and we always stayed a fortnight.' She gulped. 'Adam, if she went straight there, then...'

'She'll still be there.'

Janet nodded. 'Oh, God, Adam, I hope so.'

'So, where is it?'

'It's in Weymouth. *Sunshine Hideaway*. It's on the seafront,' said Janet, grabbing her jacket and bag. 'Come on, we need to go.'

Chapter 19

Mavis placed a tea tray laden with cupcakes onto her table. 'Here we are, Agnes. I'll be mother. You tuck in.'

'I shouldn't really,' said Agnes, helping herself to two of the largest cakes. 'Oh, by the way, I bumped into one of your guests yesterday. Warned her about the storm.' She turned what was left of the cupcake around in her hand, examining it with care. 'It was a cracker, wasn't it?'

'It certainly was,' remarked Marvis.

Agnes popped the remaining piece into her mouth and gulped it down, before adding, 'She was a lovely woman. She seemed sad though. Always the way, isn't it? Can't wait for some peace and quiet and then, when you have it, you miss the hustle and bustle.'

'Who was that then?'

'Don't think I got her name.' Agnes took a bite from the second cupcake, closed her eyes, chewed methodically and swallowed. 'She was small, a brunette, pretty little thing, wore a red jacket.'

'Oh, that'll be Judy, Judy Smith,' said Mavis, handing Agnes her tea.

'So, what's her husband like?'

'Whose husband?'

'Mavis, do pay attention, dear. We were talking about your guest, Judy.'

'I've no idea, Agnes. I didn't even know she was married.' She took a delicate bite of cake and swallowed. 'Come to think of it, I don't recall seeing a ring. Still, doesn't mean a thing these days, I suppose.'

'She said her husband was looking after the child.'

'What child?'

'Well, theirs presumably.'

'Are you sure we're talking about the same person?'

'How many red-jacketed brunettes do you have staying here?'

Mavis took another small bite from her cake and chewed.

'Well?'

Dabbing at her mouth with her napkin, Mavis replied. 'Just the one. She arrived late last Tuesday, odd day to arrive really. Anyway, she booked a fortnight in a *single* room. She's quiet. Spends most of her days out and about.'

'That's odd,' said Agnes, peering at the remains of her second cake. 'I was telling her how my Frank used to take charge of the little ones, God rest his soul, and what a kind man he was, and she...' Agnes blinked back tears.

Mavis reached across and patted her arm. 'I expect you just assumed, I mean, did she actually say her husband was looking after their child?'

Agnes pulled a handkerchief from the sleeve of her cardigan and wiped her eyes. 'Now I come to think about it, I'm not sure she did, you know.'

Mavis pushed the plate across the table. 'Have another cake.'

'Is there any more tea in that pot?'

Lifting the lid, Mavis squinted. 'I'll make a fresh one.'

Pouring the boiling water into the teapot, Mavis chattered on. 'They say it's going to be warm and sunny for the rest of the week, so that's good, what with it being the school holidays. The children do love to spend time on the beach building sandcastles, bless them.'

'She had a red plastic bucket and spade.'

'Sorry, who had a red plastic bucket and spade?'

'Your brunette, when I met her, sitting on that bench across the road, there was a child's red plastic bucket and spade by her side.'

Driving down to Weymouth from London, Adam sat in the front passenger seat next to Simon. Evie and Janet were in the back. 'I can't find a B&B called *Sunshine Hideaway*,' said Evie, scrolling down her phone. 'Are you sure that's what it was called?'

'Positive,' said Janet.

'It *was* back in the late '70s, as in over thirty years ago,' said Adam, craning his head around. 'Maybe it's closed.'

'Oh, God, don't say that,' cried Janet.

'Can you remember where it was? A street name, anything?'

'No.' Janet screwed her eyes shut. 'I remember it was a short walk to the beach and it was painted a bright sunshine yellow, hence the name, I suppose. Anyway, when Alice saw it she cried and cried saying she wanted the yellow plastic bucket and spade and I said it was too late she'd already chosen the other set; I was quite nasty to her really, oh, God. Give me a few road names, it might jog my memory.'

'The road running alongside the seafront is Preston Road,' said Evie, 'there are loads of B&Bs on it.'

'Doesn't ring a bell.'

'What about Crescent Street, Victoria Street, Lennox Street or Queen Street?'

Janet sighed. 'No, none of those sound familiar.'

The heavy traffic in London meant it was nearly nine o'clock when they arrived in Weymouth, and the sun was setting.

'Maybe if we drive down along the seafront I might recognise something,' suggested Janet.

'Or, even better,' said Evie, 'we may spot a B&B painted bright yellow. Surely we couldn't miss that.'

'OK, executive decision,' said Simon, drawing up alongside the curb. 'Assuming Alice…'

'Simon, I keep telling you, she's been Elspeth for over twenty years now. Both Janet and I…'

'Fine, assuming *Elspeth* came here a week ago, and assuming she's going to be here for the rest of this week, I suggest we find a hotel. I don't know about you, Janet, but the rest of us haven't eaten since breakfast. We've been on the road for what seems like forever and I'm knackered. We can make a start looking for this B&B in the morning. Deal?'

In London, over breakfast at Julia's on Tuesday morning, Paul checked his phone again.

'He said he'd ring you when he had news.'

'I know that, Julia, but it's been over a week now.'

'Only just. Give him a chance.'

'It's the cost, Julia, it's mounting up. Shit; I'm going to call him.'

'Oh, Paul, how's that going to help?'

'Well, I won't know unless I try, will I?'

'Suit yourself,' said Julia, as Paul hit the call button for Simon Trent.

'Mr Trent, look, I'm sorry to bother you, but...'

'You wondered if we'd made any progress?' said Simon, leaning back in his chair, as the hotel waiter poured more coffee.

'Is it Paul?' mouthed Janet, putting her toast and marmalade down.

Simon nodded.

'So, have you?' asked Paul.

Wiping her fingers, Janet waved her hand. 'Let me talk to him.'

'Mr Trent, are you still there?'

'Yes, sorry, Paul. I'm actually with Janet at...'

'Aunt Janet?' exclaimed Paul.

Julia's eyes widened. 'Janet's there?'

Paul nodded.

'The very same,' replied Simon, as Janet's arm-waving became more frantic. 'And she'd like a word.'

Janet snatched the phone away. 'Paul, it's me, Aunt Janet. Listen, now don't worry, but...'

'Oh, God, what? Has something happened to Mum?'

'Paul, I said don't worry. The thing is she's, well, she's run away again.'

'But Mr Trent found her, did he?'

'Sort of.'

'You're not making sense. Has he found her, or not?'

'He, well, he discovered where she'd been living recently.'

'Right, and where was that?'

'Down in the south-west.'

'Whereabouts in the south-west?'

'That's not important, given she's not there now, is it?'

'No, I suppose not. So, where are you now? And why are you with Mr Trent?'

'I'm with Simon, Mr Trent, because I think I might know where she is, but...'

'Oh, God; just a minute.' Paul clasped the phone to his chest. 'Julia, Janet thinks she knows where Mum is.' He put the phone back to his ear. 'Where?'

'Look, I'm not sure, it's just a possibility. Give us a few hours and we might know more. Can you do that?'

'And you'll ring as soon as you know?'

'Yes, Paul, we'll ring.'

'Promise.'

'Promise, and...,' she stood up and moved away from the table, 'I don't know what Simon charges, but you mustn't worry. I'll pay. It's the least I can do in the circumstances.'

'What do you mean?'

'Oh, Paul, it's too complicated to explain over the phone. But you're a grown man now and, in my opinion, you deserve to know the truth. All of it.'

'Aunt Janet, what's going on? What truth? Truth about Mum? What do you mean?'

'Paul, we'll speak soon.'

'Hello, hello,' yelled Paul. He stared at the phone, frowned, and looked up at Julia. 'She's hung up.'

'What was that about 'truth'?' asked Julia.

'I've no idea. But it seems Aunt Janet might know where Mum is. And do you know what?'

'What?'

'I've got a feeling she's known all along.'

'No! Why would she have kept such a thing secret for all this time? No, it doesn't make sense.'

'Not at the moment it doesn't, I agree,' said Paul. 'But she said she'll pay all Mr Trent's fees. She said it was the least she could do in the circumstances.'

'What circumstances?'

'She wouldn't say.'

Returning to the table, Janet said, 'OK, are we all ready?'

'Listen, Janet,' said Simon, 'I'm concerned that if Elspeth is here in Weymouth and she spots you or Adam it might send her running again.'

'She's seen photographs of you, Simon,' said Adam, 'so she mustn't catch sight of you either.'

'Shit. OK, let's think,' said Simon. 'We know three main things about the B&B; one, it's within walking distance of the beach; two, it was called *Sunshine Hideaway* and three, it was painted yellow.' He glanced at Janet. 'Anything else?'

'No, sorry, that's it.'

'I'll ask at reception, see if anyone remembers such a place from back then.'

Minutes later, he bounded back to the table. 'It was taken over by Mavis and Charles Clifford in the '90s. They'd been looking for a B&B for some time and they snapped it up because, if you can believe it, Mavis loved the colour.'

'So, it's still painted yellow?' said Janet.

Simon nodded. 'A subtler shade apparently, but still yellow. They renamed it *Sunflowers*. I suggest Evie takes a look, makes a few enquiries and then we can take it from there. Is that alright with everyone?'

'Fine with me,' said Adam. 'Janet?'

'Fine.'

'Excellent.' Simon handed Evie a slip of paper. 'Here's the address. Outside the hotel, take a left into Queen Street then a dogleg into Victoria Street. At the end turn right into Lennox Street and keep going towards the Esplanade and then do a right and a quick left and you should see a footpath that takes you directly to Brunswick Terrace...'

'Brunswick Terrace; that's it,' exclaimed Janet.

'...*Sunflowers* is on the corner.'

Janet turned to Evie. 'I assume you know what she looks like these days.'

Evie nodded and patted her handbag. 'Adam gave us an up-to-date photo.'

Julia leaned across the breakfast table and squeezed Paul's hand. 'You don't really believe that your Aunt Janet has known where your mum is all along, do you?'

'I don't know what to think. It was such an odd thing for her to say. And the way she said it, Julia.' He shoved his phone into his pocket. 'I think I should talk to Dad.'

'Do you want me to come with you?'

'Would you mind?'

'Of course not. I'll tell Mum we're off to see...'

'The Wizard.'

Julia thumped him with the back of her hand as she passed him. 'Mum, Paul and I are off out. Leave the breakfast stuff. I'll sort it out when we get back.

Chapter 20
Weymouth and London, Tuesday 28th May 2013

In a small café opposite *Sunflowers,* Evie sat on a high stool by the window sipping her coffee; her attention mainly fixed on the entrance to the B&B as she flicked through a crumpled tourist leaflet that had been abandoned on the counter.

The front door of the B&B opened, and Elspeth appeared with a holdall slung across her shoulder. She stood for a moment outside the gate, looked left and right, wandered across the road to the coastal path and stepped down onto the beach. Evie snatched up the tourist leaflet, downed her coffee and followed.

Sat on the beach, Elspeth removed a red plastic bucket from the holdall and, using a red plastic spade, began to fill it with sand.

'Never loses its fun, does it?' said Evie.

Elspeth shaded her eyes and looked up. 'Sorry?'

'I was just saying, making sandcastles never loses its fun.'

'Oh, I see. No. You're right.'

'Mind you, I was useless at making them when I was little.'

'I was never very good at it, either. They always collapsed.' Elspeth nodded towards her current effort. 'As this one is about to; hopeless.'

'The sand needs to be wetter, I think,' said Evie, pointing towards the sea's edge. 'I bet you could make a decent castle over there.'

'I probably could, but it's pathetic at my age, don't you think?'

'No, I don't as it happens,' said Evie. 'There are 'sand-artists', you know. I've seen pictures of some of their creations and they're amazing. Mind you, I expect they have special equipment, although I don't know that for sure. Maybe they just use a plastic bucket and spade.'

'Yes, I think I can remember seeing those years ago.'

'There's an indoor place now, where the sculptures are protected from the weather.'

'Yes, Mavis, the owner of the B&B where I'm staying, was telling me about it.'

'So, have you been?'

'No, not yet.'

'I've read that it's definitely worth a visit,' said Evie, handing her the crumpled tourist leaflet. 'The information's all in here. It's just up the road, in Lodmoor Park.'

Elspeth tapped the remaining sand from the bucket and packed it back into her holdall. She struggled to her feet and smiled. 'Thank you. I think I'll pop along and have a look now. You never know, I might get some ideas for future creations.'

The moment Elspeth turned away, Evie scrabbled for her phone. She noticed three missed calls from Alex. Annoyed that he hadn't left any message, she scrolled through for Simon's number.

'Hi,'—'Yes, she's off to Sandworld,'—'Because, oh, it doesn't matter. The point is, it'll give me time to make a few enquiries at the B&B. Talk later.'

Evie felt a gentle tap on her shoulder.

'Looks like Judy's off on a mission.'

Evie swung round to see a little old lady smiling at her. 'Sorry?'

'Your friend, Judy,' said the little old lady, pointing towards the retreating figure of Elspeth.

'Oh, right, *Judy*, yes. She hasn't visited here for ages. Never been to Sandworld, so I suggested...'

'Not going with her?'

'No. I've been several times and, sorry, you are?'

'Agnes, I'm a friend of Mavis who runs the B&B where Judy's staying. I hope you don't think I'm being nosey but, well, your friend seems sad. I do hope everything's alright.'

'Oh, yes, everything's fine,' said Evie. 'I was quite surprised to bump into her, actually. As I said, she's not been here for ages. She's visiting old haunts from her childhood.'

'Strolling down memory lane.'

'Yes. Anyway, lovely to meet you, but...'

'You have to dash,' said Agnes. 'Young people these days, always in such a tearing hurry.'

'Yes, sorry. Things to do, places to be and all that.'

'Hopefully you'll have time to catch up with her another time. She's here until next week, Tuesday, I think. That's what Mavis told me anyway.' Agnes's face became serious. 'She spends a lot of time on her own. I think an old friend is just what she needs at the moment. None of my business, I know, but I hate to see someone so sad. Life is too short, don't you think? My Frank was a great believer in grabbing any opportunity that came his way. Said the first time he laid eyes on me he wasn't going to let me get away. Mind you...'

'I really *am* sorry, and I don't wish to be rude, but I do need to be going.'

'Yes, I know, I ramble on. Mavis is always telling me. She's been a good friend. She was a tower of strength when Frank passed on.' Agnes waved her hand and smiled. 'There I go again. Hopeless case.'

'Not at all, it's been lovely to meet you.'

'Oh, go on with you. Hopefully see you again. Perhaps at the B&B?'

'Yes, perhaps. Bye now.'

In London, Paul fumbled with the front door lock and, dragging Julia behind him, he stumbled into the hallway.

'Dad, Dad it's me. He's found her. He's actually found her. Dad!'

James rushed out from his study and immediately collided with Barbara. He grabbed her arm, steadying her. 'Jesus, sorry—are you alright?' he cried.

'Yes, yes, I'm fine,' said Barbara. 'What's happened?'

'It's Mum, she's been found.'

'Are you serious?' asked James.

'Hardly something I'd joke about.'

'Where is she?' asked Barbara.

'He's not actually sure at the moment.'

'So, he hasn't found her,' said James.

'He has, well he did, but she ran off again. Anyway, the thing is, Janet said…'

'Janet?' exclaimed James.

'Yes, Janet. You know, Mum's sister.'

'Yes, thank you, Paul, I'm perfectly aware who Janet is. I had no idea she was involved in the search as well.'

'She wasn't originally. I'm assuming Simon contacted her.'

'Who's Simon?'

'Simon Trent, he's Adam's brother.'

Barbara held up her hands. 'OK, why don't I put the kettle on and Paul can start from the beginning.'

'I'll help,' said Julia.

James sat at the kitchen table drumming his fingers while Paul fiddled with his phone.

'Here we are,' said Barbara, setting the coffees down. 'Now, come on, Paul, explain.'

Paul took a deep breath and outlined how he and Julia had met with Simon and Evie in Northallerton.

'So, I was right and, as I told you before you started out on this wild goose chase, Adam Trent *did* retire.'

'Yes, but as I've just explained, his brother, Simon, agreed to take up the case. And it hasn't been a wild goose chase because she *has* been found.'

'And lost again,' said James.

'Yes and no,' said Paul. 'Janet said she knew…'

'Thought she knew,' corrected Julia.

'Alright, yes, *thought* she knew where Mum might be.' He glanced at his phone again.

'I take it you're expecting her to ring,' said James.

'She said to give them a few hours and they'd get back to me.'

'By 'they', I take it you mean, Simon and Janet.'

Paul nodded. 'And Evie.'

'Where are they now?'

'Haven't a clue.'

'So, where was your mother? Before she ran off again, I mean,' asked James.

'Down in the south-west.'

'Where exactly?'

'Janet didn't say.'

James sighed.

Barbara concentrated on her coffee.

Paul's phone began to vibrate across the table. He grabbed for it, knocking his mug over. Jumping up to avoid the flood of coffee heading towards him, he sent his chair flying. Barbara scrabbled for the few sheets of crumpled kitchen towel that always seemed to be stuffed in her apron pocket and was dabbing at the coffee almost as soon as the chair hit the floor.

Paul threw an apologetic glance towards Barbara as he put the phone to his ear.

'Hi, any news?'—'God, really?'—'I'm with Dad and Barbara at the moment.' Julia nudged his arm. 'And Julia.'—'Yes, OK, right.'—'Uh, huh, I see, yes, yes, right away. See you in a few hours, then.'

Paul slid his phone into his trouser pocket. 'Wow!' He took a deep breath and looked up.

Three people were staring intently at him. 'That was Simon,' he said.

'So we gathered,' said James.

'They've found her.'

Still clutching the sopping wet kitchen towel, Barbara froze.

James covered Barbara's hand. 'Leave that.'

'Oh, Paul, that's brilliant,' exclaimed Julia. 'Where?'

'Weymouth.'

Barbara gasped.

'You alright?' said James.

Barbara cleared her throat. 'Yes, yes, fine. Did Simon say where in Weymouth?'

'Some B&B. He's suggesting I should join them. I can't believe it, I really can't. It's amazing; you'll come with me, won't you, Julia?'

'Try stopping me.'

'You're going straight to *The Sunshine Hideaway*? Do you really think that's wise?' said Barbara.

'The where?' said Paul.

Barbara fell silent.

James frowned. 'Barbara, Paul asked you a question.'

'Yes, thank you, James. Isn't that the B&B where your mum is, then?'

'I've no idea,' said Paul. 'I told you, Simon just said, *some* B&B.'

'Barbara?'

'Oh, James, I don't know, it's just a name that sprang into my head. A vague recollection, something Alice said. It was years ago; I could be wrong.'

'What did Alice say?'

'Well, I think she mentioned staying in a B&B in Weymouth called *The Sunshine Hideaway* with her mum and Janet when she was little.'

'And you didn't think to mention this before?' snapped Paul.

'Don't speak to Barbara in that tone.'

'Sorry, Dad,' mumbled Paul, 'but given that we've been looking for her.'

'I know,' said Barbara, 'but it never crossed my mind she'd go back there. It must have been what, thirty-odd years ago. Anyway, I thought you said they'd found her in Devon.'

'No, I didn't,' said Paul. 'I said they'd found her *somewhere* in the south-west.'

Barbara closed her eyes. 'Devon's in the south-west.'

'I *know* that, Barbara, but so are lots of places.' Paul's gaze took on a steely appearance. 'You know something, don't you? Something about Mum.' He turned towards James. 'What's going on, Dad?'

James flicked his eyes towards Barbara and frowned. 'I've absolutely no bloody idea.'

That same morning, Alex rang Evie's number for the fourth time. 'Good God, you've answered.'

'Isn't that the generally accepted protocol?'

'Very amusing. Listen. I've, well, I've...'

'Is this going to take long, Alex? I'm working on a case at the moment, so...'

'Where are you?'

Without thinking, she replied, 'Weymouth.'

'I need to talk to you and I'd rather do it face to face.' He glanced at his watch. 'If I left now I could be with you this afternoon. Whereabouts are you staying?'

'*Shit, shit, shit,*' thought Evie.

'Evie, are you still there? It's important. You see, I spoke to your dad on Saturday.'

'About what?'

'Oh, don't be bloody ridiculous,' exclaimed Alex. 'What do you think I talked to him about, the current sorry state of the music industry?'

'You told him about your affair?'

'And about Charlotte, he's, um, he's a bit upset.'

'Jesus, Alex, I wonder why?'

'Please, Evie.'

Evie thought for a moment. An idea flashed into her head. 'Actually, you could be useful.'

'Useful?'

'Yes, yes, right, OK, listen. I'm staying at *The Station Hotel*. Give me a call when you get here.'

'Evie, Evie.' Alex stared at his phone. The screen informed him that the call had ended.

Back at the hotel, Evie explained how she'd chatted to Elspeth. 'I was about to go over to the B&B when this woman, Agnes, popped up out of nowhere and asked me about Judy.'

'Who's Judy?' asked Adam.

'Elspeth,' said Evie. 'That's the name she's using now. Anyway Agnes is a friend of Mavis, Mavis owns the yellow B&B place, and Agnes told me that Judy, well Elspeth, is booked in until the fourth of June, so we've got time to form a plan. Then Alex rang and...'

'Sorry to interrupt,' said Adam, 'but who's Alex?'

'He's a friend, was a friend, oh, it's not important. The thing is, I suddenly thought he could be useful as a way of luring Elspeth out of hiding.' She glanced towards Simon. 'You know, because of what he told us when he came for that meal.'

Simon's eyes widened. 'Brilliant. I say, that's inspired.'

'Is anyone going to explain what the hell you two are talking about?' said Janet.

Evie explained how Alex had recognised Alice from the photograph supplied by Paul.

187

'So you're saying he knew her as Elspeth?' asked Adam.

Evie nodded. 'Yes, always had done. It was because of him that we were able to establish that Alice had changed her name to Elspeth. Obviously, he doesn't know that.'

'And he still doesn't know that Elspeth's birth name was Alice?' said Janet.

'No, he hasn't got a clue,' said Evie. 'And, of course, Elspeth hasn't got a clue who I am either; obviously I didn't introduce myself when we 'accidently met' at the beach. And she certainly doesn't know that I work with Simon or that both Simon and I know Alex.'

'Oh, I see—I think,' said Janet.

'And she also won't know that Evie and I know that she changed her name from Alice to Elspeth,' added Simon.

'My head hurts,' said Adam.

'Anyway, has Alex agreed to your plan?' asked Janet.

'I haven't told him the plan yet. I simply said he could be useful.'

'But he's coming here?' asked Adam.

'Yes.'

'From?'

'Ripon.'

'So, he should be here by about five o'clock?'

Evie nodded. 'And Paul should be here around three o'clock.'

'Yes, and on that point,' said Adam, 'I'd rather Paul didn't know about the name change issue until I've had a chance to explain.'

'But Paul's already worked that out, Adam,' said Evie. 'He was the one who supplied us with a list of possible aliases; Elspeth Mitchell was one of those names.'

'Yes, but he doesn't know about my involvement in that name change or in my relationship with his mother, come to that, does he?'

'Well no, but…'

'Let's cross that bridge when we need to,' said Simon. 'I'd better go and sort out room availability because I expect Paul will bring his girlfriend with him. Then I'll do the meet and greet and then, well, then, we'll see.'

'And who's going to brief Alex?' asked Janet.

'Oh, don't worry about Alex. I'll sort him out,' said Evie.

Simon was waiting in the foyer when Paul and Julia arrived. He waved. 'Good journey?'

'Not too bad,' said Paul.

Another couple entered directly behind Paul. 'So, you must be Mr Simon Trent,' said the man.

Simon frowned and nodded. 'You have me at a disadvantage.'

'Dr James Sharp, husband of Alice Sharp and Paul's father.' He nodded towards the woman by his side. 'And this is Barbara Philips.'

'Hello,' said Barbara.

'Um, hello,' said Simon, throwing a glance towards Paul.

'Dad drove us down,' declared Paul, with a shrug.

The hotel manager smiled graciously as Simon approached the reception desk. 'Ah, I see we have more than expected. No problem, no problem at all,' he said, tapping at the reception desk computer. 'Now, let me see.'

'I'm sorry about this,' whispered Paul. 'But Dad and Barbara insisted.'

'It's fine.'

'Is my aunt still here?'

Simon nodded. 'In the lounge, we're…'

'Here we are,' said the manager. 'Now then, is it single or double rooms?'

'Two doubles,' said James.

'And how many nights is that for?'

James glanced towards Simon.

'Better make it until the end of the week, if that's alright with everyone,' said Simon. 'But we may need to extend.'

'That can be arranged. There is, however, one small problem.'

'What's that?'

'We only have one standard double remaining. The other double is our Suite and therefore more expensive. It has a lounge, bathroom, bedroom and...'

'That'll be fine,' said James.

'Excellent. So, that's the Empire Suite and one double booked until Friday, the thirty-first.' After a final flourish on the computer, the manager handed them their keys. 'Have a pleasant stay.'

'Could you do the same for the other guest,' said Simon.

The manager glanced at the computer screen. 'The one arriving later on today?'

Simon nodded.

'We only have single...'

'A single's fine.'

'And he'll be staying until the thirty-first as well, will he?'

'Probably.'

'And might he too need to extend his stay with us?'

'Possibly,' said Simon. 'I'm sorry to be so vague, but...'

The manager held up his hands. 'It's not a problem,' he said, as he entered the details into the computer. He glanced up. 'There we are, all done. A family reunion is it?'

'Something like that,' muttered James.

'Why don't you freshen up and then join us in the lounge,' said Simon. 'We're having tea.'

'Might as well,' said James, bending to pick up their bags.

'Don't worry about your luggage, sir,' said the manager, ringing the desk bell, 'I'll have those taken up to your rooms immediately.'

Simon crashed through the lounge doors. 'We've got a problem.'

'Has Paul backed out? I wouldn't blame him, it's a...'

'No, Janet, Paul's here...'

'So, what's the problem?' asked Adam.

'He's not alone.'

'Well, we assumed Julia would...' began Evie.

'Not just, Julia,' gasped Simon. 'James Sharp and Barbara Philips are here too.'

'Shit,' exclaimed Adam.

'We haven't got long,' continued Simon. 'They've gone up to their rooms. They'll be joining us once they've freshened up.'

'So, shall I hide, or...?'

The lounge doors swung open again. James strode in with Barbara by his side. Paul, gripping Julia's hand, followed. 'Paul couldn't wait,' declared James. 'He wanted to...good God! Adam Trent?'

'Yes, hello. Good to see you again, Mr Sharp,' said Adam.

'I thought you'd retired,' said Paul.

'I have.'

'And yet, here you are,' said James.

'Yes, here I am.'

Janet stood. 'Paul, hello. I'm your aunt. Lovely to finally meet you.'

Paul gave a curt nod. 'And good to meet you, too.'

She turned towards Julia and smiled. 'And you must be Julia.'

Julia smiled back. 'Yes. Hello.'

Janet cleared her throat before turning towards James. 'James, Barbara. You've obviously met Simon, Adam's brother,' she said, her smile now fixed in position. 'And this is Evie Morgan, Simon's assistant.'

James continued to stare at Adam as he responded to Janet's introductions. 'Miss Morgan, good afternoon, pleased to make your acquaintance. Now then, Janet, I understand from Paul that Alice has been found.'

'That's right,' said Janet. 'She's staying at a B&B. It's...'

'One that Barbara knew all about it seems,' said Paul.

'That's enough, Paul,' said James.

'Well, for...'

'Paul! Enough.'

Julia flinched.

'Tea anyone?' asked Evie.

'Lovely,' said Barbara. 'Shall I order some more?'

'I'll see to it,' said Adam, scrabbling to his feet. 'Tea alright? Or would anyone prefer coffee?'

A general muttering that tea would be fine sent Adam scurrying off.

James frowned as he watched Adam retreat from the lounge. 'I'm somewhat confused by the presence of Adam. I understood from my son that you,' he said, nodding towards Simon, 'had taken the case.'

'That's right, I did, I have. It's just, well it's...'

'We needed the old files,' said Evie.

'That's right,' said Simon.

'So we contacted Adam,' said Evie.

'Whatever for? He'd retired, so why would he have kept them?'

'Um, well, as it happens...'

'Look, does it bloody matter?' said Paul. 'The important thing is, Mum's been found. So, what do we do now?'

'There's nothing we can do until the morning,' said Simon. 'Evie has a plan.'

Paul looked at Evie, his eyes wide.

Evie glared at Simon. 'It's not a fully-formed plan, Paul. I'll explain once I'm clear in my own head about how to proceed. OK?'

'OK. But it's to be tomorrow?'

Evie nodded.

'And who's the other arrival, Mr Trent?' said James.

'Sorry?'

'The one the gentleman at reception mentioned. The one arriving later today.'

'That'll be Alex,' said Simon.

192

And he is?'

'An old friend of my family,' said Evie. 'Happens to be popping down to Weymouth for a couple of days, heard I was here and hoped we could meet. Catch up on old times, that sort of thing, you know.'

'No, I don't know. Surely you explained that you were busy.' said James.

'I did, but, oh, look, here comes Adam with the tea.' She jumped up. 'I'll give him a hand.'

As expected, Alex arrived just after five o'clock. Evie was waiting for him in the foyer. He strode towards her, dropped his overnight bag and raised his arms for an embrace.

Evie swerved away.

Alex sighed and lowered his arms.

'Simon's organised a room for you,' said Evie, her tone icy.

'Right, excellent. Good.'

'Dinner's at seven o'clock. You'll want to freshen up I expect.'

'Evie, I really need to talk to you about...'

'Not now, Alex.'

'I never meant...'

'Alex, I said, not now.'

'Fine. Have it your way. So, come on, what did you mean on the phone when you said I could be useful?' He gave her a weak smile. 'I mean, let's face it, it'd make a pleasant change.'

'Wouldn't it just.'

'Well?'

'It's perfectly simple. Simon and I will explain what we want you to do as soon as possible.'

'Right, look, when *can* we talk about...?'

'Alex, for God's sake, we're working on a case and it's reached a critical stage.' She leaned towards him and lowered her voice. 'There are going to be several people joining us for dinner. Our client for one, his girlfriend, his father and... oh, it doesn't matter, just keep the conversation general, do you understand?'

'So, you don't want me to confess about my affair with your mother in front of these strangers, is that it?' he hissed.

'Don't be childish, Alex.'

'Have you got a list of acceptable topics for conversation, then?'

Evie waved her hands in the air. 'Just don't mention Leeds, or that you met Elspeth there...'

'Elspeth, why the hell would I mention her?' exclaimed Alex, looking around. 'Oh, bloody hell, don't tell me, is she here too?'

'No, yes, oh, it's complicated, OK?' exclaimed Evie, as the corner of her mouth turned upwards.

'Oh, good one, Evie.'

'I don't mean to be mysterious, but it really is best if you know as little as possible at the moment. I promise, I'll explain everything later.'

Alex narrowed his eyes and tapped the side of his nose. 'Got it, old bean.'

'Have you?'

'No, haven't a clue what you're talking about.'

'Good. Reception's over there. I'll see you in a couple of hours.'

Chapter 21

Dinner the previous evening had passed without incident. The conversation had been stilted and, at times, forced. Alex had made his excuses early and retired to his room.

Evie had given Simon's leg a nudge beneath the table.

Simon stood.

'Oh, are you off too?' Evie had said.

He'd nodded.

'Right, well, I think I'll call it a day as well. Good night all.'

Walking nonchalantly from the dining room, Simon and Evie had then made their way up to Alex's room where they'd outlined their plan.

Alex had listened with growing fascination. 'And that's it, is it?'

'Essentially, yes,' said Simon.

'You want me to lurk in…'

'No one said anything about lurking,' said Evie.

'Alright, so, you want me to *loiter* in…'

Evie raised her eyes.

'…in this café opposite *Sunflowers*, bursting out through the doors the moment I spot Elspeth, re-establish contact and lure her back to this hotel, is that it?'

Evie lowered her head into her hands and gave a muffled scream.

'Putting aside your somewhat lurid description of the proposal,' said Simon. 'Yes, that's basically it.'

'And am I to be told why?'

'Not just yet,' said Simon.

Alex left the hotel before breakfast that morning and, as instructed, made his way to the café opposite *Sunflowers*. He ordered toast and coffee, sat back and waited. The moment he spotted Elspeth, he pocketed the recent photograph that Evie had given him, downed his coffee and headed towards the exit.

'Elspeth, good grief,' he called, rushing towards her. 'It is you, isn't it? Well, well, well, it's a small world. I haven't seen you since, let me think, about twelve or thirteen years ago, at a conference in Leeds, at the Mansion House. You haven't changed a bit; well, apart from your hair. Not that there's anything wrong with it. It suits you.' He swept his hand down to his midriff. 'I, on the other hand, have gained a few pounds. How the devil are you?'

She stared, open-mouthed.

'Sorry, no reason at all why you should remember me. You must have met hundreds of us conference types while you were working in Leeds.' He extended his hand. 'I'm Alex Brown, Professor, York University.'

A flicker of recognition showed in her face. She smiled. 'Oh, yes. Professor Brown...'

'Alex, please.'

'Alex. Yes, of course I remember you. You were always playing practical jokes on your colleagues; jokes that most of them didn't appreciate,' she smiled. 'And, I believe you tried to chat me up.'

'Guilty as charged. Never could resist a good joke or an attractive woman; gosh, sorry, no, I'm not trying it on again,' Alex spluttered.

'So, what brings you to Weymouth? Another conference?'

'Good grief, no; the university continues to make cutbacks, so no more jollies to seaside resorts. I'm here for a reviving blast of sea air. You?'

'The same.'

'Ah, right.' He took in a massive lungful of sea air, gave a hacking cough and patted his chest with vigour. 'And bloody good stuff it is, too,' he croaked.

'It seems you haven't changed that much, either,' smiled Elspeth.

'Look, please don't take this the wrong way, but I'm at a loose end, well, totally bored if I'm honest. I don't suppose you'd like to join me later for afternoon tea. I'm staying at *The Station Hotel.* It's not the most exciting of venues, but they do a rather scrumptious cream tea. Go on, Elspeth, what do you say?'

She peered out towards the sea, as the cries of delighted children drifted up from the beach. 'They seem to be having fun.'

Alex followed her gaze. 'Give a child a bucket and spade, some sand and sea and life is bliss. Would that it was as simple for adults.'

She nodded.

'So, what do you say, Elspeth?'

'Sorry?'

'To a cream tea at *The Station Hotel.*'

She continued to watch the children while Alex waited by her side. After a few moments she turned, smiled again and said, 'Do you know what, I think I'll say yes. It will make a pleasant change.'

'Splendid.'

'What time?'

'Cream teas are served at three o'clock.'

'Lovely. Well, I'll see you soon, then.'

Back at the hotel, following breakfast, coffee was being taken in the lounge.

In the far corner, a pianist played a medley of classical tunes.

James tapped his foot as he stared at Adam.

Adam sipped his coffee.

'I'm still wondering why you need to be here,' said James.

'He's Simon's brother,' said Janet.

197

'I'm well aware of that. It still doesn't explain why he needs to be here.'

'I wrote to him, Dad.'

'But he didn't reply, did he?'

'You know he didn't,' said Paul.

'Because he'd retired, you said.'

'That's what we were told,' said Julia.

'Does it really matter why Adam's here?' asked Barbara. 'The important thing is we know Alice is here.'

'At a B&B that you had knowledge of, it seems,' said James.

'I've already explained that it had slipped my mind.'

'Yes, so you said.'

Janet's coffee cup rattled in its saucer.

James turned and caught a look of panic in her eyes.

'More coffee, Janet?' said Evie.

Janet shook her head.

'Dr Sharp?'

'What's going on?' asked James.

'Going on?' said Evie, her voice pitched higher than normal. She cleared her throat. 'Nothing. I was simply wondering if you wanted more coffee.'

Adam closed his eyes and swallowed.

'Dry throat?' asked James. 'I'm sure Evie here will be happy to replenish your cup.'

Adam gave Simon a pleading look.

'*I* contacted Adam,' said Simon.

'Why? What possible use could he be? Given that he'd already failed?'

'He didn't fail,' said Paul, 'he found her.'

'And then he lost her again,' said James. 'Isn't that right?'

'Well, yes, I did and then I, well; oh, hell, I...'

James's stare was now fixed on Adam. 'And then you what?'

The clattering sound of a passing train filled the room, momentarily drowning out the sound of the pianist.

Pulling at his T-shirt neck, Adam blurted, 'I can't explain how, it just, well it just happened. And we both knew immediately.' He shrugged, adding, 'Almost as soon as we clapped eyes on each other.'

James sat motionless.

Janet shifted in her seat.

Simon and Evie gazed at the carpet.

Adam took several deep breaths.

'Sorry, who, what?' exclaimed Paul.

Barbara reached out to take James's hand, but he catapulted himself from the sofa and loomed over Adam. 'Are you saying what I think you're saying?'

'It depends on what you think I'm saying.'

'Think you're funny, do you?' Leaning down, his face inches from Adam, he spat out his words. 'Did you steal my wife?'

The pianist struck a wrong note.

'Well, she'd already left, so…'

'Don't get bloody cocky with me.'

Barbara rushed across to James and pulled at his arm. 'Come and sit…'

He pushed her away. 'I don't want to fucking sit down, Barbara. I want fucking answers,' he yelled.

The pianist glanced up from the keyboard, sighed and played louder.

'Hang on a second, Simon. Let me get this straight,' exclaimed Paul. 'Am I to understand that your brother, Adam, the guy Dad hired to find Mum, has been with Mum all along. Is that what's being said here?'

'That's exactly what's being said, Paul, yes,' said James, leaning in towards Adam again. 'So where?'

'Where what?'

'Don't push it. Where have you been living with Alice, my *wife*, all this time?'

'Jesus, Simon?' croaked Paul, 'did you know about this?'

'No, Paul,' said Evie, 'of course he didn't know. He only found out a few days ago when we traced your Mum to...'

'Evie, not now,' exclaimed Simon.

'It's alright, Simon, they have to know,' said Janet, turning towards Adam and giving him a wan smile. 'Go ahead, tell them. It's time.'

'It's time? Time for what?' exclaimed James.

'Aunt Janet? Do you know where they've been living?'

She gave a small nod.

'Where?' said Paul

'I um, we um...' stuttered Adam.

'For the love of God, will someone just give me a straight answer?' said James.

'They're living in Devon, James,' said Janet. 'In the cottage that I, or rather Alice and I, inherited from Grandma Lee.'

'Un-fucking-believable,' said James.

The pianist hit several wrong notes.

James closed his eyes, took a deep breath and collapsed back into the sofa. 'Will someone, anyone,' he began, his voice rising in volume as he spat out each word, 'tell that pianist to shut the fuck up.'

The music stopped immediately. There was a moment of silence before the piano lid was slammed shut. The sound of a stool scraping across the floor, followed by hurried footsteps, indicated that the piano recital was over.

Barbara adjusted her hair and straightened her skirt. 'We can't carry on with this discussion down here. I suggest we retire upstairs.' She eased James up from the settee. 'Come on, darling, let's get you back to our room.'

Alex wandered back towards the hotel along the Coast Path. Stopping at a bench, he sat and looked out across the sea. Surrounded by the gentle hum of buzzing insects, he closed his eyes. Small tears crept down his face as he relived the time he and Jean had spent together. He tried to imagine how his life would have been if he'd made the decision to stay in England with Jean. He sighed. It was a pointless exercise. He wouldn't have stayed, he knew that. He'd been too selfish back then. But, when he returned. When they met again. How different could it have been? Had she known that he was Charlotte's father? And, if she did, why hadn't she told him? He clenched his fists as the thought reverberated around his head. She hadn't told him because she hadn't loved him. Not as much as she'd loved Gerry. He shook his head as an insect of uncertain pedigree landed in his ear. He glanced at his watch and gasped.

Alex dashed back to the hotel, entering the lobby as the clock struck noon. The young lady at the reception desk looked up. 'Can I help?'

'I hope so. I was supposed to be meeting Evie Morgan in the lounge, but I'm rather late and she's obviously given up on me. Would you be kind enough to ring her room and let her know I'm here?'

'Of course,' said the young lady, 'and you are?'

'I'm Alex, Alex Brown.'

Replacing the receiver, the receptionist said, 'I'm sorry, there's no answer.'

'She might be with her colleague, Simon Trent, would you...?

'It's ringing now—sorry, no answer there either.'

Alex frowned. 'Where the hell is she?'

'I'm sorry, sir, I...'

'Oh, hang on, I had dinner last night with a whole gaggle. Let me think. There was a young couple, Paul and Julia something; some woman called Janet, no idea what her surname is. Oh, and an older bloke, I think he said he was Paul's father; he was with a rather splendid-looking woman, his wife I assume. He was a doctor, not sure if he was the medical type or...oh, I remember now. It's quite an appropriate name, assuming he's a medical doctor, of course. He's called Sharp, you see? *Dr* Sharp.' He looked pleadingly into the receptionist's eyes.

'I'll try his phone, shall I?'

'You're a treasure.'

'It's ringing—ah, good afternoon, Mrs Sharp? It's— sorry—you are—oh, right, how fortuitous. I have an Alex Brown with—yes, no problem, I'll let him know.' Replacing the receiver, she smiled across the vast expanse of polished mahogany. 'That was Miss Evie Morgan. She asked me to send you up to the Empire Suite. It's up the main stairs to the top floor, turn left and...'

'Smashing, thanks. Don't worry, I'll find it.'

Alex knocked on the door, ready to announce the success of his morning mission. The sound of anguished sobbing as the door was flung open by a pale-faced Evie wiped the grin from his face. 'What's happened?'

'Quite a lot, Alex,' said Evie, 'We won't be long,' she added, as she grabbed Alex's arm and stepped out of the room.

'Evie, what...?'

'Is she coming?'

'Yes. Look, what's going on?'

Leaning back against the wall, Evie took a deep breath and spoke at speed.

Alex's eyes grew wider at each new revelation.

'So, as you can imagine, it's all come as rather a shock,' concluded Evie.

'Hang on, let me make sure I've got this right,' said Alex. 'You're telling me that Elspeth used to be called Alice?'

Evie nodded.

'And she was married to James...?'

'Well, she still is, I suppose, technically.'

'And she ran off soon after having Paul?'

Evie nodded again.

'And Adam was hired to find her. And then, when he found her, he shacked up with her after first sorting out her name change?'

'Yes.'

'Did Simon know?'

'No.'

'But then Paul hired you and Simon to find her and you discovered that she'd been with Adam all along? Alex glanced at the door to the Empire Suite and then back at Evie. 'Am I right in assuming that Elspeth is unaware of everyone's presence in that room?'

Again, Evie nodded.

'Bloody hell.'

Chapter 22

'Daddy, what's the matter?'

Gerry looked up from his study desk to see Charlotte peering at him, her face clouded with concern.

'The matter?'

'Yes, I'm not a child, you know.'

Gerry smiled. 'No, you'll be twelve soon.'

'I shall be twelve in three months, Daddy. So, what is it? Is it Evie? Are you worried about Evie?'

'In a way.'

'Not because of Simon, surely,' said Charlotte. 'He's lovely. If you ask me he's a keeper.'

'*A keeper*,' spluttered Gerry. 'Where did you learn that phrase?'

Charlotte raised her eyebrows. 'Oh, Daddy, get with it. He's great. Don't you agree?'

'Well, yes, as it happens, I do.'

'So, what's to worry about?'

Gerry shook his head. 'Nothing. Well, not about them anyway.'

Charlotte frowned. 'So you *are* worried about something!'

'It's just boring grown-up stuff.'

'Why don't we ring Uncle Alex? We could all go to the park for a picnic or something, that'd cheer you up. Can we?'

'I don't think that's a very good idea.'

'Why not?'

'I just don't.'

'Oh, Daddy, what is it? Have I done something?'

'No, sweetheart, of course not. I'm sorry. It's just, well, I've got a lot on my mind at the moment, work stuff, as I said, all very boring. Why don't you ask Mandy to take you to the ice rink?'

Charlotte jumped up and clapped her hands. 'Ooh, yes. We could all go. Uncle Alex is brilliant at skating.'

'I said with Mandy, Charlotte, *not* Alex,' snapped Gerry.

'But Uncle Alex is...'

'He's not your bloody uncle, Charlotte.'

'Daddy!'

'Sorry, sorry, I didn't mean to snap, but I've got work to finish,' said Gerry, ruffling Charlotte's hair. 'Mandy will take you. Now, off you go.'

'Right, are you ready?' asked Evie.

Alex took a deep breath and nodded.

Evie gave a quick knock on the door to the Empire Suite and, taking Alex's hand, strode in.

All eyes turned towards them. Alex gave a half-hearted wave.

'Did you find her? Is she coming? How is she?' said Barbara.

'Yes, I found her.'

'So, is she coming?' asked Simon.

'Yes, she, Elspeth, Alice, Paul's mum, will be arriving at three o'clock for afternoon tea with me.'

James glanced at his watch. 'So, she'll be here in a few hours,' he said. 'Do you fancy a drink? Barbara has managed to organise for several bottles to be sent up.

'One of the advantages of occupying the Empire Suite,' said Barbara.

'Is there any whisky?'

James nodded.

'I wouldn't say no.'

'I'll do it,' said Evie. 'Ice?'

'Yes, thanks.' His eye's flicked towards the bedroom, where faint sounds of sobbing could be heard.

Evie handed Alex his drink. 'Just a small one, OK?'

'Fine; thanks.' Eyes still fixed on the bedroom, he took a sip.

'Do you think I should see if Janet's alright?' asked Barbara.

Alex leaned towards Evie. 'Remind me, where does Janet fit into this scenario?'

'Not now,' hissed Evie, with a quick nod towards Paul, who was slumped in an armchair just beside them.

'Janet's my aunt,' said Paul, he took a deep breath, 'and she's just informed me that my grandfather used to beat the shit out of her, my grandma and my mum. Lovely, isn't it?'

Julia, perched on the arm of his chair, rested her hand on his shoulder.

Paul dragged his hand through his hair. 'Why no one saw fit to tell me about my grandfather, I've no shitting idea.'

The bedroom door creaked open, Julia glanced up to see Janet leaning against the door jamb. She rushed across to take her arm. 'Paul's just upset,' she whispered.

'Of course he is, of course he is.'

Paul jumped up from the armchair to take Janet's other arm. 'Sorry, Aunt Janet.'

'Nonsense, Paul, not your fault. I'm fine.' Catching sight of Alex she asked, 'Is she coming?'

'Yes, Janet,' said Evie. 'Alex spoke to her and she's agreed to meet him for a cream tea.'

'Would you like something to drink?' asked Paul.

'I could do with a brandy,' she said, as she collapsed into the sofa between Simon and Adam.

Adam took hold of Janet's hand. 'Alright?'

She nodded. 'Sorry.'

'For what?'

She shrugged. 'Everything.'

Paul handed his aunt her drink.

Janet took a sip and said in a gentle voice, 'Your mum was never as strong as me, Paul. You mustn't blame her.'

'Blame her? I don't blame her. I just don't understand why she abandoned me.' He glanced across the room to where James and Barbara were standing by the open balcony door, a voile curtain billowing into the room. 'Dad says he doesn't understand either, but I think he knows more that he's saying. And, Barbara, well it seems she knows stuff too.' His voice, now full of venom, filled the room. 'I'm just sick of being kept in the dark. I'm not a bloody child.'

'I tried to warn you, Paul. I simply wanted to avoid all this,' said James.

'Avoid all what exactly?' He began pacing the room. 'Avoid telling me that my mum was beaten by her father. I mean, I don't wish to sound callous, but is that *it*? How the hell does that explain her running away from you, abandoning me, unless oh, I don't know, unless maybe you beat her too?'

'Don't be bloody ridiculous, Paul.'

Barbara reached for James's hand. 'Don't…'

Pulling away, James retorted, 'Jesus, Barbara, didn't you hear what he said?'

'Yes, but he's upset, he doesn't know what he's saying.'

'Yes, I bloody do, Barbara. He's hiding something, and I demand to know what it is.'

'Listen to me, Paul, I…'

'And don't say you have nothing to hide, because I know that's a lie.' He took another deep breath, shoved his glasses up onto his head and rubbed his eyes with the heels of his palms. 'I asked you when I first started looking for Mum if she wrote you a letter and you said no, but there was something in your eyes, you were lying. She did write a letter, didn't she?'

James bowed his head.

A train whistle blew, and a rush of children's laughter drifted in on the gentle breeze that wafted the curtains further into the room.

'Did she write you a letter?' asked Janet.

James nodded.

'I knew it,' exclaimed Paul. 'So, what did she say?'

'It confirmed what I already knew, Paul, and she begged me not to tell you.'

'Tell me,' demanded Paul.

Janet's eyes widened. She glanced up at Barbara who gave a small shake of her head.

Janet sighed.

Alex put his hand up. 'Excuse me, but...'

'What?' snapped James.

'Well, given that the lady in question will be here soon, wouldn't it be best to ask her?'

'Can you be patient for just a little while longer, Paul?' said Janet. 'And then I promise you, whether your mother agrees or not, I'll tell you everything.'

'Janet, I don't think...' began Barbara.

'*Everything*, Barbara. Paul deserves to know the whole truth, as does James.'

James gave Janet a penetrating stare. 'Are you telling me there's more? More than Alice told me?'

Another train whistle, a hoot of childish laughter and the faint strains of a brass band now drifted into the room. Paul swore and slammed the balcony door shut, muffling the sounds. The curtains billowed and then fell, lifeless, against the glass panes.

Barbara reached out towards James again, her voice quavered. 'It was too much for her, she...'

James whirled around. 'What was too much for her?'

Barbara closed her eyes.

'Janet?'

'I'm sorry,' said Janet. 'It's not for me...'

'Barbara, for God's sake, look at me; what was too much for her?'

Barbara squeezed her eyes shut tighter.

'Barbara!'

Her eyes snapped open. 'I'm so sorry, really I am, but I can't say; I promised.'

'Jesus fucking Christ!' exclaimed James.

Paul stared at Barbara, his eyes full of confusion and pain. He turned to his father. 'Dad?'

'I don't know, Paul. It seems I haven't known any fucking thing for a long time,' and, with an icy glance towards Barbara, he wrenched the balcony door open and fought his way through the curtains out onto the balcony.

Chapter 23

Evie and Alex made their way down towards reception.

'And I thought our situation was complicated,' he quipped.

'Are you going to be able to do this?'

'Credit me with some ability for God's sake, Evie.'

'You just need to tell Alice…'

'Elspeth, you mean.'

'Yes,' snapped Evie, 'Elspeth. Just mention that when you returned to the hotel you met a woman who you mistook for her, you know, keep it simple, don't overexplain.'

'And I'm to inform her that this woman, whose name I later discovered was Janet, is also staying at this hotel, right?'

'Right.'

'Look, far be it for me to criticise this plan, but it strikes me that Elspeth will…'

'Will see right through it instantly, yes, she will. That *is* the plan.'

'Sorry?'

'Alex, just do it.'

'Fine.' He checked his watch. 'She'll be here any moment.'

'OK. Don't forget the signal.'

'The signal?'

Evie groaned. 'Loosen your tie, when…'

'Yes, loosen tie. Got it.'

Elspeth entered the foyer and waved as she caught sight of Alex, who was sitting, legs crossed, in a large, leather armchair facing the main door. He jumped up, adjusted his face, forcing a wide smile and rushed towards her. 'I'm so glad you came,' he gushed. 'I was convinced you'd change your mind once you'd had time to think about it. You know, bloke you haven't seen for over thirteen years pops up out of the blue and invites you back to his hotel.'

'For a cream tea, you said.'

'Oh, yes, absolutely, a cream tea, gosh I wasn't trying to suggest anything more, I mean…'

'Are you alright? You seem rather flustered.'

'Flustered, me? No, no, not at all,' said Alex, his face flushing. 'It's just, well, the strangest thing. When I got back here earlier, you know, after bumping into you, I saw a woman and, well…'

Elspeth looked around. 'Are women not allowed in here, then?'

'What?'

'You seem shocked that you saw a woman.'

'Oh, right, yes, hah! No, it's just that this woman looked rather like you, and…'

'I've been told that I have one of those faces.'

'One of what faces?'

'Mobile, a face that can look like several different people and yet, when you compare these people to each other, they look nothing like each other, if you know what I mean.'

'Not really, no,' mumbled Alex. 'Anyway, shall we go through to the dining room?' He took hold of Elspeth's arm and guided her towards a set of double doors with a sign above them.

'Welcome to the *Palace Room,* a rather grand name,' said Alex. 'Don't get too excited, it's called that because someone, no idea who, painted a mural on the far wall that bears some small resemblance to that palace in Brighton. What's it called?'

'The Pavilion?'

'That's the one.'

'But we're in Weymouth.'

211

'Yes. I don't get it either. Still, ours not to reason and all that.' He pointed to a small table by a window. 'That's my designated spot. Look, the scones have already been delivered, frightfully efficient these waiters. Gosh, they look tempting. I expect they'll bring the tea when we sit down, they wouldn't want it to get cold I suppose. Here we are.' Alex, glancing around, pulled a chair out and settled Elspeth. 'I even dashed up to her, most embarrassing it was.'

'Sorry, dashed up to whom?'

A waiter pushed a trolley up to their table. 'Your tea, Professor Brown. Shall I pour?'

'What, oh, yes, lovely. Elspeth?'

'Milk, no sugar, thank you.'

'And for you, sir?'

'The same, thanks.'

'So, you dashed up to whom?' repeated Elspeth.

Alex, eyes darting left and right, took a sip of tea. 'Ah, yes, the woman, the woman who looked a bit like you. I called out to her, started blathering on about her being early and that the cream teas weren't served until later, but it didn't matter, I was thrilled to see you, except, as I drew closer to her, I realised it wasn't you, it was, oh dear. It was her.'

'It was who?'

'What?'

'You said it was her, and then you stopped.'

'Did I?' Alex closed his eyes and took a deep breath.

'Yes, you did. Look, are you sure you're alright?'

'What? Me? Yes, why?'

'I'm getting concerned, Alex. Your behaviour is verging on the manic.'

He rubbed his forehead and, scanning the dining room once again, he finally spotted Evie and sighed. 'Me, manic? No, absolutely not. I'm fine, completely fine; just a little warm,' he said, as he loosened his tie.

Evie approached the table on cue. 'Goodness, hello again,' she said. 'Fancy seeing you here. Did you get see the sand sculptures?'

Turning her attention away from Alex, Elspeth looked up at Evie. 'What? Sorry?'

'The sculptures, made of sand, did you get to see them?'

'Oh, those, yes I did,' said Elspeth, before turning back to face Alex. 'This woman, the one who looked like me, did you...?'

'And what did you think?' Evie continued.

'They were amazing; sorry, I just need to check something with my friend here.'

'Oh, I do apologise, I didn't mean to interrupt,' said Evie, giving Alex a wide-eyed stare.

'Ah, right, yes,' mumbled Alex.

Evie's eyes widened further.

In a voice several octaves higher than normal, Alex gabbled, 'Gosh, that's weird, well not weird, a coincidence I suppose. Anyway, fancy you two knowing each other.'

'Have you inhaled nitrous oxide?' said Elspeth.

Alex wiped his forehead with his napkin and, in a voice still higher than normal, continued, 'No, I,' he cleared his throat. 'I was just saying it's weird. Sorry, I've already said that, haven't I?'

'And, as it happens, we don't know each other,' said Elspeth. 'We only met yesterday.'

'Did you? Right, so that means introductions are in order. Elspeth this is Evie...'

Elspeth's face paled.

'...an old family friend of mine. Evie, this is, Elspeth. I knew her years ago when she worked in Leeds.' He swallowed. 'Evie, why don't you join us? You wouldn't mind would you, Elspeth?'

'No, I, no of course not,' she said. 'Please sit.'

Evie sat.

Alex handed her a plate. 'They always put four plates out. No idea why; still, useful for when an unexpected guest pops up, I suppose.'

'Yes, most fortuitous,' said Elspeth, peering at Evie across the rim of her cup. 'And your name is Evie?'

Evie nodded.

'Such a pretty name. I don't know many Evies.'

Evie smiled as she began to spread a generous helping of clotted cream over a scone. 'Now, shall I have strawberry or raspberry jam?' she said, picking up the little pots from the centre of the table.

'Strawberry's traditional, I believe,' said Elspeth. 'It's what we always had as children when we came to stay in Weymouth.' She replaced her cup onto its saucer. 'I'm not an idiot you know.'

'Sorry?'

'I assume you're the Evie who works with Simon Trent.' Turning towards Alex, she continued. 'And I also assume that bumping into me this morning wasn't happenchance.'

Alex exchanged a furtive glance with Evie.

'And there I was, actually happy to have met you again, Alex, an old friend, or so I thought. Someone who knew nothing of my past life, but here you are conniving with...'

Alex reached out and touched Elspeth's forearm. 'I knew nothing about you being a 'runaway' or whatever the politically correct term is. I really am just a family friend of Evie's.'

'Well, that's a moot point,' muttered Evie.

'Not now, Evie.' Alex tightened his grip on Elspeth's arm. 'I honestly thought you were Elspeth,' said Alex. 'I only found out a few hours ago that you were originally named Alice, and...'

'And our 'accidental' meeting?'

'That was down to me,' said Evie.

'Right, and this woman, this woman you saw; the one who looks like me.'

'That was…' said Alex.

'Janet, my sister, obviously.'

Alex nodded. 'Yes, and I only found that out a couple of hours ago. I've been played too.'

'Don't expect sympathy from me,' said Elspeth, pulling her arm free.

'No, fair enough,' said Alex, 'but your sister's in a terrible state, well everyone is actually, and they—Ow! Evie, that bloody hurt.'

'Everyone? What everyone?' exclaimed Elspeth.

'It must have been awful for you both,' said Alex, rubbing his shin.

'What's Janet been saying?'

'No wonder you bolted. But Paul's a smashing young man—Ow! bloody hell, Evie, what's the matter with you?'

'For God's sake, Alex. It's alright, Elspeth, he just wants to meet you,' said Evie.

'I can't face him, really I can't,' said Elspeth, jumping up, sending her chair crashing to the floor.

The waiter appeared from behind a pillar and caught her as she stumbled. 'Alright, madam, I've got you.'

'Leave me alone. I need to get out of here.' Struggling free, she made a dash for the exit.

'Oh, bloody well done, Alex,' said Evie. 'Get back up there. Tell them what's happened. I'll follow Elspeth.'

Alex sat frozen as he watched Evie dash through the doors in pursuit of Elspeth.

'Now!' screamed Evie, as the doors swung shut.

Alex burst into the Empire Suite. 'Elspeth, Alice, has bolted again. She knows Paul's here. My fault I fear, sorry. I'm not cut out for this undercover work. Anyway, she panicked. Evie's run after her. She, Evie I mean, sent me up here to let you all know.'

Paul jumped up.

Simon snatched hold of his arm. 'I think we should leave it to Evie,' he said. 'She'll calm her down.'

'And then what?' demanded Paul.

'Once we hear from Evie, I think it would be best if I spoke to your mum first. Is that alright with you?' said Janet.

Paul slumped back into the chair. 'I suppose so. Oh God, please don't let her disappear again, not now.'

Chapter 24

Evie found Elspeth sitting, rigid and upright, on the bench opposite *Sunflowers,* looking out across the beach towards the sea. Plonking herself beside her, Evie sighed and pointed. 'Oh, look at that little girl with the yellow sun hat, she's made a lovely sandcastle.'

Elspeth glanced at Evie, and then looked to where Evie was pointing. She smiled. 'I see it. Yes, it is rather good.'

'It's even got a flag. Somewhat out of proportion to the tiny castle, though.'

Elspeth gave a little giggle. 'I think it must be the old man's polka-dot tie. Her granddad, I assume.' She turned towards Evie, her face pale and drawn. 'Fancy wearing a tie to the beach.'

'It's a generational thing.'

Elspeth nodded. 'Yes, I suppose so.'

'My granddad always wore a tie, even when he was gardening,' said Evie.

Elspeth smiled. 'So did Granddad Lee.'

The sound of the Harry Potter theme music startled them.

'Sorry, that'll be my little sister,' said Evie. 'Do you mind?'

'No, I won't run away. I'm tired of running.'

'Hi there, Charlotte, what's up?'

'It's Daddy.'

'What's the matter with Daddy?'

'He's miserable, and he won't tell me what's the matter and I know something's the matter, I can tell. He went all weird when I suggested we could all go for a picnic with Uncle Alex. I've tried to talk to Uncle Alex, but he's not answering his landline. I've left a message for him on his mobile. Can you come over?'

'Not really. I'm in Weymouth.'

'At the seaside?' exclaimed Charlotte. 'Without me?'

'Yes, but it's to do with work, I'm not...'

'Everybody's working, it's not fair. All my friends are away with their parents for half term and I'm stuck here, on my own, as per.'

'Sorry.'

'Perhaps Uncle Alex will pick me up and take me to the seaside when he gets my message.'

'I don't think that's very likely.'

'Why not?'

'It's just that things are difficult between Daddy and Alex at the moment.'

'Has Daddy had a row with Uncle Alex?'

'A sort of row, yes.'

'About what?'

'I can't really say.'

'I'm entitled to know,' yelled Charlotte. 'He's my daddy too, you know.'

Evie clenched her jaw. 'Charlotte, look, the thing is, Uncle Alex is here with me.' She glanced at Elspeth and mouthed an apology. 'He's helping me and Simon with a case we've been working on, and...'

'So, he's at the seaside too! That's simply *not* fair.'

'It's not a case of being fair or not; as I said, he's working.'

'Fine,' snapped Charlotte. 'I'll go out somewhere exciting and fun with Mandy, on my own; but *something* is really wrong with Daddy, and I'm worried about him. Still, if you're *on a case,* then that's that.'

'Charlotte, listen, I'm ...'

'She sounded rather cross,' said Elspeth. 'I could hear her from here.'

'She's hung up. And yes, you're right, she is cross. Very cross.'

'With you?'

Evie nodded. 'Well, with everyone actually. With me, with our dad *and* with Alex.'

'Is everyone cross with poor old Alex?'

'Less of the 'poor',' snapped Evie.

'Sorry; have I hit a raw nerve?'

'It's complicated.'

'Now, that's a good one,' snorted Elspeth. 'I think I can trump you on whatever complication scale you care to select.'

Evie giggled as her eyes began to fill with tears.

'Oh, I'm really sorry. I didn't mean to trivialise whatever...'

'No, it's alright, it's...' Evie wiped her eyes roughly with the back of her hand. 'I, well Simon and I to be exact, uncovered the fact that Alex had an affair with my mother, years ago and then, recently, Charlotte was in an accident, nothing serious, but it was while she was in the hospital that Dad noticed her blood group didn't match his. So he knew he couldn't be the father. It was really awkward because I already knew, you see, knew that Charlotte wasn't his; because of the affair. She's Alex's child. Alex didn't know, well not at first, he knows now because I've told him. Anyway, I think he's confessed all to Dad. That's why Alex came down to Weymouth, and now Charlotte's saying she's worried about Dad, and I, oh shit!'

'Life's never easy, is it?'

'Oh, God, sorry. I don't know where all that came from, sorry.'

'Don't apologise,' said Elspeth, handing Evie a tissue. 'Are you alright?'

Evie sniffed as she took the tissue. 'Thank you. Yes, sorry.'

'Stop apologising.'

'Sor…'

'Evie,' exclaimed Elspeth.

'Sor—oh, dear,' said Evie, blowing her nose.

Looking back out towards the sea, Elspeth said, 'Back at the hotel, Alex said something about 'everyone' being here.'

Evie blew her nose again.

'So, who's everyone, Evie?'

Evie took a deep breath. 'Right. Well, apart from me, there's Alex, obviously, then there's Simon and Adam; he's…'

'Is Adam alright?'

'He's worried about you.'

'And how did Simon deal with, well, you know.'

'With finding out that Adam wasn't in Ireland?'

Elspeth smiled. 'Tactfully put.'

'Suffice it to say they're alright now,' said Evie.

'Is James here too?'

Evie nodded.

'And, dare I ask, how did *he* react to the news that Adam and I were together?'

'Um, how can I put this?'

'Not well, then?'

'Not particularly, not at first,' said Evie. 'But, that's not surprising really, is it?'

'No, I suppose not.'

'They're alright now, though. Not exactly bosom buddies but, as James pointed out, it was all a very long time ago.'

'And, Barbara, is she here as well?'

'Yes, they came down from London with Paul and Julia; Julia's Paul's girlfriend. She's a lovely girl, you'll like her. She's been incredibly supportive, you know, with helping Paul search for you.'

'So, is that it?'

Evie nodded. 'It was only supposed to be Paul. He was the one who hired us in the first place. He doesn't blame you. He just wants to meet you, but he'll understand if you don't want to meet him. He wrote you a letter, just in case. He gave it to Simon.'

'How much does Paul know?'

'Janet told him, well, she told all of us, about the beatings.'

'And that's all she's told you, is it?'

'Yes, but she implied there was more.'

'Oh, there is,' said Elspeth, 'much more.'

'Janet thinks it's time for the whole truth to be told.'

'Yes, I know, and I think she's probably right,' said Elspeth, standing and brushing her skirt down. 'I assume everyone's waiting at the hotel.'

Evie nodded again.

'Come on, then, we'd better get back.'

Evie scrabbled in her bag. 'I'll just ring Simon to let them know we're on our way, is that alright?'

'Fine.'

Janet was waiting for them in the foyer. She stood up the instant she caught sight of Elspeth and gave a tentative wave. The three women stood in silence while guests and hotel staff bustled around them, then Janet smiled and asked, 'Are you alright?'

Elspeth nodded.

'Has Evie explained, well, has she told…?'

'Told me who's here? Yes, Janet. She has.'

'I thought we could have a chat in my room first, you know, before…'

'Before I'm thrown to the wolves?'

'Don't be silly, it won't…'

'Sorry, I didn't mean—oh, hell, what a bloody mess.'

'I'll leave you to it,' said Evie. 'And I'll see you both later, yes?'

Janet nodded as she took Elspeth's arm. 'We'll join you in the Empire Suite as soon as we're ready.'

Evie watched the two women as they trudged up the stairs towards Janet's room. She sighed and headed towards the lift. Watching the arrow as it descended towards the ground floor, Evie felt a gentle tap on her shoulder. She turned. Alex stood, head cast down.

'Oh, for God's sake, don't look so miserable. Panic's over, I found her, and…'

'Yes, so I saw. How is she?'

Evie shrugged. 'Hard to say. Janet's going to talk to her and then they're going to join us in the Empire Suite to, well, I'm not sure really; to explain everything, I suppose.'

'I thought you should know now I've done my bit, as it were, I thought I'd head off. I just wanted to say, I just…'

'Are you getting in, or what?' demanded a stick-thin woman.

Evie muttered an apology and stood aside.

The stick-thin women swept into the lift, the doors closed, and Evie watched the arrow move up one floor and then stop.

'Surely she's not used the lift to go up just one floor,' she exclaimed, as she punched the lift button.

'Evie…'

'Yes, I heard. You've done your bit. You're off home. Fine. Thanks.'

'Oh, Evie. I really am so very sorry. I didn't know Charlotte was mine, really, I didn't. It just never entered my head.'

'And that's supposed to make me feel better, is it?'

'No, obviously not, but Charlotte's caught in the middle of this mess.'

Evie closed her eyes. 'Yes, I know.'

'She sent me a message. She's confused and upset, Evie. She doesn't understand why Gerry and I aren't talking anymore. She wanted me and Martha to take her ice skating.'

'I know, she rang me. She told me she's worried about Dad.'

'He threw me out. I mean, I understand why, obviously, but we can't leave it like this.'

'No, you're right, we can't. But I can't deal with this right now, I…'

The lift bell dinged.

'I know, I know. You go and join the others and I'll see you when you get back.' He reached out and gave Evie's arm a brief squeeze.

The lift doors opened.

Evie stepped inside.

Alex held the doors open. 'It'll all be alright in the end. It simply *has* to be.'

Janet flung open the window in her room before joining Elspeth, who was perched on the edge of the bed. She took hold of her sister's hand. 'I know this is difficult and I know how hard this has been for you, but I'm just not prepared to keep it a secret anymore, Elspeth. It's already been too long. Everyone needs to be told what a monster Mum's been living with for all these years.'

'You don't need to convince me, Janet, not any more. I agree with you, but we can't tell Mum.'

'But…'

'Think about it, Janet. She'll blame herself, she'll say she should've seen the signs, she'll feel responsible. It's such an awful thing for her to…'

'And what about, Paul?'

'What about him?'

'Do you imagine he'll want to allow his grandfather to get away with what he did to us?'

Elspeth shrugged as tears began to roll down her face. 'Oh, I don't know, Janet. I'm just so tired of it all.'

'So am I, Elspeth, so am I.'

'We've buried it for so long.'

'I know.'

'I'm scared.'

Janet squeezed her sister's hand. 'He can't hurt us, not anymore.'

Sniffing and wiping her eyes, Elspeth said, 'No, you're right, he can't.' She stood and looked down at Janet. 'Come on, let's do this.'

Up in the Empire Suite, Paul had been out on the balcony, pacing back and forth, clenching and unclenching his fists. He was now slumped in what had become his usual armchair, his face pale. 'Do you think she'll want to see me?'

'I'm not sure, but I think she's had enough of hiding from the truth, whatever that truth is,' said Evie.

'So, what do we do now?' asked James.

'We wait,' said Simon.

'Janet said she and Elspeth would join us up here as soon as possible,' said Evie.

'Shall I ring down for tea and sandwiches?' said Barbara.

'Oh, good idea. I'm famished,' said Evie.

'Me too,' said Julia.

'What about everyone else?'

'Yes please,' they all chorused.

'Any preferences?'

'Just order a selection,' suggested Julia.

As the last sandwiches were being eaten, there was a gentle tap at the door. Evie jumped up, rushed over and opened the door to reveal Janet and Elspeth standing side by side holding hands.

'Can we come in?'

Evie turned to face the group. 'It's Janet and Elspeth.'

'We can see that,' said Adam, dashing towards them. 'God, you had me so worried,' he said, as he enveloped Elspeth in a hug.

'I'm afraid we've just finished the sandwiches, but I...'

'We're fine, Barbara,' said Janet.

'Well, come in, come in,' said James.

Adam released Elspeth from his embrace and she locked eyes with James across the room. She gave a diffident nod.

James rubbed his forehead and took a deep breath.

Barbara gave a nervous cough.

'I'm not sure what the conventional greeting is when one finds oneself in a situation such as this,' said James.

'No, I shouldn't think there is one,' said Elspeth.

'You look different,' said James. 'But, I suppose that's to be expected after all this time.'

Elspeth ran her fingers through her hair. 'I have had my hair cut.'

'It suits you,' said James.

'Thank you.'

The sound of the lift door clanging shut, and a high-pitched cry of, 'Don't want to. Don't want to,' penetrated the silence in the room.

'Someone doesn't sound too happy,' said Evie in a forced, bright voice.

Adam took hold of Elspeth's hand and led her towards the armchair where Paul was still sat. He stood, held out his hand, let it drop again, smiled, swallowed and sat back down.

Elspeth knelt by his side. 'Hello.'

'Hello,' replied Paul, his voice husky and cracked.

'I'm your mother.'

'I'm your son.'

'Well, yes, so I gathered.'

Paul smiled. He lifted his left arm and took hold of Julia's hand. 'This is Julia, my girlfriend.'

Elspeth smiled across at Julia. 'Hello. Evie's been telling me that you've been a great support to Paul. Thank you.'

Julia flushed and cast her eyes downwards. 'I'm so glad he's found you.'

Elspeth smiled. 'And I'm pleased he found me too.' She reached out and stroked his face. 'You look just like Granddad Lee.'

For a moment, all was still. Everyone focused on the vignette being played out in front of them. Traffic noise drifted up from below, car horns blared, people laughed, a train whistle blew and, in the distance, the faint sound of a police siren competed with the silence of the room.

Barbara cleared her throat. James shuffled from foot to foot. Tears began to well up in Evie's eyes, Simon gave her a warm smile as he put his arm around her. Janet hugged herself and Adam, face radiant, rested his hand on Elspeth's shoulder. The sound of a door slamming shut and a woman screaming out, 'Fine, just sod-off then,' induced a hysterical giggle from Evie, which quickly spread through the room.

James, recovering his composure first, asked, 'Right then, would everyone like a drink?'

'That would be lovely,' said Barbara.

'Tea, coffee or …?'

'Tea would fine.'

'What about everyone else?'

'I'll have whatever's on offer,' said Evie, wiping her eyes.

'Me too,' said Janet.

Simon picked up the phone.

Room service arrived, cleared away the sandwich trolley and replaced it with a tea trolley. Pulling the door to with a gentle click, the waiter departed.

'Shall I be mother?' said Barbara.

'Lovely, thanks,' said Janet.

Barbara poured several cups and handed them out.

Hand shaking, Elspeth accepted her tea. She cleared her throat and glanced at Janet who, with great care, took the cup from her and placed it on the table.

Taking another deep breath, Elspeth said. 'This isn't easy, but...'

Everyone held their breath.

'...I can't go on, not like this. Not anymore.'

'It isn't a pretty story,' said Janet.

'We gathered that,' said James, with a nervous laugh, 'what with the dramatic build-up.'

'Do you want me and Simon to leave, you know, so that it's just...?'

'No, no,' said Janet, glancing towards Elspeth, 'Unless...'

'No, Evie, it's fine, stay.'

Janet and Elspeth were sat on the sofa, their bodies touching, their faces pale. Janet reached out for Elspeth's hand and gripped it. She closed her eyes as tears began to trickle down her cheeks.

Adam eased his handkerchief into Janet's free hand.

She rubbed her face dry, took a deep breath and gave Elspeth's hand a squeeze. 'It started a long time ago,' she began. 'Every summer, when I was little, Mum and I used to spend a fortnight away from London. Here, in Weymouth. Dad stayed home. After Alice was born, it'd be the three of us. I remember hot sun and sand, buckets and spades. I had a yellow bucket,' she glanced at Elspeth. 'And you had a blue one.'

'No, I had a red bucket.'

'Are you sure?'

'Yes, I've still got it.'

'Strange. The things we hold onto to. I've still got my yellow bucket, you know.'

'Oh, Janet, I don't think I can...'

'We have to. We agreed.'

'I know, but...'

Janet gave Elspeth a quick smile as she pressed on. 'When I was eight, Mum announced that she'd be going away with just Alice. I was to stay at home and look after

Dad.' She balled Adam's handkerchief tightly in her hand. 'He said we'd have such fun. I could play at being the mistress of the house and do all the things that Mummy did. I asked him if I'd be allowed to go to the shops on my own and he said of course, that's what grown-up ladies do. It was all great until, until...'

'Oh, God,' said James.

Evie gasped, 'No, oh no,' she murmured.

Simon reached out and put his arm around Evie's shoulder. He held her tight.

'Dad said I could stay up late. He drank a lot of beer. He made me a hot chocolate, said he'd added something special for his favourite little girl. He carried me upstairs, said it was like I was his new fresh bride. I remember feeling dizzy and I remember giggling. Next thing I remember was him laying me on the big double bed and starting to undress me, saying we could play a game. A tickling game. He ran his hands up the inside of my thighs and stroked and tickled me, saying I was his beautiful princess. Then I remember his rough unshaven face scraping against my legs. I kicked out. Said I didn't want to play anymore. He got cross then; he held me down. I closed my eyes, his breath stank. He grabbed my hand and held it tight. I tried to pull away, but he gripped it tighter. He bent down, his face inches from mine, contorted into a grotesque expression. He spat out the words, words that I'll never forget; *You belong to me, little one. You will do as I say, otherwise I'll get the leather strap and we don't want that, do we?*'

'Jesus, the bastard,' croaked Evie.

'Then, when I was twelve, he sat me on his lap and said he had a very important job for me. I remember feeling proud. He said I would always be his best little girl, but it was time for Alice to join in. He said it would be fun because I could help train her. He said it was very important that she did as she was told and, because I was *so* good at being Daddy's best little girl, he was going to trust me to judge her performance.'

'Jesus, you mean he expected you to watch?' gasped Evie.

Janet nodded. 'Can you fucking believe it? But, that wasn't the worse thing, no...'

'Oh, God,' cried Adam.

Elspeth averted her eyes from Paul, as a low moan escaped her lips.

Paul gripped the arms of the chair.

'...the worse thing was, I was jealous,' continued Janet, her voice thick with emotion. 'Jealous that Alice was going to be the special one now. How sick is that?'

Paul buried his head in Julia's arms and sobbed.

Adam staggered backwards, his face drained of all colour. Simon guided him towards a chair.

'I need a proper bloody drink,' said James, snatching up the phone. 'Yes, hello, could you send up some drink?'—'I don't know, whisky, gin, wine, whatever,' he yelled, as he slammed the phone down and marched across to Elspeth. 'Why the hell didn't you tell me?'

Releasing Janet's hand, she stood and faced him. 'I'd have thought that was obvious. I felt dirty.'

'If I'd known I'd have, I'd have...'

'You'd have what, James? There was nothing you could do. It was too late. Oh, Janet, can't we stop now? I'm so ashamed.'

'He raped us, Elspeth. *Raped* us. We were children, for God's sake, just children.'

'The sick, evil bastard,' yelled James.

Elspeth howled, collapsed back down into the sofa, hid her head in her hands and rocked back and forth, mumbling incoherently.

Adam made to push himself up from his chair, but Janet shook her head as she gently rubbed Elspeth's back until the rocking ceased. 'Alright now?'

Elspeth nodded.

'I'm going to carry on, OK?'

Elspeth nodded again.

Janet took a deep breath and continued. 'Four years later, I was pregnant. And suddenly I wasn't daddy's special little girl anymore. He became incandescent with rage. He slapped me; told me I was a slut. He said I was no use to him anymore. I said I'd tell Mum what he'd been doing to us. I remember, he laughed in my face. I can hear his words now, full of malice and contempt; his expression smug, such was his confidence in his own invincibility.

He grabbed my long hair and pulled me towards him so that I could feel his breath on my face. *You do that, and we'll see what happens, shall we?* he said. *In fact, why don't I fetch Mummy now? She's just got back from her WI meeting. You go and fetch Alice, she's in Mummy and Daddy's bedroom, we've been having a little fun while Mummy was out. Alice is such a good little girl. We'll see what they both have to say, shall we?* I just stood there, head bowed, and he patted me on the head. Of course, he knew I couldn't say anything. Oh, Elspeth, I...'

Elspeth threw her arm around Janet and pulled her close. 'I'm so sorry.'

'Don't be ridiculous. It wasn't your fault. None of it was your fault. If anyone should be apologising it should be me...'

'Now that really *is* ridiculous,' cried Elspeth.

'I abandoned you. Left you, when I knew, I knew what he was doing to you.'

'I was twelve, Janet. I could look after myself by then. Anyway, what choice did you have?'

Janet shrugged. 'None, not really, I suppose.'

'Oh, this is awful,' said Evie. 'So, when you left home it was to have an abortion?'

Janet tore her eyes away from Elspeth and gave a curt nod. 'That's right, yes. Granddad Lee was a GP and

Grandma was a nurse. I had the abortion at their local clinic.'

James stared, open mouthed, at Elspeth. 'And you too?'

Elspeth nodded.

'This is unbelievable,' said James.

'Mum doesn't know it was Jack,' said Janet.

'And what about your grandparents, did they know?' asked Simon.

Janet shook her head. 'No, but I think Granddad had his suspicions.'

'But why didn't your grandfather say anything to the authorities?' demanded Evie.

'What *could* he say?' said Janet. 'We both told Mum that we'd had sex with our boyfriends in the woods. And that's what she told Granddad.'

'It was a plausible explanation,' said Elspeth, wiping her eyes with the back of her hand. 'We spent a lot of time in those woods, didn't we?'

'Yes we did. It was the only way we could keep out of Dad's way. We used to hide in an old shed in the woods and wait until we thought he was in bed before we ventured back home. Poor Mum, she despaired of us.'

'That's terrible,' said Evie.

'It was all we knew,' said Janet. 'When I moved out, Mum told the neighbours I'd gone to live with her parents so I could attend college; a lie that materialised into a truth. She told everyone the same story when Alice moved away. She certainly didn't want the neighbours to know that both her children had got themselves pregnant.'

'It broke Mum's heart,' said Elspeth. 'She thought it was her fault. She thought she'd failed us. She said she still loved us but, and this is the bit that nearly made me tell her the truth...' Elspeth closed her eyes and she clenched her fists. 'After it had been arranged that I would be joining Janet in Devon, Mum swore me to secrecy. She said *Daddy* must never find out that both his beautiful innocents had been with boys. She said it would destroy him.' Elspeth choked back a hysterical laugh. 'She was worried about how my bloody Dad would deal with the news; can you believe it? I swear I wanted to tell her there and then. Tell her everything. Tell her what that evil bastard had done to us, but I just couldn't. She wouldn't have believed me anyway so, what was the point?'

'And you're saying she still doesn't know it was Jack who got you both pregnant?' said Simon.

'No, and she must never find out. It'd kill her.'

Adam pushed himself up from his chair and went to Elspeth. He took her in his arms. 'I love you and that's it. Nothing else to add.'

There was a gentle tap at the door.

All eyes turned towards the sound.

The knock came again, this time lounder. A cheerful male voice called out, 'Room Service.'

'Enter,' called James.

A waiter popped his head round the door. 'I've bought a selection of drinks up for you. They're on a trolley. Where would you like them?'

James swept his arm round the room. 'Wherever.'

The waiter hesitated a moment as he surveyed the scene. Leaving the drinks trolley outside in the hallway, he entered. 'Have you finished with the tea?'

'Yes, yes,' said James, with a dismissive wave of his hand.

'Thank you,' said Simon. He gave the waiter a warm smile. 'We seem to be keeping you busy.'

With all eyes fixed on him, the waiter bustled around, collecting cups and loading them onto the trolley. He gave a brief nod as he wheeled the tea trolley from the room and replaced it with the drinks trolley. 'There are glasses on the bottom shelf,' he said. 'If you need anything else…'

'We're fine now, thank you,' said Simon.

Paul sat quietly, Julia standing by his side, as James picked up various bottles on the trolley. 'Well, we seem to have most things here,' he said. 'What would you like, Paul?'

'A vodka and tonic please.'

'Barbara?'

'I'm alright, thanks.'

'Elspeth?'

'Is there any gin?'

'A Gordon's.'

She nodded.

'Adam?'

'A whisky, please.'

Holding onto Adam's arm, Elspeth shot Paul a hesitant smile.

Paul looked across into his mother's eyes. 'I can't believe it,' he said. 'You here, with me and Dad—it's alright, I know you're with Adam now, I just mean, well, you know.'

James held a glass aloft. 'Would you like ice in this gin, Elspeth?'

'No thanks.'

Handing Elspeth her drink, James called out, 'What about you, Adam? Ice?'

'Yes, please.'

Elspeth took a sip of her gin. Blinking back tears, she took a deep breath. 'Paul, I need to tell you—well, I'm so very sorry, but I'm afraid there's more to tell.'

'More?'

'About your father.'

James dropped three cubes into a glass, poured the whisky and handed the drink to Adam.

'Smashing, thanks,' said Adam.

Paul glanced across at James. 'What about him?'

'You don't know, do you?'

'I don't know what?'

James turned from the drinks trolley and handed Paul his vodka and tonic. 'Your drink,' he said.

Paul snatched the glass from his father's hand. 'What is it that I don't know, *now*, Dad?'

James frowned.

'I take it you didn't show Paul my letter.'

'You asked me not to,' said James.

'He told me it confirmed what he already knew, but that's obviously not true, is it?' said Paul, propelling himself from the chair and glaring at James.

Elspeth swallowed and glanced across towards Barbara. 'And you haven't said anything to James about what really happened?'

Barbara shook her head. 'Of course not. You told me in confidence.'

James's frown deepened. '*What really happened?* What do you mean by *what really happened?* In the letter you said...'

'I know what I said in the letter, James,' said Elspeth.

His face contorted in confusion, James turned to Barbara. 'Well?'

'I, I'm sorry, James, I...'

'Oh, for God's sake!' He whirled around to confront Adam. 'What's going on?'

Adam shrugged. 'I've no idea.'

'I couldn't tell you, Adam, I just couldn't.'

'It's alright, Elspeth. It was a long time ago. I knew there was something else, more than the beatings, but I also knew you didn't want to talk about it. I respected your right to keep whatever happened to yourself, but you've told us about the abuse now; so, that's that, isn't it?'

Elspeth shook her head.

Paul took a gulp of his drink, slammed the glass down, folded his arms tight across his chest and stared at his mother. 'So, you're saying there's more we don't know, more secrets never to be told?'

'No, Paul,' said Elspeth, her expression strangely serene. 'I'm telling you that there is one final secret, but now it's time for it to be told.'

'Elspeth, please, don't,' said James. 'Not now. I've kept my promise all these years.'

'I know, and I'm sorry James, but he needs to know the *whole* truth,' said Elspeth, her voice faltering. 'And you need to know too; only then will you fully understand why I ran away.'

Another wave of confusion crossed James's face. 'But, I *do* understand. You know I do.'

'Jesus, your own father abused you when you were a child,' said Paul. 'Surely there can't be anything worse.'

'I'm afraid there is,' she said, as she reached out for Adam's hand and held onto it.

Paul locked eyes with his father.

'I just wanted to protect you from what your mother wrote in her letter. I didn't want it to alter how you felt about me, and...'

'What does that even mean?' demanded Paul.

James turned towards Elspeth. 'I don't know what to do. I don't know what to say. I was trying to protect Paul from the knowledge of the beatings, I mean, that was bad enough. But the sexual abuse; I had no idea, really, I didn't. To keep that secret for so long, it must...'

'It's alright James, I'll explain everything now.' Elspeth gave Adam's hand a squeeze. 'I need to be close to my son,' she whispered.

Adam nodded as he released her hand.

She smiled up at him.

He smiled back.

Head held high, she made her way across the room towards Paul. 'When I told James about the abortion he was amazing. He...'

Paul whirled round to face James. 'What? You just said you didn't know about the abuse.'

'I didn't, I...'

'No, Paul, he didn't,' said Elspeth. 'No-one knew. I told him the same as I'd told my mum; that it'd been my boyfriend.'

'I don't understand,' said Paul, blinking back tears.

Elspeth stared down at him. 'I'm so, so sorry.'

James took a deep breath. 'It was the year after your mother and I met,' he said. 'She'd already told me about her abortion, well, her version of it as it now turns out. Anyway, I knew I wanted to marry her, but she was young and vulnerable. I didn't want to take advantage, but then, in the summer of 1990, she told me she was pregnant again. I confess I was angry at first, but when she explained what had happened, I…'

'Hang on,' said Paul. 'Are you saying I'm not yours?'

'Not biologically mine, no. It was some fucking art student who'd slipped something into her drink. Probably did it for a laugh. Nothing could be proved, of course, and so…'

'Stop, James…'

'I thought you said he needed to know the truth.'

'He does,' said Elspeth, her voice unnaturally calm. 'As do you.'

'But, I *do* know…'

'No, you don't know, James. That's the problem. You see, it wasn't a student,' she said.

'I beg your pardon?'

'I said it wasn't…'

'Yes, I heard what you said, Elspeth, I'm not deaf. Nor am I senile. I distinctly recall you telling me about it at the time. It's also what you said in your last letter to me. You said you couldn't bear looking into Paul's eyes because it bought back terrible flashbacks of the rape and all you could see looking back at you were the evil eyes of…'

'My father, James,' said Elspeth. 'All I could see looking back at me were the evil eyes of my father.'

'What, sorry, you what?'

'It was when Jack travelled down to Plymouth looking for you,' said Barbara.

James started. 'I, I...'

'He came to the college and told you to keep your hands off me. He accused you of cradle-snatching,' said Elspeth, her voice trembling.

'Yes, thank you. I know what he said to me—but, hang on—how do you *know*? I never told you about his visit.'

'It's just that, well, it's just that...'

'It's just that, what?' snapped James.

'James, let Elspeth speak,' said Barbara.

'Sorry.'

'I knew about his visit because he came to find me first, James,' said Elspeth.

'You're not saying, Jesus. You're saying he raped you again?'

Elspeth nodded.

He stared at Barbara, veins throbbing in his neck. 'And you knew?'

'She told me in confidence, James. I couldn't tell you.'

'You know what a state I was in after Paul was born, for God's sake, that's why you hired Barbara,' said Elspeth. 'And she was so kind, so understanding that it all came out in a rush. And the moment I told her what had happened to me when Jack came to the college looking for you, I regretted it. It wasn't fair on her. I had to beg her not to tell you that it'd been him and not a student. You mustn't blame her.'

James stared, wide-eyed. 'I don't understand. Why couldn't you have told me the truth?'

'I just couldn't. I should have fought him off.'

'Don't be ridiculous, Elspeth,' retorted Janet. 'His raping you was not, I repeat not, your fault.'

'Oh, God, Paul, I never wanted you to find out any of this. It's all so sordid,' said Elspeth, her composure now evaporated. 'I did try. I tried so hard but, every time I looked at you all I could see was my father's grotesque sweaty face swimming above me, his rough stinking hand over my mouth and I'd feel the bile rising, the panic spreading through me. I was terrified, terrified that I'd harm you.'

'She loved you, Paul,' said Barbara. 'That's *why* she had to leave; do you understand?'

Paul snatched his glasses off as tears slid down his face. He dragged his hand across his cheek and nodded.

James rushed to Paul's side and grabbed hold of his shoulders. 'Listen to me, Paul. This changes nothing. I'm your dad. I always have been and I always will be.'

'Oh, James, I am so, so sorry,' said Barbara.

'Will everyone stop bloody apologising,' yelled Paul. 'The only person who should be apologising in this scenario is my *darling* Granddad.' He gave a hysterical laugh, as his voice rose. 'No, sorry, my mistake; my fucking father, it would seem.'

The following morning, Simon and Evie methodically worked their way through breakfast, glancing up every now and then as the swing doors of the dining room banged shut.

'Do you think they'll be alright?'

Simon swallowed his mouthful of scrambled egg, dabbed at the corner of his mouth and shrugged.

'Helpful as ever.'

'Well, sorry, but how am I supposed to know? Oh, watch out, here they come now.'

Evie twisted around to see Elspeth, Paul, Adam and James chatting together as they walked in, while Janet, Julia and Barbara followed, giggling amongst themselves.

She turned back and gave Simon a warm smile. 'Well, that looks hopeful.'

'What does?'

'The fact that they're all together, chatting and laughing. Honestly, sometimes you can be incredibly slow. God knows how you've managed without me for all these years.'

'I know. Remarkable, isn't it?'

Twisting around again, Evie gave a wave.

Adam waved back, leaned down and whispered something into Elspeth's ear, before making his way over. Pulling up a chair, he closed his eyes and let out a long, deep sigh. 'Well, that was a night and a half,' he said, glancing at his watch. 'Two hours sleep I estimate, if that.'

'And?' said Evie.

'Well, we're all still talking, and I have to say James has been remarkably understanding, you know, all things considered.'

Evie glanced across towards the buffet area. Elspeth turned and smiled as she handed Paul a tiny glass of orange juice.

Evie gave a small gasp and grabbed Adam's arm.

'What?'

'I hope someone thought to contact Mavis.'

'Who?' asked Simon.

'The owner of *Sunflowers*, because, if not, she's probably rung the police to report a missing guest, and...'

'All sorted. Barbara spoke to her last night.'

Evie sighed and released Adam's arm.

'What about Janet and Elspeth?' said Simon. 'How are they?'

'Now that the truth's out, I think they're going to be fine.'

Evie shuddered. 'Their own father. It doesn't bear thinking about.'

'I know. They're remarkable women,' said Adam. 'Simon?'

'Yes?'

'What are you going to do about your fee? Janet's said she'll cover it, but...'

239

Simon held up his hand. 'There is no fee.'

Adam thumped Simon on his back. 'Splendid, splendid.'

'Hardly seems ethical, under the circumstances.'

'No, quite; I did offer to refund James my fee, you know, given that I'd, um...'

'Given that you'd been shacked up with his wife.'

'Yes, yes, alright, I think we've covered that,' said Adam, his face twitching. 'Anyway, he wouldn't accept it.'

Evie jumped up and planted a kiss on Simon's cheek.

'Good to see that you and your partner have such a close working relationship.'

Evie giggled as she turned and kissed the top of Adam's head.

'What's that for?'

'For being Simon's brother.'

'That's a dubious honour.'

'Oh, most amusing,' said Simon, his eyes twinkling. 'So, I assume you and Elspeth are off back down to Devon, then.'

'Yes, but not immediately. Janet's come up with a humdinger of an idea.'

'About?' said Evie, settling herself back down.

'Amy.'

'Oh?'

'Yes, she's going to see if she can persuade her to leave Jack and move in with Elspeth and me.'

'They're going to tell her that Jack raped his daughters?' gasped Evie. 'I thought Elspeth was dead against that.'

'She was, well, still is,' said Adam. 'No, the thing is Jack still knocks Amy about and Janet's worried that one day he'll go too far. Amy's not as strong as she used to be.'

'Not physically maybe,' said Evie, 'but, Jesus, to put up with that sort of violence for all those years well, I can't imagine.'

'So, what's the plan?' said Simon.

'Wildly ambitious in my opinion, but there you go.'

'So, come on,' said Evie, 'tell us.'

He glanced over his shoulder before continuing in a whisper. 'She's going to arrange for Amy to meet Elspeth and Paul.'

'Where?'

'Not sure yet.'

'And will you be there?'

'Yes, and Julia, too.'

'And then what?' said Simon. 'Is Janet going to say, *Look, Mum, everyone's fine. Meet your grandson. Oh, and here's Alice— she's changed her name to Elspeth by the way—and she's been living with Adam for over twenty years in your parent's old cottage, and now they'd like you to move in with them.*'

'Something like that, yes.'

'Good luck with that,' said Simon. 'And, keep in touch.'

'Of course, I will,' he said, giving Simon's shoulder a gentle squeeze. 'And I'll let you know how Janet's master plan pans out.'

'Oh, before you go,' said Simon, reaching into the inside pocket of his jacket. 'This is the letter that Paul instructed me to give to his mum, you know, if she hadn't wanted to see him.' He handed it to Adam. 'I'd appreciate it if you could return it to him; then he can decide what he wants to do with it.'

Chapter 25
York, Mid June 2013

Charlotte was sat alone in her bedroom. Her toys were divided into two groups. She picked up a scruffy, short-haired rag doll and shook it. 'This has got to stop. Whatever nonsense started this, it has to end now.'

She turned and picked up a battered Action Man. 'And you, well, you should know better. You know Raggity can be silly, he always has been. You need to man up.'

She reverted to a high-pitched voice. 'I'll sort them out, Charlotte, don't worry.'

'Please do,' said Charlotte to a stuffed rabbit sat next to Raggity.

'And I can help,' said a teddy.

'I should hope so. You're supposed to be a private investigator,' said Charlotte.

The sound of the creaking gate sent Charlotte dashing to the window. 'It's Aunt Martha, hurrah,' she exclaimed, as she snatched her bedroom door open. 'I'll get it, I'll get it,' she yelled, running downstairs.

'Steady on, Charlotte,' said Mandy, 'you'll fall.'

'It's Aunt Martha.'

'Calm down,' said Mandy, grabbing hold of Charlotte's hand. 'Come on, let's see what she wants.'

'Perhaps she's got a message from Uncle Alex.'

'Perhaps,' said Mandy, as they made their way towards the front door.

The doorbell rang just as Mandy opened the door.

'Gosh,' exclaimed Martha. 'You must be psychic.'

'I heard the gate,' exclaimed Charlotte. 'Do you want to talk to Daddy?'

'Is he in?'

'Yes, yes, yes. He's in the study,' said Charlotte, snatching her hand free, 'I'll get him.'

Mandy grabbed hold of Charlotte's blouse. 'Hold on there, poppet, let's...'

'But...'

'But me no buts,' said Mandy. 'Come in, Martha. Would you like some tea?'

'That would be lovely, thank you. I'm sorry to turn up like this but, well, we can't go on like this.'

'That's just what I said to Raggity,' declared Charlotte, with pride.

Martha gave Charlotte a quizzical glance.

'Raggity, the rag doll,' said Mandy.

'Ah, I see, and what did Raggity have to say on the matter?' said Martha.

'Nothing, she's a rag doll.'

Martha bit her lower lip.

'Daddy, Daddy,' yelled Charlotte, breaking free again and running down the hallway. 'Aunt Martha's here. Mandy's making tea.' She banged on the study door. 'Daddy! Daddy, Aunt...'

Gerry snatched the door open. 'Charlotte, what in God's name are you...?'

'Martha's popped over,' said Mandy in a quiet voice. 'I was just about to make tea. Would you like some?'

Charlotte took hold of her father's hand. 'Daddy?'

Looking down into Charlotte's wide blue eyes, he sighed. 'Fine, I could do with a break.'

Charlotte jumped up and clapped her hands. 'Come on, Daddy,' she said, dragging at his arm.

'Alright, alright, give me a moment,' said Gerry. 'I just need to finish the sentence I was in the middle of. You go on. I'll join you in a moment.'

'Promise?'

'Promise, now go on.'

Mandy carried the tray out onto the patio. 'The weather's lovely, isn't it?'

'Beautiful,' said Martha.

'It's the summer,' said Charlotte, raising her eyes.

Gerry came out onto the terrace. 'Right then, to what do we owe the pleasure?'

'I need to talk to you about, well, about the situation.'

'I think everything that needs to be said has already been said, don't you?'

'No, Gerry, I don't. That's why I'm here.'

Mandy cleared her throat. 'I don't think, well, I don't know, obviously, given that I don't know what you're about to say, Martha. But what about?' Mandy flicked her eyes towards Charlotte.

'Charlotte, would you be a good girl and do Daddy a favour?'

Charlotte stamped her foot. 'I want to stay here.'

'The thing is, poppet, I rather think Martha needs to speak to Daddy in private,' said Mandy.

Charlotte's bottom lip quivered.

'It'll only take a moment,' said Martha. 'And then...'

'And then perhaps I could take you to the ice rink,' said Mandy.

'With Aunt Martha and Uncle Alex?'

'We'll see,' said Mandy.

'That means no,' growled Charlotte.

'Not necessarily,' said Martha.

'Daddy?'

'We'll see.'

Charlotte stamped her feet again and flounced off.

'I'll see to her, don't worry,' said Mandy.

'Shall I pour you a cup?'

Gerry nodded.

'He's in a terrible state,' said Martha.

'My heart bleeds.'

Martha slammed Gerry's filled cup down. 'For God's sake, stop acting like a petulant child.'

'Did you add sugar?'

'No, do it yourself.'

Head down, he measured out half a teaspoon, poured it into his cup and stirred.

'Gerry, you've known me for a long time. Jean and I were close. She never wanted to hurt you.'

'Good to know. So, is that it? Is that what you came to tell me?'

Closing her eyes and taking a deep breath, Martha pressed on. 'She never expected to see Alex again. She loved you. You know she did. Seeing him again shook her.'

'Enough to send her into his arms again, it would seem.'

'She tried, Gerry, she tried so hard. And then when you went off to Africa…'

He pushed his cup away. 'Ah, right I see,' he snarled. 'So it's my fault.'

'No, Gerry, I'm not saying that, for God's sake, stop feeling so bloody sorry for yourself for just one second.'

'How you've got the nerve to, well, it beggars belief. You colluded in the whole thing, Martha. I know about the letters.'

Martha rubbed her forehead. 'I haven't come here to excuse my involvement in that arrangement, or to apologise for that matter; I've come here to tell you one very important fact.'

'Fine. Tell me. Then you can leave.'

'Jean never once suspected that Charlotte wasn't yours, she…'

'Oh, give me a break, Martha.'

'Gerry,' Martha yelled. 'Jean genuinely thought that Charlotte had arrived a few weeks early. She put it down to stress.'

'Stress?'

'Yes, Gerry, stress. She'd been in love with Alex at Cambridge and she was pissed off when he upped and left for America. When she met you, she couldn't believe it. She

245

told me you were poles apart from Alex. You were kind, caring and completely unselfish; she said she'd been a fool to fall for the empty charms of the feckless Alex…'

'And yet…'

'I *know*, Gerry, I know, but his ten years away improved him. You took to him immediately, didn't you? You said he was a decent chap, intelligent and fun to be around.' She smiled. 'Come on, you can't deny that.'

Gerry shrugged.

'Jean told me the day before she left for that last trip to Wales that she was finishing it. She said Alex had asked her to make a choice, you or him.'

Gerry clenched his fist and struck the table.

Martha reached out and covered his fist with her hand. 'We were sat in the corner of the University library and I remember how she laughed. I said to her that I didn't really see what there was to laugh about. She looked me straight in the eye and said, *But, don't you see, Martha, the moment Alex said that to me, the moment he asked me to make that choice, I realised the truth. It hit me hard in the chest. My heart flipped. I love Gerry, Martha, love him with all my being. My feelings for Alex aren't real, not really; probably just trying to recapture what we'd had all those years ago; stupid, stupid and naïve of me. So*, you see, she…'

'And you're telling the truth this time?'

'Yes, Gerry, yes,' said Martha. 'Please, I can't bear to see you or Alex so miserable and it's so upsetting for Charlotte. She doesn't understand why you two aren't speaking.'

Gerry gave a curt nod. 'No, I know. She's rather cross with me.'

Martha laughed. 'Yes, and her expression when she's angry, well, she looks just like Jean.'

'Doesn't she just,' exclaimed Gerry. 'It's unnerving.'

Martha stared out across the garden. 'The magnolia you and Jean planted when Evie was born is looking splendid.'

Gerry followed her gaze and smiled. 'She always loved magnolias. The pink flowers are supposed to represent youth, innocence and joy; a load of psychobabble in my opinion, but Jean believed in it all.' He pointed over to the side of the garden. 'We planted that one when Charlotte arrived. It's not much to look at yet, is it?'

'No, but it'll look splendid in a few years.'

'Charlotte needs to be told the truth.'

'I know, Gerry, I know, but not yet. When she's older, when her magnolia flowers.'

Chapter 26
London, Late June 2013

'What's this all about, Janet?'

'What do you mean, Mum. It's not *about* anything. I'm simply taking you to see my latest exhibition.'

Amy buttoned her coat and picked up her handbag. 'And we'll be back before Jack gets home?'

'Yes, Mum. I said, didn't I? Now, have you got your keys?'

Amy rummaged through the contents of her bag. 'Oh dear, I'm sure—oh, yes, here they are.'

'Right then, off we go.'

Janet parked her car outside her studio. Amy looked around and frowned. 'I don't wish to sound discouraging, dear, but there don't seem to be many people. Are you sure you've got the right date?'

'I'm hardly likely to get the date of my own exhibition wrong, Mum.'

'I know, dear, but...'

'It's a private exhibition. Invitations have been sent out to a small and exclusive group.'

Amy glowed. 'Goodness.'

'Now, give me your arm and I'll help you up the stairs.'

'Am I dressed alright, Janet? You never said it was to be a select affair.' She looked down at herself. 'I feel dowdy.'

'You look fine, Mum, don't worry.'

They climbed the stone steps at a slow, gentle pace, with Amy taking regular stops to catch her breath.

'Here we are,' said Janet. 'We're early. I thought I'd get you settled with a drink before the other guests arrive.'

'Give me a chance to get my breath back,' Amy puffed, as she struggled with her coat buttons. 'Where shall I...?'

'Give it here. Now, what would you like to drink; I've got wine, sherry, whisky...?'

'A nice cup of tea would go down a treat, love.'

Taking a sip, Amy asked, 'So, who are these other guests? Will I know them?'

'Yes, you'll know them.'

Amy raised her eyebrows. 'So, who are they then, dear?'

'You'll see.'

'Janet, what's going on?'

'Nothing's going on.'

'Janet Isabella, you're up to something, now, come on, tell me.'

'Are you sure you wouldn't prefer a sherry, or some...?'

'For goodness sake, Janet, I'm your mother, I know...'

'Alice is one of the guests, Mum.'

'Alice,' exclaimed Amy. 'Alice is coming here?'

Janet nodded.

'Oh, Janet, I, oh; here, take this.'

Janet took the cup from Amy's shaking hand. 'She's coming with Adam and...'

'Adam? Adam who?'

'Adam Trent.'

'That private detective chap?'

'Yes, Mum,' said Janet. 'She's, um, well, she and Adam are together.'

Amy frowned.

'They're a couple, Mum. They live together.'

'In the same house?' said Amy, her frown deepening.

'Yes, Mum, in the same house.'

'Well, I never.' She lowered her voice. 'Probably best not to mention that detail to your father.'

Janet shot her mother an incredulous glance and pressed on. 'I've also invited a young man and his girlfriend, a lovely girl called Julia. She's been helping,' Janet cleared her throat.

'She's been helping this young man find his long lost mother.'

Amy's hand flew to her chest. 'You mean, do you mean? Oh, goodness me, are you saying Paul's coming too?'

'Yes, Mum.'

'Oh, my, my.'

'And, just one other thing I should add before everyone arrives.'

Amy's eyes widened.

'It's nothing awful; it's just that Alice changed her name. She's called Elspeth Mitchell now.'

'Elspeth Mitchell,' repeated Amy.

'Are you alright?'

Amy gave a hysterical giggle. 'I think so. Goodness, what a thing, my Alice, I mean Elspeth, coming here.' She stood, adjusted her hair, hugged herself and collapsed back down into the sofa. 'Living with Adam; gracious. And Paul, I...' She closed her eyes and took a deep breath. 'I think I will have that drink now.'

'What would you like?'

'A sherry, dear; a large one.'

Amy, even though she was sitting down, swayed a little. 'I don't know what to say, really I don't.'

'It's simple,' said Elspeth. 'Just say yes.'

'And you say you're living in Grandma Lee's old cottage, the one Janet said she'd sold?'

Elspeth nodded.

'They needed a place where they could be together, where they could be left in peace, Mum,' said Janet.

'It was rather awkward for Adam,' said Elspeth. 'He obviously couldn't tell Simon about, well, you know.'

'No, I suppose he couldn't, yes, I see.'

'So, what do you say?' said Adam.

'I don't really think Jack would approve, and he certainly wouldn't want to leave London.'

Janet took Amy's hand. 'They only want you to move in with them, Mum.'

'But what about Jack? I can't leave him on his own. He wouldn't be able to cope.'

'He'll be fine,' said Janet.

'Mum, he mustn't know where I am and so, if you agree to move in with us, you wouldn't be able to tell him where you'd gone,' said Elspeth.

'But that's silly, dear,' said Amy. 'Why don't you want your father to know where you are?'

'Oh Mum, you know why,' said Elspeth.

'I can't just leave.'

'You can't stay with him, not anymore,' said Elspeth.

'She's right,' said Janet.

'Gran, please say you'll leave him, please,' pleaded Paul.

Amy shot a confused glance towards Janet.

'He'll go too far one day, Mum, he'll really hurt you. We're all worried about you.'

Amy's eyes widened. 'Janet, be careful what you say. Paul's...'

'Oh, for God's sake, Mum, he knows about the beatings; they all know,' said Janet.

'But he's much better now,' said Amy, smiling and nodding. 'Yes much better.'

'Only because you pander to his every need and never question him.'

Amy's shoulders dropped.

'I don't wish to be impertinent,' said Julia, her tone gentle. 'But, why *do* you stay with him?'

'He doesn't mean it, dear. He can be a lovely man. It's the drink. Normally he's kind. He wouldn't hurt a soul.'

'You've got to be joking,' exclaimed Paul.

'Paul,' said Julia, grabbing his hand.

'She needs to know the truth,' said Paul.

'What truth, dear?'

'About the man you're living with, Gran. He's evil.'

'Paul, don't,' said Elspeth.

'Oh, dear sweet boy, no, he's not evil,' said Amy. 'Weak perhaps, yes weak. He found it very difficult when the girls left. That's when he started drinking more, and well, he sometimes gets a bit cross and he can be rather...'

Paul pulled himself free, and fell at Amy's feet, sobbing.

Amy patted Paul's head. 'Now, now, don't upset yourself. I'll be fine.'

'You won't be fine,' spluttered Paul.

Adam rested his hand on Paul's shoulder. 'Come on, enough now.'

Paul shook himself free and dragged his hand through his hair. 'He's my father, Gran.'

'Oh, don't be silly. How could Adam possibly be your father?'

'Not, Adam,' he screamed, 'Jack. Jack's my father.'

Amy froze. She squeezed her eyes shut.

Paul covered his mouth and, as his outburst died away, everyone became aware of a dripping tap. Each drip hitting the stainless-steel sink base sounded disproportionately loud in the stillness of the studio.

Elspeth knelt and eased Paul away. She whispered, 'Adam, take him.'

Adam wrapped his arms around Paul and held him tight.

Elspeth sat on the sofa and took Amy's hand into hers. 'Mum?'

Amy began to rock back and forth. A low growl rumbled deep in her chest.

'I didn't mean to; oh hell, what have I done?' cried Paul.

'It's alright, Paul,' said Adam.

'No it bloody isn't.' He pushed his head backwards into Adam's chest, shook himself free and rushed towards Julia's open arms.

Amy stopped rocking. She took a deep breath and turned to face Elspeth. 'Is it true?'

Elspeth nodded.

'I see.'

'Oh, Mum, I...'

'Janet, tell me the truth. Your pregnancy. Was that,' she swallowed, 'was that your father?'

Janet nodded.

'And when you left home to join Janet?'

Elspeth nodded again.

'I see.'

'Are you alright, Amy?' said Adam.

'Perfectly fine, young man, thank you for asking,' said Amy. She glanced at her watch. 'Goodness, look at the time. It's almost four. I really should be getting back. Janet, my coat please.'

'But, Mum...'

'Coat, please. It's been lovely to meet you, Paul. You seem to have grown into a fine young man. And you; Julia, isn't it?'

Julia wiped her eyes and nodded.

'Look after him, there's a good girl.'

'Mum, Adam and I are going home in a few days. Please say you're going to come with us,' said Elspeth.

'I can't think about that now. I'll let you know.'

'We could delay our return,' said Elspeth, 'then we could all go down together, that'd be alright, wouldn't it, Adam?'

'Of course, it...'

'Nonsense, you two need to get back home,' said Amy, patting at her hair and smiling a bleak smile. 'After all, we wouldn't want you bumping into Jack, not after all this time.'

'But you will come?'

'I'll see.'

'But...'

'Don't fuss, dear, I'll be fine,' said Amy, glancing at her watch again. 'Now, I'm sorry, but I really *must* get going. Janet *do* come along.'

Janet unhooked Amy's coat from the coat tree and stood, clutching it to her chest. 'Mum, I really think…'

'Jack will be home in half an hour.'

'Right, as you wish.'

'I do. Now, come on.'

At the door, Janet turned. 'I'll be back shortly. Help yourselves to drinks.'

'Janet!'

'I'm coming, Mum, I'm coming.'

'Do you think she understood?

'Oh, I think so, yes,' said Adam.

'But, she seemed so calm,' said Elspeth.

'It was spooky,' said Julia.

'Will she be alright?' said Paul.

'I'm not sure,' said Adam.

'Oh, Adam, I don't think she'll leave him,' said Elspeth.

'No, I think you're probably right,' said Adam.

'But she can't possibly stay with him, not knowing what she knows now,' exclaimed Paul.

Elspeth clutched at the back of her neck as she tipped her head backwards. 'I just don't know, Paul. I can't deal with how calm she seemed. It was surreal.'

'Well, there's nothing more we can do,' said Adam. 'She knows the truth now. We've made the offer; it's up to her.'

'Drink anyone?'

'Oh, yes please, Julia, a whisky,' said Elspeth.

'I take it I'm driving, then. So, I'll have a coffee,' said Adam, reaching for his phone.

'Who are you ringing?' asked Elspeth.

'Simon. I said I'd let him know how it all went.'—'Ah, hi, it's me.'—'Not sure really.'—'It all came out.'—'Yes, she knows everything.'—'Well, like I said, difficult to say.'—'I've no idea. She said she'll think about it. I'm worried, Simon. I'm convinced she understood, but her reaction, well, it was odd.'—'Yes, OK, talk later, bye.'

Chapter 27
London. One week later

'Hello, dear. I'm all packed,' said Amy. 'When can you get here?'

'What, sorry?'

'You said I could move in with you and Adam.'

'Yes, yes, I, we did, but…'

'I see, you didn't mean it, oh, well, never…'

'No, of course we meant it. Your room's all ready for you. I'll ring Janet, she'll bring you down.'

'Why can't you come and get me, dear?'

'Because I'm in Devon, Mum, it'll take me…'

'Oh, yes of course you are; silly me. Don't worry, I'll call Janet. So, it's alright then? I can come?'

'Yes, Mum, of course you can. Have you, well, have you told Dad?'

'Don't worry about Jack, dear. I've sorted all that out.'

'Right, great. Well, see you soon, then.'

'Yes, darling, see you soon.'

Janet crunched up to the front door and rang the bell. She looked up and down the street and rang the bell again. She crouched down, opened the letterbox and called out. 'Mum, I'm here.'

She banged on the door, stood back and looked up towards the bedroom window. The curtains were drawn shut. She tutted and stepped along the path towards the living-room window. She frowned as she realised these curtains were also closed. 'Oh, for goodness sake,' she muttered, as she struggled with the side gate.

She tried the back door. Locked. Shielding her eyes, she peered through the kitchen window. Banging on the glass, she called, 'Mum, where are you? You rang, you said…'

'Oh, Janet, it's you.'

Janet whirled around to see Amy pulling the shed door shut. 'Mum, what on Earth were you doing in there?'

'In where?'

'In Dad's shed. He'll have a fit if you've disturbed anything.'

'It doesn't really matter anymore, does it?'

Janet smiled. 'No, I suppose not. Anyway, are you all packed?'

'Yes, dear, but I'm afraid I couldn't manage the bags down the stairs. They're still in the bedroom.'

'That's alright, I'll get them.'

'You'll need these,' said Amy, digging into her apron pocket and tossing Janet a set of keys. 'Jack labelled all the keys. The long key is the one you need for the back door.'

'I know that, Mum.'

'Yes, of course you do. And, as I said, Jack labelled them all.'

'Anyway, why is it locked?'

'Security, dear.'

'But you're home.'

'I'm aware of that, Janet, but you can never be too careful. That's what Jack always says.'

'Yes, fine. Anyway, we really need to get going,' said Janet, glancing at her watch. 'He'll be back soon.'

'Oh, he's already back.'

'What? Where?'

'He's in his shed.'

Janet flinched. 'So, he's just letting you go, is he?'

'Yes, dear,' said Amy, striding towards Janet. 'Now come along. I just need to wash my hands and then we can get going.'

'Mum, you're hurt. Did Dad…?'

'I'm fine, don't fuss. Just get the bags.'

'Mum, let me look.'

'Janet,' exclaimed Amy, 'we need to leave.'

Janet swallowed. 'Mum, there's blood all down your arms and, oh, God, Mum, what's happened?'

'Nothing at all. Now do come along,' said Amy, snatching hold of Janet's arm.

'Alright, Mum. Let's get you cleaned up,' said Janet, glancing over her shoulder towards the shed.

With a shaking hand, Janet unlocked the back door and guided Amy into the downstairs toilet. 'Here we are, and look, there's plenty of soap in the dispenser.'

'Yes, Lily of the Valley. Jack always buys it for me, and I've always hated the bloody stuff.'

Janet stiffened. 'Right, I'll, um, I'll bring your bags down. Will you be alright?'

'I'm perfectly fine, thank you. Don't fuss.'

'You ought to go to the loo, too, it's a long journey,' said Janet, as she stepped outside. 'I'll close the door, give you some privacy.'

Janet turned and quickly made her way back to the kitchen. Clutching the bunch of keys, she took a deep breath and stepped onto the patio. She glanced behind her and then dashed towards the shed. She rested her hand on the warm, wooden door as she began to sort through the keys, but there was no need; the door creaked open. It was the smell that hit her first. The metallic smell of fresh blood, mingled with the smell of engine oil, compost and weed killer. She took a tentative step inside.

And there he was, wedged between his wheelbarrow and his brand new Hozelock hose reel. His prized mattock, not cheap but worth every penny, was embedded in his back. The blood oozed from the gaping wound and flowed across the concrete floor.

Janet's hand flew to her mouth. She staggered backwards, crashing into the swinging shed door. She snatched hold of the door and slammed it shut. With shaking hands, she fumbled with the keys and dropped

257

them. Swearing, she fell to her knees, scrabbled in the grass and, chest heaving, she searched the bunch for the correct key. It was clearly marked in Jack's neat script with the single word, *Shed*. She gave a manic laugh as she pushed herself upright, shoved the key in the lock and turned it. She leaned against the door for a moment, her breath rapid and shallow. She clutched her stomach, bent forward and vomited.

'Janet, I asked you to fetch my bags. Just leave him. He can't hurt us anymore.'

'Mum...'

'I've washed my hands. I'll wait in the car, shall I? Yes, that's what I'll do. I'll wait in the car.'

Janet swayed and dragged her hand across her mouth.

'Don't be too long. Alice will be waiting,' said Amy. 'Don't forget to lock all the doors. I've done the windows.'

Janet staggered into the kitchen, rushed to the sink and vomited again. Leaning over the sink, she turned on the tap, closed her eyes and rinsed her mouth. Lifting her head, she opened her eyes and was confronted by the sight of the shed. A basic wooden shed; well-weathered now, with ivy growing up the side and tree branches overhanging, it looked welcoming. She reached for the window-blind's pull cord and yanked. The view vanished.

She took a deep breath, locked the back door and trudged up the stairs. In her parents' bedroom, she shuddered. The framed picture of Jack and Amy on their wedding day sat on the dressing table, as it had done for as long as she could remember. On either side were photos of her and Alice as children. One showed them smiling in the sun, clutching their red and yellow buckets and spades. The other showed them sitting on Jack's lap, his loathsome grin wide and grotesque.

Hands shaking, she reached for her phone.